A SLIGHT CASE OF ARSON

R. E. G. Davies

Published by

MELROSE BOOKS

An Imprint of Melrose Press Limited
St Thomas Place, Ely
Cambridgeshire
CB7 4GG, UK
www.melrosebooks.com

FIRST EDITION

Cover designed by Jeremy Kay

ISBN 978 1 907732 20 1

Printed and bound in Great Britain by:
CLE Digital Solutions. St Ives, Cambridgeshire

FSC
www.fsc.org
MIX
From responsible
sources
FSC® C019549

Contents

Contents (cont.)

Prologue

Being restricted by the conditions of the Official Secrets Act, the full account of the international negotiation and events of 1975 that provide the background of this book cannot be published. This fictional narrative is based only on reminiscences and recollections of the persons involved.

Chapter 1

Codswallop

'Codswallop!'

Elizabeth Lloyd's single-word ejaculation shattered the morning serenity of the Scotland Yard office of Detective Inspector Michael Bridgeman of the Criminal Investigation Department's Arson Squad. He not only raised his eyebrows but raised his whole torso by several inches as he jerked upright in his chair. He was not accustomed to being spoken to in this fashion, at least not at Scotland Yard.

'I beg your pardon?'

Miss Lloyd was unrepentant. 'What you have just told me is a load of old codswallop.'

Mike Bridgeman was not exactly sure of the derivation of the term but he knew what it meant. Translated into contemporary vernacular, he knew that the lady sitting opposite meant "bullshit" but was polite enough not to use quite such a harsh epithet. He glanced at Detective Superintendent Jim Marshall, who had accompanied his friend's daughter to Bridgeman's office. He tactfully left her to fight her own battle.

'Hang on a minute,' Inspector Bridgeman felt that a slight cooling-off period was called for, 'let us have a cup of coffee, and review the facts again.' He had started the dull March day in a good mood. He had looked forward to a quiet morning, with nothing special except a 10 a.m. appointment with a young lady, requested by an old friend in the force, and one that he had expected to clear up with a few words of friendly advice.

Indeed, he had put his feet up, literally, on the corner of his desk, and the height of his interest so far had been the outcome of a minuscule patch of blue sky that, in true British fashion, was destined to disappear at any moment. He had reflected that the claims of a good view of London from his office window were exaggerated. Nine-tenths of the horizon consisted of chimney-pot-strewn rooftops, and the distant glimpse of St Paul's had to be pointed out carefully to interested visitors.

The Times had done little to relieve the flatness of a Monday morning. The 1975 February General Election already history. Minor weekend incidents had included some civil disturbances by warring football supporters, another demonstration by the Wessex Nationalist Party in Trafalgar Square, and the front page headline made the best of an international situation, declaring "Strait of Hormuz closed". The only incident that was relevant to his job was a small item reporting a fire of apparently little consequence in west London.

He had started the day by dutifully scanning the few paragraphs. Nothing beyond the bare bones of a reported incident in which some old huts had burned down, nothing of value, no lives lost, in fact, nobody there. But he had made a mental note that this was the fourth such un-newsworthy incident of its kind that had come to his notice within the last few weeks. The occurrence had been unexplained and although arson was half suspected, all that had happened was the destruction of some worthless buildings. Nobody seemed concerned about the damage, and enquiries had been cursory, at best.

In his diary for Monday there was nothing more demanding than to do a little homework in preparation for a small delegation from the Japanese Police Department which was accompanying a team of high-level trade negotiators. They were taking the opportunity of

2

paying Scotland Yard a courtesy call, and Mike was mildly flattered at the attention. But he had been relieved by a telephone call from Detective Chief Superintendent Jim Marshall, of Special Branch, who had asked for a favour.

'Can you have a chat with an attractive young lady in about an hour's time, if you are not too busy? I don't want you to chat her up, just give her some advice, and at least you can thank me for lightening the gloom of the morning. She's the daughter of an old friend. You may even know him yourself. Remember Haydn Lloyd? Retired last year. He and I were very close in the early days, and we still are, even if he has taken leave of his senses and gone to raise mink in the wilds of the Welsh mountains. We used to walk the beat together in Chiswick in the late Thirties, when we had to venture out in pairs.

'Anyway, Haydn's daughter, Elizabeth, works in London for a big insurance company, as assistant to one of their investigators, and she came round to see me last night. She has her knickers in a twist about some fire in Hammersmith – that's H Division territory – and she thinks her boss is neglecting his duty in not putting the entire force of Scotland Yard on to the job immediately. In a weak moment, I promised to see her. But really, it's arson-related, so that's where you come in, or to be exact, where she comes in to you.'

'Is that all?' Bridgeman had mused that his thoughts on the fires had stimulated some ESP activity.

'Liz is a sensible girl, and I don't want to short-change the daughter of an old friend. So can you listen patiently, and then check up with H Division, if you think she has a point?'

'Righto, Jim. Doesn't sound too world-shattering. I noticed something in this morning's paper. Leave it to me – I'll let you know the story.'

Mike Bridgeman was beginning to feel that he was becoming the Universal Aunt depository of all the humdrum jobs that nobody else wanted. Japanese delegations, chairman of the non-uniformed staff welfare committee, counsellor to over-imaginative young ladies: they'd be asking him to serve biscuits and tea next.

His colleagues would have been kinder. Jim certainly qualified by conventional criteria as a Good Chap. In his mid-fifties, he was a non-smoker, moderate drinker, and retained the marks of an athletic youth. Sharp-featured, blue-eyed, losing a little of his dark brown hair, he could have been mistaken for a successful businessman who jogged every morning. He owned a house in Wimbledon, where his wife, Carol, shared his love for two daughters, a collection of records of early English composers, and a loathing of jogging. His main weakness was a dedication to the fortunes of the Chelsea football club, at whose Stamford Bridge ground he spent many a Saturday afternoon, and endured the consequential ribaldry every Monday morning.

He had taken the precaution to ask Sergeant Green to check up with Hammersmith for a few more details. Coffee had arrived from a denizen of the cafeteria, and noting that the description of the visitor as attractive was correct, Mike felt he could begin, cautiously. 'If you don't mind, Miss Lloyd, before you present your problem, it might be a good idea if we reviewed the facts. I must confess that I know practically nothing about this west London fire, but Sergeant Green is checking it out for me with H Division. I am somewhat surprised that you are so concerned, as apparently it seems to have been some kind of accident. Nobody was hurt, nobody was there, nothing of value lost, and the property seems to have been almost worthless, and therefore of little interest for insurance purposes.'

Sergeant Green had made his statement with reluctance, as the H Division report said nothing that *The Times* had not reported. So Miss Lloyd must know something that the newspaper and the Hammersmith Division did not.

The fire had taken place on the previous Thursday night, at an abandoned warehouse site belonging to the Hammersmith Borough Council. The wooden-built premises occupied about an acre on a site bordering the Central London Underground line off Wood Lane, near Wormwood Scrubs, and were earmarked for early demolition, preparatory to the erection of a multi-storey block of flats. The Council was unperturbed about the loss. The Chief Clerk had been heard to observe that the £325,000 for which the wooden shacks had been insured, and for which sum he was making a claim to Messrs Martin, Smith, and Jenkins, was a better deal than paying a demolition contractor to do the job. Whoever had dropped a cigarette or incendiary device had done the Hammersmith Council a favour.

Several local residents had reported the smell of smoke at about 10.30 p.m.; the fire brigade was on the scene within half an hour, having been delayed momentarily by an immobilized lorry parked right outside the gates to the warehouse yard. This was not unusual as discarded lorries in this area were commonplace. But by the time they arrived at the site, the dry timber of the warehouses had burned to the ground.

'Nothing extraordinary, I would have thought,' the Sergeant observed as he closed his notebook.

Elizabeth Lloyd begged to differ. 'I repeat... codswallop. It may not seem extraordinary to you, but to an insurance investigator specializing in fire, there is something distinctly odd about it, because I have reviewed the situation with specialized knowledge, if you like.'

Miss Lloyd had a captive audience.

'The odd aspect of this fire is the speed at which the whole warehouse area was gutted. Of course, I know that the buildings were all of decayed wood, ideal for kindling, and vulnerable. Places like these have gone up in flames from the concentrated heat of the sun beamed through a piece of broken bottle glass. In this case, too, if it had been one hut, the speed of the burning would not have been surprising.'

Elizabeth looked Mike Bridgeman directly in his eyes, and knew that she had his attention.

'But this was on Thursday night, there was no wind to fan the flames, it had rained all day Thursday, and not one, but ten buildings burned down, simultaneously, and no two buildings were nearer than 25 feet apart. It was too quick and efficient to have been accidental.'

The audience was now more than captive. It was captivated.

Elizabeth continued. 'I've suggested to Mr Braithwaite – he's the man I work for – that this is distinctly odd, but he thinks that I'm given to an excess of imagination, and he can't get too excited about £325,000, which is a trivial sum in our line of business. We have it well covered and we do not wish to upset the Hammersmith Council, which will soon be demanding some heavy insurance for its development plans. Anyway, he's too busy preparing his speech for the Fire Insurance Underwriters Convention in Madrid next week to worry about a small warehouse fire.' Miss Lloyd paused for breath, and Bridegeman grasped the opportunity to get a word in edgeways.

'May I clarify one or two points, Miss Lloyd? I take it that Mr Braithwaite has no objection to your freelancing, as it were, and possibly making a mountain out of a molehill? Isn't his judgement worth taking into account? What did he say when you expressed your doubts?'

Elizabeth's attitude visibly hardened. Her tone was cold and deliberate. 'This is no molehill. Mr Braithwaite wasn't entirely negative. I am his assistant and, in his absence, I am his deputy. He agreed that, if there was no wind on Thursday, it would look suspicious. A gang of delinquent youths out to start a bit of bovver, perhaps? But what if the fire was started deliberately. Under our policy, it could make a difference to the insurance liability. Anyway, he sent Mr Stratton, one of our experts, down to the scene on Friday, and has agreed to pursue the matter if anything suspicious is discovered.

'But I don't like it. I had a look at the large-scale ordnance map and those huts could have been laid out by someone who was fanatical about fire prevention. They were so well spaced apart. My boss's gang theory would only apply if they were well disciplined and highly organized. I cannot get it into anyone's head…' Elizabeth put her coffee cup down smartly enough to spill some of the contents, and caught Mike's eye again, 'that the speed with which this well-soaked collection of huts burned down was uncanny in the almost scientific way in which they all went at once.'

Sergeant Green grinned. 'Sounds like a little intuition, if I may say so, Miss. Are you sure about the spacing of the huts being a sufficient deterrent to the spread of the fire?'

Miss Lloyd glared icily, and spoke through clenched teeth, restraining herself from repeating her introductory expletive. 'Positive. The spaces could not have been better fire-breaks, if they had been lined with asbestos fences. Indeed, the fire would not have spread, even if there had been a wind. But let me pursue my intuition, as you call it. Why should a gang of youths start the fire in the first place? I am also looking at the question from the psychological angle,' she glanced menacingly at the audience of two. 'I used to read the subject at college. Petty vandalism is invariably spontaneous. But this was methodical. For God's sake, there was nothing to be gained from setting fire to a lot of empty, derelict, useless, huts.'

This time, the Inspector did not wait for the pause, as Elizabeth now had her second wind, and was at full canter. He had to assert a little control, otherwise they were going to be here all day. Also, a small department in his memory cells reminded him that perhaps he ought to have looked more carefully into those other unexplained fires.

'Perhaps we could summarize? We are faced with a mysterious fire, which might be a case of arson. The only people who will apparently profit by it are the ratepayers of the Borough of Hammersmith. It is most unlikely that they would have gone to such lengths as to start this fire. But the Arson Squad cannot move in such a case – and I assume that you wish us to do so – without a great deal more definite evidence. Far more important, it is under the authority of H Division until such time as they feel they need support from us. But I will gently make a suggestion or two. How does that strike you?'

At that moment, the Detective Chief Superintendent returned, looking at his watch. 'How have you been getting on, Liz? Any luck?'

'These gentlemen have reservations about the reliability of women's intuition, but at least they listened, and the Inspector has promised to investigate.'

'Has he, indeed? I hope, Mike, that this doesn't mean that you're going to tread on some divisional toes.' The tone of his voice indicated more of an instruction than a statement or question.

Bridgeman reflected that he was damned if he did, and damned if he didn't. He reassured the Superintendent that he would be Discretion Personified, at the same time expressing the opinion that Miss Lloyd had presented her case well, and that he would not be pursuing the matter at all if he did not think that the facts justified the action.

Mike decided that he should pour some oil on potentially troubled waters, and this time looked Elizabeth in the eye. He also thought that the opportunity to take a young and attractive lady out to lunch did not come his way too often. Elizabeth Lloyd was in her late twenties, and wore a dress that was stylish enough for a cocktail party yet not too ostentatious as a working outfit. It concealed a 5' 6" figure that the inspector felt was extremely well distributed, and its soft green material heightened the dramatic effect of her auburn hair. Her alert eyes were green to perfection. This was no dumb redhead who was going to be palmed off with platitudes.

He successfully poured oil on the waters with, 'May I suggest a light lunch and perhaps a drink? Who knows, our bar may even have some codswallop.'

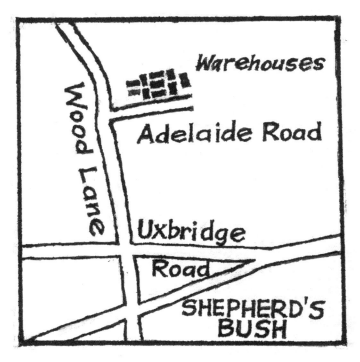

Ten "empty, derelict, useless huts"

Chapter 2
There'll Be a Hot Time

On the following afternoon, Mike Bridgeman sat facing Jim Marshall across the latter's desk, watching his superior fussing with his pipe, going through a complicated ritual of rubbing tobacco into shreds, packing these into the bowl of the pipe, along with sundry dross from the desk top, and expending half a box of matches in setting light to an instrument that his colleagues claimed to be a threat to the environment, and possibly a case for the Arson Squad. Mike meanwhile observed the generous, uninterrupted view of the River Thames, the wall-to-wall carpet, the warm furnishings, and the general air of opulence. This, he felt, was less of an office than a den where a chap could enjoy work solely because of the suggestion of ease, comfort, and relaxation.

'Did you enjoy your lunch with Elizabeth?' Marshall broke the silence.

'I did indeed, not only because Miss Lloyd is a fascinating young lady, but because she is quite concerned with her ideas about this fire. She is back in her office, incidentally, helping to prepare her boss's speech to be delivered in Madrid. She relishes the chance to do something on her own initiative.

'I must admit, grudgingly – and I hope I did not give her cause for over-enthusiasm – that her analysis of the apparent lack of motive, or proof of accidental cause, as she calls it, has the merit of common sense, at least; but I told her that we need hard evidence, not psychology, to prove arson. But when she charged me to offer any explanation that would fit the circumstance, I had to plead ignorance.

'We are not absolutely sure that it was deliberate, but one fact seems firmly established. The Met. Office confirms that, uncharacteristically for March, there was no wind, not even a slight breeze on Thursday night. And there was a steady drizzle during the 24 hours previous to the outbreak of the fire. Worst possible conditions for a fire-raiser, which is what Miss Lloyd correctly emphasizes.'

'Has H Division come through with anything further than we know already?'

'They have, and they haven't. Their Detective Superintendent Sanders telephoned a few minutes ago to say that he had asked a Detective Inspector to look into it, and that they would let us know if they wanted our help. He was polite but firm... and I can't say I blame him. It's a bit early for us to be sticking our noses in.'

Marshall chuckled. 'True to form. I would have predicted it. They're right of course. None of our business yet, anyway. You did say Sanders?'

'Yes, but I don't know him. Why?'

'Just a hunch. It's not like Guy Sanders to do his own telephoning. Not about a routine matter. Which just makes me wonder if there isn't more in this than meets the eye.'

* * *

Marshall's instincts were on target. As they were talking, Guy Sanders had been conducting a conference in his paper-strewn office at H Division Headquarters in Hammersmith. The others present were Mr Stratton, from Martin, Smith, and Jenkins, the insurers; a Hammersmith Fire Brigade sergeant; three uniformed constables;

and Detective Inspector David Thomas. Sanders was pacing up and down in front of a large wall-map of London, all of four steps in each direction, somewhat incongruously, as his well-groomed moustache and upright bearing stamped him as an ex-sergeant-major who would have been more at home in the wide open spaces of a barracks square. Stratton and the Fire Brigade were deployed, seated upright, on the right flank; the three constables, respectfully, stood in echelon on the left; and Thomas held the centre stage.

Sanders opened the discussion, like a machine-gun burst. 'What's all this bloody nonsense I've been hearing about this fire up Wood Lane? Straightforward case of a few vandals with nothing better to do. Why the hell are you lot wasting everybody's time... including mine?' He glared at Thomas who, to his credit, glared straight back.

'I think you ought to hear what we have to say, Sir. Mr Stratton, representing the insurers, came down last Friday to look around – this is normal procedure – and he and the fire brigade have found some interesting items of evidence that point to a deliberate and planned case of arson.'

'Well, let's have it man.' Sanders almost barked the words at Stratton who would have taken a step backwards, had he not been sitting down. Sanders belonged to the type who habitually gave orders. Stratton habitually took them.

'I have my report here.' Stratton reached for his briefcase, but was halted in mid-reach.

'Do you need to refer to your report? Is this so complicated that you cannot tell us without notes?'

Stratton looked hurt, but made an effort to preserve the dignity of Messrs Martin, Smith, and Jenkins. He was a small man, sallow of complexion, and drab of suit; but he had a job to do which included taking orders, but not submitting to intimidation. 'In our business, we endeavour to record the facts, and hesitate to paraphrase or depend on memory, because of the risk of liability. A word out of place and ten thousand pounds can go down the drain.'

He paused, coughed, and paused again, scrutinizing the pages of the file. Sanders raised his eyes to heaven, in silent prayer and unspoken oaths. Finally, the insurance investigator decided that he could go ahead, without self-incrimination. 'The essence of my conclusions – and they agree with those of the fire department – is that arson has been committed, on a planned, even scientific, basis.'

'What the hell do you mean by that?'

'There were ten old wooden huts, and all of them burned down very quickly, in spite of the wet weather. I am not surprised. We have found no less than seven identical contraptions, one in the charred remains of seven of the ten huts, and I have little doubt that we shall find similar contraptions in the other three. Although I cannot positively identify the type of instrument, it is somewhat similar to others in my experience, and I am sure that further scrutiny and examination will confirm my opinion that they are incendiary devices.'

Although Sanders acted like a sergeant-major, he was possessed of a great deal more intelligence than is normally credited to Her Majesty's non-commissioned ranks. He did not waste time arguing with a specialist.

'What do they look like?'

The Fire Brigade sergeant produced a package, like a conjuror producing a rabbit out of a hat, from some bottomless concealed pocket. 'Here is one, or leastways, what's left of one. It's the best example we could find so far.' He laid the brown-paper package on Sanders's desk.

Stratton's word "contraption" had been well chosen. The device, dulled and blackened by the fire, consisted of a light metal tube, about 20 inches long, and about 1½ inches in diameter. At the end was a small mechanism, now clogged with charred debris, similar to the working parts of a flint-type cigarette lighter. Stratton explained, gaining confidence as his audience gathered round the desk to listen to the expert.

'You see, it's quite simple. We sometimes call this a pipe-bomb, although this is thinner than the usual ones we have seen. The tube contains inflammable material, like a firework, which is ignited by this apparatus at the end here. Looks like a simple flint or cap that would be able to produce the necessary spark for ignition. The device would then burn furiously like a Roman candle, giving off intensive heat, and setting alight anything near to it that would burn.'

'But how did ten of these infernal machines go off at the same time?' Sanders enquired, having been briefed on the speed of the minor inferno.

'Do you see this hole here?' Stratton pointed to a small hole bored into the pipe at the detonator end. 'The device was spring-loaded, kept in tension by a peg through these holes. When the peg was pulled out – a piece of long cord would have been enough – the ignition took place, rather like pulling the pin of a hand grenade. And all ten could have been jerked out together. The pegs could have been simply pencils, and they would have gone up in flames too. In short, a very simple booby trap.'

Sanders grunted. 'That seems sound enough. Now, Thomas, who or what do you think is behind this lot? Don't tell me the I.R.A. in Belfast are reduced to this minor stuff. And incidentally, what are Faith, Hope, and Charity doing here?' He looked belligerently at the three constables, still lined up respectfully, awaiting their turn, massively patient, and enjoying their chief's characteristic performance.

David Thomas was 28 years old, about six feet tall, clean-shaven, of athletic build, and with good sharp-featured looks. He knew Sanders of old, tolerated his idiosyncrasies, and was confident that, in spite of the bluster, he would get a fair hearing.

14

'They are here because they have what I believe to be some evidence relating to the warehouse fire. I admit it is rather slender and entirely circumstantial, but I would like your permission to check it out. Perhaps Constable Cheeseman could make the first statement?'

Sanders stared intensely at the constable, a mannerism that he had employed for many years to judge whether or not he was hearing the truth, but in this case, to imply that brevity and accuracy were demanded.

'On Thursday evening, 12th March, at 10.15 p.m., Constable Baverstock and I were proceeding in our Panda car down Adelaide Street – that's just behind where the fire took place, Sir – and observed a stationary vehicle – a private car – parked on the roadside, with nobody in sight. I put it down to a spot of the other going on in the nearby waste ground, except that it was a wet night, which would have been very uncomfortable. Also, it was a queer place to park a car, even in the daytime. And when we returned just after 11.30, it was gone.'

'Description? And what the hell has all this got to do with the fire?'

Cheeseman knew his job. 'Red Rover 2000, registration MTU 658H.'

Thomas interjected before Sanders could comment further. 'Constable Michelmore is next.'

'I was on duty at the same time as Constables Cheeseman and Baverstock, but on the other side of the tracks, as it were. They were in Adelaide Street, at the side of the Council site, while I was patrolling the main road, Wood Lane, which skirts the front of the site where the main entrance is. It's a double gateway, in a high brick wall, lying back from the road. At about 10.15 – though I couldn't place the time exactly, because I didn't think it important at the time – I noticed two men hanging round the gateway, leaning against a lorry, minding their own business, so to speak, and it only struck me later that I more or less recognized them.'

Sanders was sarcastic. 'You're not sure of the time, you more or less recognized two men, and all they were doing was minding their own business. Give me a break.'

'Well, Sir, it was only when Inspector Thomas happened to mention the fire that I thought more about it. I realized that they looked like two men who also belong to the Old Comrades Association of the Hammersmith Regiment, which I also belong to, and they usually go there on Thursdays, early evening, and then at about 9.30 they always go on to the pub, for a bit of supper I would think.'

'You do know them, then?'

'Only by sight. They were in the Second Battalion.' Constable Michelmore implied that this placed them on a level with the Chelsea Pensioners, and he would not be seen to mix with such rabble.

'So what's the bloody point?'

'Their habits, Sir. They were usually with two others, and the four of them seldom leave The Three Crowns until it closes at eleven. I've had to caution them once or twice, in a friendly way, for threatening to disturb the peace around midnight, as they often felt like singing, like a barber's shop quartet, and the local residents used to complain.'

Sanders was getting impatient. 'Thomas, this is a load of bloody nonsense. What the hell have four drunks singing got to do with a fire?'

David glanced at Michelmore, who nodded. 'I agree, it doesn't add up to much, except for something most unusual. On Thursday night, the quartet was only a duet. They'd had a few beers but they didn't seem all that drunk. They were not exactly disturbing the peace. And they weren't singing your typical barber's shop song book. They were singing "There'll be a Hot Time in the Old Town Tonight".'

16

Chapter 3

Two and Two Could Make Four

Guy Sanders digested this statement, glared at the assembled company, and tried to decide if he could believe his ears. The uniformed trio beamed with apparent satisfaction. Mr Stratton shuffled papers thoughtfully. The fire brigade fiddled with the evidence. After what is often described as a pregnant pause, Sanders finally spoke.

'Let me get this straight,' he said grimly, conveying the impression that he was suffering fools not very gladly, and that he was keeping calm in the face of grave adversity. 'A fire took place on Thursday night. It was probably arson. But are you trying to tell me that, because a car was parked nearby for an hour or two, and two men were minding their own business, and two other men were singing a song that only distantly had any relevance, then there is a case to investigate?'

David Thomas took up the cause. 'With your permission, Sir, I would like to follow this up. If nothing else turns up in a day or two, we'll put the thing on ice. There is something rum about it. Why should anybody go to so much trouble?' He pointed to the device on the table. 'That's not just a Guy Fawkes banger. It may look a bit primitive, but there seems to have been a production line. And somebody had to be on that line.'

Stratton spoke up. 'You cannot buy these, or anything like them. Certainly not do-it-yourself. They are normally produced in a back-street workshop, but their manufacture needs some knowledge of metalwork and pyrotechnics. I share the Inspector's doubts, especially the idea of a production line.'

The ball was in Sanders's court. 'Thomas, I'll give you 24 hours. Send these gadgets to forensics. If you can't come up with anything more, we'll have to drop it. See if you can prove any connection between the car and the drunks. But if you start harassing locals who do nothing worse than sing, I'll have your guts for garters.'

Left alone in his office, Detective Superintendent Sanders congratulated himself that, at least, he had been right to stall off the inquiry from the Yard, and by not closing the case, he had kept his options open. He made a mental note to ask, diplomatically, why the Yard was so interested in an apparently trivial matter.

* * *

Early on Tuesday evening Inspector David Thomas walked up the stairs behind Montague Burton's tailoring establishment at the end of Wood Lane and discreetly opened the door which exhibited a fine, if misspelled, example of the sign-writer's art, stating succinctly "Hammersmithian Old Comrades' Asociation, Members Only". Through a small hallway he came to a larger room which, except for a bar at one end, and some framed advertisements for various alcoholic beverages, presented all the austere desolation of a wartime N.A.A.F.I. canteen. Fifteen formica-topped tables were distributed in columns of three, sporadically attended by men drinking purposefully. Two games of darts were in progress, and the murmur of conversation was accompanied by the clink of glasses and tankards and the staccato rattle of dominoes. At the bar, a few dedicated professional drinkers had placed themselves strategically close to the beer-pumps. The barman looked questioningly at Thomas as he approached.

'You a member of the O.C.A.?'

'Well, no. As a matter of fact, I'm a police officer and I would like to ask you one or two questions, that is, if you can spare the time.' He produced his badge.

The men at the bar suddenly became intensely interested in the game of dominoes three tables away, and two of them did a vanishing act through the door marked, unnecessarily, "Men". The barman was less self-effacing.

'I'm Charlie Woodhouse. I keep regular 'ours, I've got a current licence, and I don't have no trouble.' A weather-beaten, sinewy man of about 60, he was obviously an old sweat, had seen many years of regular army service, and his confidence was born not so much from a record of ethical conduct, but from never having committed the worst crime of all, that of Being Found Out. He prided himself on a thorough knowledge of King's Regulations, and he was not about to be brow-beaten by a plainclothes copper.

Thomas smiled. 'No need to be on the defensive. I'm not investigating you or the O.C.A. But I am interested in some of your club members; in particular, four men who I believe are what you would call regulars. They come on Thursdays. Can you help me?'

'Depends. What 'ave they done? We don't have no trouble 'ere. This is a respectable club.' Charlie felt a certain loyalty to his clientele, if only to retain their business.

'I'm not at liberty to tell you at the moment. Let me put it this way. Do any of your Thursday regulars enjoy a sing-song? I assume that your licence includes singing?'

Charlie Woodhouse took offence. 'Course it includes singing. No law against that.' As if to confirm the liberal qualities of the club, almost on cue, a party at the end table, pint mugs aloft, began to acquaint anyone within a radius of about 100 yards with *What A Soldier Told Them Before He Died*.

'You haven't answered my question.'

'What question?'

'Were people singing last Thursday?'

'Course they were singing. That's why they come 'ere. Some pubs don't like it. Don't like the words. Offends the ladies, they say.'

'Quite. Can you remember what they were singing?'

'Blimey, do you think I keep a list? I'm 'ere to sell beer, keep order, and see there's no fighting. But there's no 'arm in army songs.'

'You misunderstand me. I'm not here to judge the morality or the taste of the singing. I'm interested in a special type of song, a sort of jazz number, actually.'

'We don't 'ave no jazz here. Go round the Palais for that.'

Charlie's record of 12 years ("seven and five") of undetected crime had been achieved largely by his ability to talk his way out of practically any situation, partly by evasion, partly by wearing down the opposition. He had not lost his touch.

David felt that sterner measures were called for.

'How would you like to lose your singing licence?'

'You can't do that.'

'I wouldn't count on it. The words of that song they're singing now would hardly be repeatable in front of a magistrate when you ask for a renewal of your licence. Incidentally, they are in the wrong key.'

The humour was lost on Charlie, but the veiled threat was not. He suspected that the Inspector was bluffing (which he was) but he was not going to chance it.

'What sort of jazz song?'

'Well, not pure jazz, but jazzy songs that were popular in the Thirties – when songs had words to them – like *Happy Days are Here Again* and *Nobody's Sweetheart*.'

'Lumme, you're going back a bit. Before your time and all that Beatles stuff.'

'That's beside the point. Answer the question. If I mentioned the title or a line or two, would it ring a bell?'

For once Charlie Woodhouse was slow with the repartee. He seemed surprised. 'How the 'ell did you know?'

Now it was David's turn to be puzzled. What was Charlie getting at? They looked at each other blankly.

Charlie smiled, for the first time during the conversation. 'You just made a joke. 'Ow did you know what Frank Eastwick and his mates were singing last Thursday?'

'What do you mean, and who is Frank Eastwick?'

'Come off it. You know what I mean. *When you 'Ear Those Bells go Ting-a-ling* – that's the first line of the song they were singing. You knew all the time they were singing *There'll be an 'Ot Time in the Hold Town Tonight*. And Frank's the local bookie.'

David Thomas suppressed his excitement at this revelation, but smiled encouragingly. 'Allow me to buy you a drink.'

Relieved at the sudden generosity, Charlie drew up two pints of Young's Best Bitter and they touched glasses.

'Bottoms up, Charlie. Let me assure you that anything you tell me will not be spread around, and if anyone asks, just say that I'm checking up on your licence. I'm sure that I can rely on your discretion.'

Hoping that Frank Eastwick hadn't been reneging on his bets, and wishing to remain on the right side of the Law, Charlie volunteered, 'All right, I suppose you want to know the rest of the words too.'

'Right first time. You're ahead of me. But first tell me about Frank the bookie.'

'Lives near King Street. Works the White City dogs. Sharp but straight. Always pays up. They say he's worth a small fortune, but he don't act like it. Comes 'ere with his mates. Usually four of 'em but

21

sometimes they don't all come.'

'Run a car?'

'Dunno. He usually walks from just across the Broadway. But I think one or two of his mates drive here. Tell you what though, they've all got it in for the Japs. Always leading off about the prison camps and that sort of stuff. The Second Battalion was out East in '42 and Frank got nobbled and spent the rest of the war up the jungle, building that railway they made that River Kwai film about. They tied him up once with barbed wire. If Frank's had a few beers and the fancy takes him, his language is enough to close the place down.'

'Did they have a habit of leaving early?'

'Depends what you call early. Sometimes they leave about nineish to go to The Three Crowns to get pie and chips; but sometimes one or two of 'em leave early.' Charlie took a long swig of Young's Bitter. He clearly regarded the eating of pie and chips as beneath the dignity of a serious drinker.

The beer was good for Charlie's memory. 'Now I come to think of it, Jim Smith sometimes stays on a bit, and he does have a car – lives up the Finchley Road. The others walk or take the chube.' Charlie gave a knowing leer. 'Big Jim (they call him) doesn't always go straight home, and he's not an Old Comrade either. Comes here as a guest, like.'

'Any idea of the sort of car he drives?'

'All sorts, I think. He's a car dealer. I got his card somewhere. He likes me to tell him if any of our members wants a car…' Charlie sifted through some well-worn cards in his drawer, '…Big Jim's Car Mart, 303, Finchley Road. New and Used Quality Cars. That's what he claims. I wouldn't buy a pair of roller skates off him.'

'May I keep this card?'

'Keep it. I only stack 'em in 'ere to do the lads a favour…' he shuffled through the cards again '… here's another one: Walter

Dudman, Television and Radio, Stereo, Tapes, 54, Putney High Street. Precision Repairs a Speciality. Now he's a riot. Always got a new story. Should have been on the stage. Proper comic.'

'Was he a Hammersmithian?'

'Same Battalion as Frank. But he was lucky. Got shot in the leg and was out of Singapore before it surrendered. Still walks with a limp. But it wasn't the Japs that shot him. If you 'eard the story, it would give you a good laugh.'

David mentally noted that he should prepare for near apoplexy if he ever interviewed Walter Dudman. But he had struck lucky, and looked forward to reporting to Sanders in the morning. He did not want Charlie to run out of steam. 'There was a fourth man?'

'Bill Castleman. I know a lot about 'im, because he done me a favour. 'E's a travel agent in Kensington High Street, and 'e got me a discount on a 'oliday in Palma for me and the wife. 'E's a good bloke, went to a good school, I think. 'Ere, look at his brosher.'

David examined the full-colour document, resplendent with bikini-clad, or rather, bikini-unclad damsels. 'Can I keep this too?'

'Enjoy yourself. I'd like that one back, though, and not because of all that flesh. Some of the lads are thinking about getting up a party this summer, and Bill's going to 'elp 'em get a bargain fare package.'

David Thomas was counting his luck and took his leave. Charlie felt that perhaps he had said too much. He didn't know what the problem was, but felt that he should defend his old comrades. 'Don't be too hard on them, Inspector. Drunk and disorderly was it? Well, they're not the violent sort, even though their language is a bit rough. They've been coming 'ere for years but never caused any trouble.'

'Thanks for the testimonial, Charlie. I'll bear it in mind. Oh, just one more thing. Does this quartet only come in on Thursdays?'

'They 'ardly ever miss a Thursday, although Big Jim doesn't always make it. Bill Castleman is a regular, and Frank and Walt sometimes twice a week. Come to think of it, this is a good night for them two. If you 'ang around, they might be in. They're more local. Like an introduction?'

David pondered over this unexpected but possibly advantageous opportunity. He could play it straight. Identify himself and proceed along the orthodox: 'Where were you on the night of the 16th?' But he was not sure which of the four had been in each of the two places on the night of the fire. In fact, so far, it was all hearsay; and any of them could deny any knowledge of the alleged activity. Big Jim could have been the driver of the car at Adelaide Street, but in any case they could all provide alibis for each other. On second thoughts he decided that, if Frank and Walter did come in, he would content himself with a long scrutiny.

'Thanks for your offer, Charles, but I shall defer that pleasure until some future occasion. But if you breathe a word of my identity, or reveal that the Law is watching them, I can close this place down. Do I make myself clear?'

By this time, the club had filled up a little, even though the men at the bar had made a surreptitious exit. Others were coming and going, and after a while, Charlie nudged David as a small furtive-looking man came in, accompanied by a jovial companion, turning only slightly towards a middle-aged spread. They ordered two beers, and took them to the table. 'Is it still raining, Frank?' asked Charlie, to confirm that David had struck lucky.

Walter Dudman did not seem to be in his usual life-and-soul-of-the-party mood. He talked earnestly with Frank Eastman for the better part of an hour, consuming three pints of Young's in the process. By the time he left, David felt he could have picked them out from a crowd. He followed them out discreetly, but apart from Walter's limp, they did nothing more than say goodnight to each other, Walter catching a No. 9 bus and Frank walking in the direction of King Street.

* * *

Next morning, Inspector David Thomas was up with the lark, although that bird had slept a little late, but by nine o'clock he was parking his car in the Finchley Road, weighing the pros and cons of whether or not to approach Big Jim Smith, without making the line of questioning obvious.

He was saved the trouble. Outside Big Jim's Car Mart, fourth in line in a group marked "Today's Snip", was a dark red Rover 2000, registration MTU 658H. Judging from the price tag, it was a bargain and unlikely to stay in Big Jim's car lot very long.

Chapter 4
Bells of Fire

Later on that morning, Detective Chief Superintendent Jim Marshall was gazing appreciatively at Miss Elizabeth Lloyd. With Braithwaite gone, she had received Mr Stratton's report, together with the exhibits of incendiary devices, and had felt that her instincts (not intuition – perish the thought) had been substantially reinforced. Stratton had disappeared into the wilds of Leicestershire, to apply his eagle eye to some further examples of the arsonist's art, leaving Miss Lloyd to deal with the matter as she thought best. He presumed that this meant waiting for Braithwaite's return; but he was wrong. She had gone straight to her father's friend, exuding determination.

'I told you there was something fishy about this. No wind, no motive, but incendiaries lined up by the dozen!' And she had elaborated on the theme while Jim used up several matches to get his personal incendiary going properly, and Elizabeth coughed politely as she avoided the smoke. He often used this ritual as a time-consuming ploy while he gave some thought to tricky problems. He knew that this chip off the old block could develop determination into obstinacy, and she would be difficult to stop, once she had the bit between her teeth. He had to keep her at a controlled canter before she broke into a full gallop.

She had threatened to go down to the scene of the crime – for he had had to agree with her original hunch that it was palpably a crime – and start her own investigation, on behalf of Martin, Smith,

26

Jenkins, Braithwaite, Stratton and the whole world of fire insurers in general. He made up his mind, pushed a button on his desk, and asked a constable to fetch Mike Bridgeman. His thoughts had drifted to the spectacle of Guy Sanders's reaction if he found someone snooping around in his territory without being informed, and he did not wish to have a head-on collision with H Division.

'Mike, this Hammersmith warehouse thing is hotting up (if you'll forgive the pun) and she wants to make further enquiries there. I have given up hope of persuading her to wait until her boss gets back, but have told her that it would be tactless, to put it mildly, to work independently of the police. So would you call Guy Sanders and tell him that Miss Elizabeth Lloyd, representing Martin, Smith, and Jenkins, would be coming down to offer help in the investigation.'

'Just like that, Sir? From what I've heard of Guy Sanders…'

'Of course not. Use tact. Tell him that she has experience and perhaps has records in her files that might be useful. Say that she's an expert in incendiaries. Play the psychology card, if you like.'

Jim Marshall was rewarded by a smile that would have justified a black lie, or even committing perjury for. If you can't fight 'em, join 'em.

Obviously useless to stop Elizabeth getting into the act, so she had better be chaperoned. Sanders would ensure that she did not get out of hand. And he had a lurking suspicion that the Arson Squad might be called in before this affair was over.

* * *

At three o'clock the same afternoon, Detective Superintendent Guy Sanders was reading Inspector David Thomas's report carefully, fingering his moustache as a form of punctuation, and registering grudging appreciation by a series of sniffs and grunts.

'Dammit, Thomas, you've made a point. You've connected the car at the warehouse with the men in the club. They've found two more of those bloody contraptions, by the way. We'll have to notify the Arson Squad, and request advice.' But Sanders clearly regarded this as a humiliating gesture, and he was not about to throw in the towel. Not yet.

He went on, 'Couldn't it have been just a coincidence? There needn't be a real mystery about a car parked in Adelaide Street. Look at the map – he pointed to the large map of London on his wall – it's more or less directly en route between the Wood Lane pub and Finchley Road, and what Londoner doesn't have his own short cut to avoid the main streets?'

'But why Adelaide Road?' David pointed to the relevant passage in his report. 'The car was empty. Where were the two men?'

'There you go. Christ all-bloody-mighty, how do you know for certain that there were two? The constable saw them hanging around, but he didn't see them in the car. This Smith fellow might have been alone, and after a few beers, hopped over the fence for a pee. And if that's what he was doing, he's not likely to draw a patrolling police-man's attention.'

'It won't wash. You'd be laughed out of court.'

Thomas looked deflated. 'I suppose you're right, Sir. But what else have we got? No motive, just a bunch of hand-made devices too incinerated to leave much of a clue, and about half an acre of ashes. There must be some point to all this.'

'I agree. But you can't assume that a bookie, a car salesman, a television shopkeeper, and a travel agent are all conspiring to subsidize the ratepayers of Hammersmith by substituting arson for an accident.'

At that moment the telephone rang. Sanders lifted the receiver and David observed that his manner suggested that he was speaking to a higher authority, such as Scotland Yard. Uncharacteristically, he murmured the occasional 'yes', or 'very well', and finally, 'we'll do our best, Sir'. Now it was his turn to look deflated.

'I don't believe it,' he growled.

David did not dare to interrupt Sanders's reverie.

'I must be out of my mind. Do someone a favour and you're Joe Muggins for life.'

'Something seems to be troubling you, Sir?'

Sanders erupted. 'Jesus H. Christ. If it's not bad enough trying to talk my own simple-minded force out of making fools of themselves, now I get lumbered with wet-nursing every flaming insurance investigator who fancies their luck as an amateur detective. You remember Stratton? He's gone up north somewhere, and now some woman in his outfit has got round Marshall to allow her to come down here to help us with our enquiries. "Help", he says. That was Inspector Bridgeman, of the Arson Squad, acting for Jim Marshall, who probably didn't want to ask me himself. Apparently he thinks this female is quite bright, because she read psychology at Cambridge. Psychology!' Sanders spat out the word, implying that this was not the necessary qualification for detective work, not in his book, and especially not from a woman.

'What's this woman like?' David ventured to ask.

'He didn't say. But I can guess. Thin-lipped intellectual, pointed nose, hair in a bun, wool socks, and what they call that uncertain age. But we'll have to be polite, if she's got Marshall's blessing. Her name's Lloyd, by the way, Elizabeth Lloyd.'

'Lloyd, of London? You must be joking.'

'Fact. But I doubt if she'll appreciate any of your devastating Welsh wit on that score.' Sanders paused, and looked thoughtfully at the ceiling, and turned to Thomas with a malevolent look in his eye. 'Come to think of it, it wouldn't be a bad idea if you took her under your wing. Someone's got to watch her. Bridgeman can't come, and it's not going to be me, as I don't fancy a crash course in psychology from some female blue-stocking.'

'I suppose I deserve this. Why isn't Inspector Bridgeman coming down? I would have thought the Arson Squad would have wanted to be on hand.'

Sanders smiled a happy smile. 'Inspector Bridgeman is having pangs of conscience. There have been other unexplained fires around London recently, and he hasn't bothered to enquire about them. Now he's trying to cover his tracks and he's got most of his men sorting through ashes in St Albans, Wandsworth, and Uxbridge. So you'll have to do it. Can't trust Constable Cheeseman in Adelaide Road after dark.'

* * *

The buzzer sounded. 'That'll be her now, I expect.' Sanders looked complacent. 'Miss Psychology is all yours. See that she doesn't poke her thin nose in too far, but don't give offence, otherwise we'll hear from the Yard, and you'll get a black mark on your record. She ought not to waste too much of your time, so you can use my office. Don't ever say I don't try to help.' He pressed the intercom button. 'Show Miss Lloyd in, Constable, and tell Mullins to have the Jag ready. I'm going to look into last night's robbery in the Bath Road.'

He regretted his decision immediately. Dressed in close-fitting blue slacks, a casual shirt, and a smart safari jacket, casually unbuttoned, Elizabeth Lloyd was ushered in by the Constable. Sanders was taken aback by his first encounter with, for him, a hitherto unknown species of psychology graduate. He quickly took in the full (rather than thin) lips, the pert (rather than long and thin) nose, the green eyes framed by an oval face and faultless complexion; and the cascading auburn hair that would have been wasted in a bun. He was irritated to observe David Thomas grinning as though he had just won first prize on the football pools. David took advantage of his chief's apparent consternation and spoke first.

'Good afternoon, Miss Lloyd. Welcome to H Division. I'm Detective Inspector David Thomas, and this is my boss, Superintendent Guy Sanders, who unfortunately has to go out on some urgent business, and he has asked me to look after you while you're down in our neck of the woods.'

'Hello. Thank you so much. My father's friend, Jim Marshall, assured me that I would be in good hands. I put on some casual clothes, in case we have to mess about at the warehouse site. I hope that's all right.'

David warmly reassured Elizabeth and ushered her into the best chair in the office. The Superintendent's attention, meanwhile, was caught by the driver's eye through the open door which the constable had pointedly neglected to shut. Accepting the inevitable, he made as dignified an exit as was possible under the circumstances, vowing silently that Thomas would pay for this.

David smiled. 'Pity the Super couldn't be with us, Miss Lloyd. Tell me, are you really from Lloyds? As an insurance investigator, that would make you Miss Lloyd of London, wouldn't it?'

'You are not exactly correct, Sergeant. Mr Stratton, whom I think you have met, asked me to do as I thought best, so here I am. But let us agree that you won't take down my particulars, and I won't ask you for your qualifications as a gag-writer. In other words, cool it.'

David took a firm grip. This redhead was, as the Americans say, Something Else. He was suitably humble. 'I'm awfully sorry. I should have known better. Quite improper of me, of course. When on duty, a policeman shouldn't make jokes, even bad ones, even in plainclothes...' and tried to smile disarmingly, and parodied a Welsh accent, '...look you.'

Elizabeth ran her eyes searchingly and deliberately over the representative of the Law, who she gathered was to be her companion during the next day or so, and decided that, in spite of the inauspicious start, it could have been worse. She saw a vigorous-looking young man, probably in his late twenties, with grey eyes, light brown wavy hair, and about six-feet tall. He was, she realized, quite good-looking, although not fitting into the stereotyped film star mould.

'I take it you're Welsh, with a name like that. At least we have something in common, even if it's not a very developed sense of humour or an authentic accent.'

David groaned inwardly. 'Look here, I really am sorry. No more cracks, I promise. Let me offer an excuse. I've had a hard time trying to convince my chief that there's more in this warehouse fire than meets the eye, and I'm hoping that you might be able to help, what with your experience in fire investigation, and your psychology, and all that. I apologise for the tasteless flippancy.' Seeking advice, he hoped, might not be seen as too transparent a piece of flattery, and he was pleasantly relieved when Elizabeth took his statement at face value, and seemed to thaw slightly.

'Fair enough. I'll lay my cards down too. My experience is not as extensive as might have been alleged by my father's friend. But I do know something about human behaviour – psychology, if you like – and that's the reason why I'm here. I would not pretend to be able to analyse the facts about incendiary devices, but it was my psychology that led to our looking for the evidence, simply because there was no explanation for setting fire on a wet night to a bunch of useless warehouses. Mr Stratton's report of the apparatus used confirms my suspicion – and don't call it intuition. You must agree that it doesn't make sense.'

'Any ideas on the motive, then?'

'No. But I am convinced that there is something highly suspicious here. But my boss doesn't want to pursue it.'

'Well, that is one thing we have in common. My boss doesn't think much of it either. So let us generate some mutual inspiration.' David thought that he was making progress in his rehabilitation with the lovely lady opposite him, but could not proceed as the buzzer sounded, and the duty constable said that a Mr Charles Woodhouse wished to see him.

David grinned at Elizabeth. 'Here's a bit of luck, we may get something out of this chap.' He explained briefly who Charlie was, and about the men in his club, and the funny business about the words of the song implying a *Hot Time in the Old Town Tonight*.

'Afternoon, Inspector.' Charlie was cheerful when he came in, and even more so when he saw Elizabeth. He almost ogled her.

David introduced Elizabeth. 'This is Miss Lloyd. She is in insurance. And don't say it! What brings you here?'

'Well, Inspector, after you'd gone last night, and I was clearing up the glasses and generally tidying up, I thought of something.'

'Don't tell me you've remembered the words.'

'No, but I've got evidence.' Charlie produced two grubby-looking papier-mâché table-mats from his pocket and laid them triumphantly on the table. David and Elizabeth stared at the slogans extolling the virtues of Young's Bitter.

'We give up. What the hell are you getting at?'

'They were singing different words. You know how the song goes, about bells ting-a-linging, and how sweetly you must sing, and the chorus will join in, and all that?' David nodded, although he wasn't sure of the words.

'They had different words, and there was something about fire bells.'

David looked Charlie squarely in the eyes. 'Would you repeat that last sentence again?' Charlie obliged.

'Sorry I didn't think of it last night, but my mind was on other things – like my licence; but this mat reminded me. See?' He turned the mats over and pointed to a confused scribbled inscription on the backs, written by a black felt pen.

David inspected them carefully, and was pleased to observe that Elizabeth was no less interested. The scribble consisted of several lines of long-hand, mostly over-written several times as if in correction, and one mat was almost entirely scored through in an apparent attempt at total obliteration. The other mat seemed like a re-write and some words were faintly legible, including "fire" in the top and second lines and what looked suspiciously like "Hammersmithian" in the third.

Charlie went on: 'When I was stacking the mats to see if they were too far gone to use again, I turned them over to wipe them, and then I remembered that I had seen Bill Castleman with his pen out, and his mates were laughing their heads off, and started singing *There'll Be a 'Ot Time in the Hold Town* – and I should have thought about it last night – they didn't start the first line with "When You Hear Those Bells"; they were singing "Those Fire Bells". And then I heard the same bit about fires later in the song. I thought you ought to know because you think they set fire to those warehouses, don't you?' Charlie paused for breath.

'Charlie, we have to be extremely cautious about circumstantial evidence. We have to guard against putting two and two together and making eight. But I appreciate your taking the trouble to tell us this.'

'I asked a few questions myself. Spoke to Joe Brooks – he's the landlord at The Three Crowns – and what d'you think? – Frank and the others didn't 'ave their usual last Thursday. Joe says they didn't come in. First time they've missed since he can remember. He's sure of it, because they didn't pay their subs for the Christmas orphans' fund.'

'Thank you very much indeed, Charlie, but be sure you don't mention this to anyone, if you wish to avoid a possible slander action.

But let me know if you remember anything else. Mind if I drop in for a pint next week?'

'On the 'ouse, Inspector.' Charlie felt that his licence was secure for another few years.

* * *

After Charlie had departed, with a self-satisfied grin on his face, David spoke first. 'Intriguing. But it doesn't get us any further. References to "fire" are still tenuous and could be coincidental, and "Hammersmithian" is not out of place in the Old Comrades club of that regiment.'

'You seem to accept defeat very easily.'

'My dear Miss Lloyd,' David put on his best smile, as he sensed that Elizabeth was acutely sensitive to possible patronizing. 'Intuition, hunch, call it what you will, but the police can only work on facts, unshakable evidence, and proof positive. Charlie's table-mats look hopeful to us, but are simply not good enough as evidence. They don't prove a thing.'

Then a constable knocked and walked in respectfully, handing an official envelope to David. 'This just came in from forensics,' he said. David scrutinized the report and showed it to Elizabeth. He was rewarded by a bright smile – brighter, he felt, than any that he had received so far. Succinctly, it confirmed what they already knew or had deduced. Each device consisted of a metal tube, and the contents had been a highly inflammable powder that had been sparked off by a simple detonator. This was just a thin plunger, kept in tension by a strong spring, which was released by the withdrawal of a pin or peg. The additional information was that the tubular parts were of no less than seven different diameters, and of three different kinds of steel.

'Not much significance in that, is there? Just that they weren't mass-produced.'

Elizabeth stood up, purposefully. 'For all your reservations about evidence, Mr Doubting Thomas, the vital feature about all this is the complete lack of motive. No point in inspecting the site, we know what happened. But we don't know why it happened. Why the hell should anyone manufacture primitive pipe-bombs just for fun? There must be a reason, and to take such trouble, it must have been a good reason. Motive, motive, motive, it's elementary.'

Sometimes in a man's life, a certain risk is justified. Nothing ventured, nothing gained. For purely non-professional reasons, he too had a motive: to gain Miss Lloyd's respect, at the very least. So he chose his words carefully.

'May I suggest that two heads working together might conceivably be better than two working separately? My devotion to evidence may seem exaggerated, but this doesn't necessarily imply that your approach is less important. So why don't we go and have a coffee and a doughnut, and talk it over, away from the atmosphere of H Division?'

From David's viewpoint, Elizabeth's five-second silence felt like ten. 'I suppose, Inspector, there are worse ways of proceeding. And you could do with some psychological treatment yourself.' It was her turn to call the shots. 'You could start by not addressing me as your "dear" Miss Lloyd.'

As he escorted her through the outer office, he observed a group of constables moving away from the intercom, and was red-faced to notice that he had forgotten to switch it off in Sanders's office.

Chapter 5
The Experiment

Hoping that his dark green MGB-GT might receive approval, David opened the door and warned about the low roof. For her part, Elizabeth hoped that he wasn't going to rabbit on about revs per minute, mag wheels, and gear ratios. Having lost two girlfriends already on that score, David refrained.

During the short drive, in the direction of the King's Road, where the coffee shop would be close to Elizabeth's flat, they learned a little about each other. David discovered that, although from a Welsh family, she had grown up in London, gone to school in Kent, studied at Cambridge, and had travelled in Europe for a few months before finding a job with Martin, Smith, and Jenkins. She had had the good fortune to be able to rent a mews flat in Chelsea, the property of an aunt who had gone back to Wales.

She was obviously intelligent, independent, and perfectly capable of keeping the opposite sex in its place.

For her part, she reassured herself that, if she was going to obtain the fullest benefit from the Law, an amicable gesture or two could pay dividends. Like herself, he was a non-smoker, a moderate drinker (or so he said) and rented a place in Shepherd's Bush, and spent some of his off-duty time following the fortunes of Queen's Park Rangers.

'I'm not against football…' she volunteered, '…but I do prefer cricket. My father used to drag me off to Lord's and I liked his explanations of the bowling tactics and the field placings, and the decisions of when or when not to declare,' she grinned. 'All psychology really.'

'You take your psychology everywhere, don't you? I hope you won't cross-examine me on my views of leg-side field-placings.'

Elizabeth found the conversation relaxing. 'I must sound awfully intense. But we happened to get round to sports and I used the dreaded word again. But don't you agree? Football is all instant tactics, and cricket is all cunning strategy.'

Discussion on the subject was halted as David manoeuvred his MG into a little side-street parking spot just off Chelsea's trendy King's Road, on one corner of which was The Colombian Coffee Shop. A ruana-clad waitress brought them the menu, which included seven varieties of Colombian coffee, and a good selection of pastries. Elizabeth chose a Cali Medium 'But I bet they're all the same. But at least here it will be black and strong. Which is just what I need right now.'

David ordered, adding a plateful of chocolate éclairs, and suggested that they could talk about the fire, perhaps deriving inspiration from the more casual surroundings. Elizabeth agreed, and launched forth.

'At risk of being rejected as an amateur, relying only on intuition, I would like your honest opinion on some thoughts I have had. I keep thinking about motive, and have been indulging in a little process-of-elimination approach. So here goes. First, we can eliminate revenge, because, as we know, the owners stood to benefit from the insurers – us. Second, it was not a political demonstration because the resulting ashes were meaningless. Yet this was not just casual arson, it was almost a scientifically-planned piece of arson. The incendiaries were pipe-bombs which, though primitively made, were nevertheless extremely effective, because they were planted with almost geometric precision.

'So one or two ideas crossed my mind. Suppose a gang has some incriminating evidence, in the form of documents, or had some materials that they had hidden in the disused huts, and wanted to destroy them because there was too much risk in trying to take them away. But this doesn't explain why there were ten devices, as it is unlikely that such booty or whatever would have been distributed among all ten huts.

'Also, it occurred to me that someone in the Hammersmith Council might be trying his luck at a little insurance swindle; but still, why ten, and why so thoroughly complete and well-organized? I keep coming back to this. Why ten, neatly in a row, or, to be exact, neatly arranged geometrically in rows?'

David pondered on this admittedly amateur analysis of motive. 'I'd still like an excuse to glean some evidence; specifically I'd like an excuse to examine that Rover with a spot of Sherlock Holmes detection – you know, finding in the car some clay that precisely matches the clay from the hut site. But I suppose Big Jim would have cleaned the car; and in any case, he has probably sold it by now, as one of Today's Snips. Forensics weren't much help. All they added was the fact that the pipes were all different and therefore must have been made primitively in some back-street workshop.'

Elizabeth looked up sharply, her eyebrows knitting slightly. She opened her mouth, closed it, took a breath, and ventured, 'With all due respect, as an amateur to a professional, are you sure that that deduction is completely logical?' David said he was all ears, but that he had complete faith in forensics.

'You are not following my line of thought. I don't wish to quibble, but even in a back-street workshop, an independent machinist is just as likely to simplify his work by standardizing on the tubes. Why choose different diameters every time?'

'He could have been just experimenting.'

'Exactly. The more I think of it...' Elizabeth stopped in mid-sentence. She swallowed hard, while David stared, puzzled.

'I think I've got it.'

'What, that our pipe-bomb manufacturer was experimenting?'

'No!' Elizabeth was raising her voice now, so that people in adjacent booths looked curiously at the debaters. 'It's more than that. Don't you see, the whole affair was an experiment! It explains everything. They would choose a place where there would not be much fuss – they couldn't go to a public rifle range or anything like that. And it wasn't enough to set off individual devices one at a time, as they were after something bigger. That's why there were so many. They were deliberately choosing different tube diameters and by observing the lined-up huts, they could see which type would do the most damage.'

David digested this analysis which, he had to admit, had not occurred to him, and he could see no flaw in the argument.

'Miss Elizabeth Lloyd, speaking as a professional to an amateur, as Professor Higgins would have said to Eliza in *Pygmalion*: "I think she's got it". You have given me enough ammunition to ask Sanders to keep the file open. And I'll elaborate on your theme. If this little gang is going to all this trouble, there has to be something pretty damned serious at the end of it. This is an elaborate performance for a minor experiment. And what are they experimenting for? It's got to be arson with a capital A.'

'I'm so glad, Inspector. Your psychology about the coffee-shop venue proves a point, I think. And I would like to correct a statement you just made. I, not you, have given you the excuse to pressure Sanders, so that the operative word is "we".'

David was only too anxious to oblige. 'Let's give it a shot, but on one condition for this we stuff.'

'What's that?'

'We drop the Inspector; you could even call me David, and let us celebrate our joint genius with some nourishment. This is your stamping ground, and you must have a favourite restaurant.'

Elizabeth smiled sweetly. She liked his name; it was Welsh too. 'Buy me a good cannelloni at Luigi's and I'll forget about the consultancy fee. You can also drop the Miss, but not in front of the Super, and not with a Welsh accent, look you.'

Basking in the radiance of – at last – a real smile, David would happily have treated the entire Italian army to a cannelloni dinner. And he hoped that this might not be the last opportunity.

Chapter 6
The Birds Have Flown

Next morning, David Thomas waited at H Division for Guy Sanders to arrive. He felt that, having made the connection with the Rover car, and with Charlie's table-mats, he could obtain an extension of time to continue investigation. He had promised to telephone Elizabeth if he made progress in that direction, and reflected that a whole week had passed since the fire, but only now were the police even interested in it.

They had parted at eleven o'clock the previous evening on terms that he would not have believed possible, given the inauspicious start. Basking in the joint euphoria of discovering a motive for setting fire to derelict sheds, they had vied with each other in crediting the wonders of applied psychology to the reliability of concrete evidence, and agreed to share the kudos equally. But he had warned Elizabeth that Sanders might find a flaw.

He had told her a little of his background – that although he was Welsh on both sides of the family (his mother was a Llewellyn), he had been brought up in Dorset, "Far From the Madding Crowd" in the village of Piddletrenthide, and had joined the police force to gain some excitement in the metropolis. Elizabeth repressed a chuckle at the name and David was pleased to note that she remarked on their joint Welsh heritage. Now, as he awaited his chief's arrival, he was apprehensive that Sanders might shoot their case down in flames. But, as he had hoped, for all his bluster, Sanders was not a fool. He grasped the essential features, and supported the request for further investigation.

'I did not at first share your boyish enthusiasm for making this a case of arson, but you have made your point well. If I didn't have to attend to Weinstein's diamond robbery, I'd get on to the case myself. You can do it, but proceed cautiously. Remember, we don't have the slightest grounds for charging anybody with anything right now, unless you are lucky enough to find some forensic clues in that Rover, and prove that Big Jim, as you call him, was actually in charge at the time. Eastwick and Dudman did nothing wrong, as far as we know, but at least you would recognize them now. One of the troubles with arson is that, unlike the so-called smoking gun, the evidence usually goes up with its own smoke.

'I think your best plan is to attend to Big Jim, and keep a close eye on him. A constable or two can keep tag on the others, and we'll see if they get together, and we might be lucky if they burst into that bloody song. Find out if any of them have a record.' Sanders actually beamed at Thomas, who was dutifully appreciative.

'Thank you, Sir. But there is something that I have to ask you. What about Miss Lloyd? I have more or less undertaken to keep her informed of progress in the case.'

Sanders ejaculated: 'Bloody hell, she's really done a job on you, hasn't she? Can't say I blame you, but since when has the Metropolitan Police Force had to call on the services of an amateur? This is real life, not Sherlock Holmes fiction. I suppose it's different when she is a ravishing redhead, crafty as a truckload of monkeys, and has friends in Scotland Yard.'

'With respect, Sir, I would agree with your first point, substitute "highly intelligent" for the second, and pass on the third.'

Sanders ruminated on the third point, remembering that Miss Lloyd had indeed come into the case with Scotland Yard's implied blessing, and furthermore, without mentioning the dreaded word, she had helped to provide some logic to the whole affair. Capitulation with dignity was called for.

'I suppose we shall have to go along with this for a while, and I'll give a full report to Bridgeman at the Arson Squad. From their point of view, she is still with us, and Marshall will play bloody hell if he thinks we've ostracised her. So make sure she doesn't interfere with proper procedure, and keep her amused. Off you go.'

* * *

David telephoned Elizabeth, warning her about proper procedure, and informed her of a way in which she could help, thus fulfilling Sanders's request to keep her amused. He would attend to Big Jim, the constables could find out about Eastwick and Castleman, who lived nearby, and Elizabeth could visit Walter Dudman's television shop, as she lived only a few stations from Putney on the District Line, or could catch a No. 30 bus, and she could be inconspicuous. Elizabeth was suitably pleased. They agreed that they would meet in the Colombian Coffee House at around four o'clock.

Dressed casually, Inspector David Thomas entered the showrooms of Big Jim's Car Mart, only to discover that Big Jim was out. A young salesman tried to look important, quickly launching himself into a sales pitch. 'You couldn't have come at a better time. We've just taken delivery of some one-owner cars, low mileage, and in immaculate condition.' He did not mention that the one owner had been a cut-price car-hire company, that the low mileage was because the odometer dial had been round once already, and the fresh paint covered several well-concealed areas of plastic metal. David showed interest.

'Can I see some, while we're waiting for Mr Smith?'

'I wouldn't wait. He's gone up north, to the car auctions; took the

Rover. Sometimes he's away for days. We move a lot of cars.'

'Trade is good, then?'

'It's all right, but not like it was. All second-hand... sorry, previously-owned... now. We used to have a good dealership, had the Austin-Morris agency for the whole district, but those bastards across the road pretty well killed that.' The salesman pointed to a display of foreign cars across the road, featuring German, Italian, and, prominently, Japanese models. 'They undercut him and they've pushed him out of the new family and sports car market.'

'So Big Jim is not as big as he was, then?'

'You could say that. Bloody shame, I call it. Jim's not a bad bloke, but he has to be careful with the money these days. I don't get the commission I used to. He has to watch every penny. Here he is, dragging around auctions, when he used to just lift the 'phone and the suppliers would be on his doorstep. Now he watches those Japanese cars turn over by the dozen. Sad. He gambles too – goes to the White City dogs every Thursday.'

'Does he do much driving himself?'

'Not so much now. He was a good driver, though, and still is. Used to do a bit of rallying. Could have been a pro race-driver. Might have done him more good. Hey, didn't you want to see some cars? I can handle any sale, and Big Jim won't be back for days.'

'I drove past a few days ago and saw a nice red Rover 2000. Can I see it?'

'You're out of luck. That was a real give-away. We stuck a tag on it at six o'clock Monday evening, and we sold it at 9.30 next morning. Foreign bloke walked in and took it without hardly looking at it. I told Jim it was under-priced but he told me not to interfere with his judgement.'

'Do you think Jim could find me a nice Rover?'

'He might, if you can get in touch with him. Not sure where he is right now, but you might try the auction at Cooper's Farm, near Melton Mowbray, just off the motorway. But I don't know for sure.'

Having drawn a blank, David cut his losses and returned to H Division, argued about the matter of his contributions to the coffee club being overdue, and found that the other constables on the case were back.

Constable Dennis Brooks had been sent to check on Frank Eastwick, and had also drawn a blank. He lived alone, renting two rooms from his landlady in a side-street just off King Street. When the constable called, Frank had already left for the day, and wasn't expected back. Mrs Perkins said he always went out and was late home on Thursdays, but she didn't know where he was now. Yes, he was a nice gentleman, but wasn't married. Always paid his rent regular, even in advance. She hoped that he wasn't in any trouble.

Constable Brooks had managed to elicit a little further information from Mrs Perkins, with creating the impression that the matter was more than a routine enquiry about a minor indiscretion at the track. Frank had recently entertained some foreign visitors, but they were very respectable. Might have been German, she thought, as they kept saying "ya". They had visited several times, usually in the mornings; sometimes there were two, sometimes three. She had had the impression that Frank had been negotiating something or other with them, and that he was well pleased with the result, as he had paid her quite a bit extra for the rent.

While Brooks was making his report, his colleague, Constable Stan White, who had been assigned to interview Bill Castleman, joined them. 'Looks as though we're both out of luck today,' he began. 'My man has gone away for two weeks on travel agency business. But I had a chat with his assistant, Miss Clatworthy, attractive lady, if I may say so.' He looked pointedly at David, as if to dare him to challenge the propriety of fraternizing with the opposite sex while on duty.

'What did Miss Clatworthy divulge?'

White referred to his notes. 'William Castleman is in his early fifties and looks like this.' He produced a glossy photograph, showing a man with blond hair, florid complexion, and wearing horn-rimmed spectacles. 'This is from his publicity brochure. His eyes are a gorgeous blue, according to Miss Clatworthy. He was in the Navy during the War and afterwards, then spent some time out East, and used his knowledge of the Orient to establish his travel business. Quite a cultured sort of bloke, listens to jazz music, and likes poetry, even dabbles in it himself, she says.'

'Did she say where he went?'

'Booked a flight to Paris. His Far East business has fallen off, and he's trying to work up the European trade, for the summer season. After Paris, his ticket was open-dated to Rome, and then back to London. He didn't come in this morning.'

'Today's Thursday. I wonder if he will be at the club tonight to say goodbye and join them for a sing-song. You say he likes poetry. We may have found our lyric-writer for re-hashes of old jazz tunes.'

With that hopeful speculation, David Thomas left and homed in on the Colombian Coffee Shop in the King's Road.

* * *

Elizabeth Lloyd was very proud of the little notebook she had purchased especially for her assignment. She had already written three entire pages on the subject of Mr Walter Dudman, proprietor of the radio and television shop of the same name at 54, Putney High Street. Flushed with her success in arriving at a plausible motive, she was now keen to demonstrate to David (who, she suspected, regarded her moment of inspiration as a stroke of luck) that her capabilities extended into practical, as well as theoretical, sleuthing work.

Her concern was unnecessary. By this time, David was well and truly smitten. Hitherto, he had tended to regard girls as either pretty, but not too bright; or homely types who were good cooks but boring, or intellectuals who were overbearing. But this Elizabeth! She was apparently gifted in more ways than one. For her, he would cheerfully do the cooking himself, and even make the bed.

When Elizabeth walked in, he was idly wondering how the waitress could serve all day wearing a woollen ruana, and speculated that there was probably nothing much underneath. Reading his mind, she was in a serious mood. 'Would you like to hear about Walter Dudman, or are you too busy studying the female form?' she said.

David hastily changed the direction of his attention. 'Of course… I hope you've had better luck than we have. Big Jim's gone up north on a second-hand car-hunting jaunt; Bill Castleman's gone to Europe for a fortnight; and Frank Eastwick was not at home. Did you see Walter?'

'No I didn't. What's more, he's going away tomorrow too. I went to his shop, preparing to enquire about having my television repaired, and found his wife standing in. We started to chat, and as business was not exactly brisk I was able to sit back and make mental notes. All I had to do was to say "Oh?" or "Really?" or "I know" every now and again. She seemed a little concerned about him and showed me his picture. Here he is, aged 53, thickset, overweight a bit, medium brown hair, blue eyes, heavy moustache. They have two children, who have both left home, so she misses her Walt when he's away.'

'Interesting – all our suspects are about the same age, which I suppose we could have assumed anyway, from their old Comradeship.'

'Walter and Gladys – that's her name – live in East Cheam, and have had this shop since the end of the War. Walter learned a lot about radio in the army as he was in signalling, so he started his business with Gladys in 1946. At first they did very well too, but trade has slackened off during the past few years. He doesn't believe in rentals, but the television rental business cut into his trade, or people don't have their sets repaired so much these days. They simply buy new. But they are quite happy to chug along, and Walter's repair work is all right because he's so good at it. He has a natural gift for mechanics and electronics. He should have been a scientist, according to Gladys.

'He's a happy-go-lucky chap. That's why Gladys married him. Walter is always good company. He likes to joke, and she likes his humour. But he's been more serious lately, and has spent more time with his bows and arrows.'

'His what?'

'Bows and arrows. You know what they are, surely? Archery. He was shot in the leg towards the end of the War, which curtailed his sporting activities. But he still likes to get out in the open air, and so he took up archery, which doesn't need leg-work. He became quite good at it, and that's why he's leaving tomorrow. He's off to Copenhagen as a member of a British archery team which has challenged a combined team from the Scandinavian countries. Gladys thinks he's almost up to Olympic standard. He took the whole day off today, to practise at his range in Virginia Water so as to be in good form for the match.' Elizabeth paused for breath. 'How have I done?'

'Couldn't have done better myself,' David reassured her, thinking in fact that she had probably done better. There are occasions when a girl asking questions has a definite advantage. Some women would unwind to another woman but shut up like a clam to a prying male.

David considered the situation. 'I think our best course is to check up with the barman at the Old Comrades Club, as he might know their whereabouts. Apart from Big Jim, who is up north, the other three could conceivably be in town tonight. Let me drop you off at your flat, I'll nip over to Hammersmith to see Charlie Woodhouse and, with luck, our male voice group. The club is strictly male, and in any case, I wouldn't expose you to that kind of company or their vocabulary. But then, if you are willing, I could pick you up at around 8.30 or nine, and we could have dinner again. How does that sound?'

Elizabeth frowned. 'Your idea of chaperoning an interfering insurance investigator does cover a wide field. Can you claim this on expenses?'

'Well, yes; but I don't intend to.'

'Good. Then we'll go Dutch.'

* * *

'Thought you'd be back,' said Charlie affably as, just after 7 p.m., David ordered two pints of Young's Best Bitter. 'Good 'ealth. I suppose you've come along to see our male voice choir. They're not here yet.'

'Never mind, we can chat a bit while we're waiting.'

David filled in the time by diplomatically pumping Charlie for further details of the backgrounds of the four men. Predictably, most of the information concerned their army careers and experiences. Walter Dudman had been the only regular soldier, and had met Frank Eastwick out East before the latter had been taken prisoner. Frank had met Bill Castleman, one of the few survivors of the Prince of Wales naval fiasco, because he was in hospital, in the same Japanese prisoner-of-war camp, after being captured in Singapore. Big Jim had joined the group only recently, about five years ago, because he and Walter had become friendly when they developed a business connection involving repair and installation of car radios.

As they chatted, David became a little apprehensive. He checked his watch against the bar-room clock, thoughtfully provided by Young's Brewery, and reminded Charlie that time was getting along, and didn't Frank and his pals assemble before 8.30?

'Blimey, you're right! Didn't notice the time. They're usually here by now, except sometimes Big Jim. Come to think of it, one or two of them should have been here about the time when you got here.'

'Is that unusual?'

'Can't remember the last time when at least two of 'em didn't turn up early on a Thursday. 'Ere…' Charlie assumed a mildly aggressive tone. '…'Ave you been upsetting my regulars and putting 'em off?'

'I assure you Charlie, that our enquiries have been most discreet, and even if they heard about them, which I seriously doubt, there was no way to connect the line of questioning with your club. All we are trying to do at the moment is to trace the movements of everyone who was around the area of Adelaide Street last Thursday. These four appear to be possible suspects, but we have absolutely no firm evidence. I'm telling you all this in the strictest confidence, of course.' David glanced pointedly in the direction of Charlie's licence, proudly framed, on the wall by the clock, to ensure Charlie's discretion.

The clock hands were now moving past 9 o'clock. 'Do you think they might be over at the Three Crowns?'

'Might be. But they always come here first.'

'I'd better try it out. See you later, perhaps.'

* * *

Joe Brooks, proprietor of The Three Crowns, revealed the fascinating information that not only had Frank Eastwick and company not been in for their usual that evening, but he knew for a fact that Bill Castleman was going for a dirty weekend in Paris, and two of the others had called in yesterday for a lunchtime pint, and had paid up their Christmas Orphans Fund to cover the next month in advance.

David returned to H Division briefly to make this rather negative report, and decided that it was time to apply a little more psychology to the problem. He knew exactly where to find some expert advice.

He pushed the bell marked Lloyd in the cobblestoned mews. Elizabeth lived in an upstairs flat, with sky-blue window frames setting off soft reds and browns in the old brickwork, now enriched in colour under the yellow light of a simulated gas-lamp that still added a genuine Victorian charm to the area. Elizabeth looked down from the window. 'It's almost ten o'clock. You're late.'

'I'm sorry.' David was apologetic, but pleased to note that Elizabeth had hoped for an earlier meeting. 'Our birds seem to have flown. To the four corners of the globe for all we know.'

'Come up and tell me about it. The door is unlocked.'

Settling himself in a comfortable wing-backed chair, David accepted a generous glass of Bristol Cream. Elizabeth, he thought, looked superb. She had done something to her hair (or was it the light) which brought out the richness of the auburn, tinged with chestnut; and she wore a dark green dress, cut in simple lines, which did her no harm. She was dressed for candlelight and violins, and David congratulated himself that he had put on a decent suit.

'Correct me if I'm wrong, but would it be in order to suggest some French cuisine, or perhaps Hungarian, this evening – or what's left of it? There's precious little to report from my end, and as I said, our quartet have all gone away.'

'Well, Inspector Thomas, we're both off the hook and off duty. I would fancy some real Hungarian, none of the local Irish stew laced with paprika. I know a lovely place in Pont Street.'

'I can hardly wait. Do they serve leeks?'

'Not even Hungarian leeks. Hang on a jiff. Don't you want to hear the Test Match scores from Port of Spain before we leave?'

David mentioned that he had actually had other things on his mind, and that as the West Indies were likely to pile up a huge score, he did not wish to know.

'I must see if David Gower or Ian Botham are doing anything. I think they're super – in different ways, of course. It won't take a minute – they give us a news flash just after the ten o'clock headlines.'

The measured tones of the B.B.C. newscaster were just finishing the headlines: '...three more tankers are still immobilized in the Straits of Hormuz, which remains closed to shipping. And here is a late news item that has just come in. On the Dorset-Wiltshire border, fire brigades from Salisbury, Shaftesbury, and Blandford are rushing to the scene of a mysterious fire that broke out about an hour ago at a disused army camp near the village of Ashmore. No lives are believed to have been lost, nor anyone injured, as the camp is reported to have been totally deserted for several years. But the camp will almost certainly be destroyed, so intense was the unaccountably sudden blaze. At this time, there is no information or explanation as to the cause of the sudden blaze.'

Chapter 7

Fire Over England

Early on Friday morning, David picked up Elizabeth at her flat. Their Hungarian meal the night before had ended with a quick coffee and a Tokay. They were both convinced that the fire had been started by the suspected arsonists from Hammersmith who were conspicuously absent from their customary Thursday meeting at the Club. They agreed with hearty unanimity that a prompt visit to the Dorset-Wiltshire border was indicated, and that David could provide the transport, subject to Detective Superintendent Guy Sanders's agreement.

They presented themselves at H Division before eight o'clock, hoping that Sanders might be in early. David had thought out his justification for deserting the Hammersmith beat. With his local background, he could contribute some special knowledge of the probable cause to the local police force in Dorset. This could save them a great deal of time and trouble, even though there was no further headway on the motive. He could also provide descriptions of possible suspects, but the snag was that the C.I.D. Arson Squad, in the shape of Detective Inspector Mike Bridgeman, might want to take over control of the case.

They were pleasantly surprised to learn from the Station Sergeant that Sanders had been at his desk for half an hour, and had been on the telephone continuously. At that very moment he was speaking to his opposite number at the County Police Headquarters in Dorchester. David pushed his head round Sanders's door and was beckoned in. He gently eased Elizabeth in with him.

Sanders finished his long distance conversation '...will be all right then. I'll certainly ensure that my man doesn't tread on any toes, and I'll warn him not to practise his perverted sense of humour. Oh, there's just one thing. He'll probably have a lady with him. She's an insurance investigator who has been helpful to us in our local probe that I told you about. Who knows, she might be able to help, and Thomas will see that she doesn't get in anybody's way. I would not have called you unless I thought it was serious. Yes, it could be more than a local matter. Thank you very much. I'll keep in touch and you will also hear from the Arson Squad.'

He looked up at David and Elizabeth. 'I guessed you'd be here early. I heard the news last night too, and I've already taken some action. I called the Ministry of Defence, but they're not awake yet – no need, I suppose when we don't have a war on our hands. When I do get through, I'll clear the way for you, in case you find the site surrounded by a cordon of armed infantry. Bridgeman and his boys are still following up St Albans and the other two fires, and think they are on to something, so they'll let us go along as it takes the pressure off them.'

David smiled. 'You're ahead of us. I was going to ask your permission to stay on the job, as there seems to be an obvious link through the similarity of circumstances.' Elizabeth interjected: 'Identical, not similar. Derelict, deserted, groups of wooden huts, in both cases; and both razed to the ground in short order.'

David continued: 'And although there was almost certainly at least a breeze – Ashmore is a windy area, on high ground at the edge of Cranborne Chase – it rained heavily two or three nights ago, and those huts would have been soaked. This was no accidental discarded cigarette stub.'

Sanders had moved from his previous scepticism. 'I agree. Get down there right away – you won't need much urging, but take it easy with that hot rod of yours. I don't want the Dorset Police complaining of Londoners abusing the Highway Code in their territory. As for you, young lady,' he looked seriously at Elizabeth. 'I meant what I said about your not getting in their way. As an insurance investigator, you have a flimsy reason for sticking your nose in. But I think you're smart enough to realize that you can't go tearing off on your own on a matter like this. Inspector Thomas has got the message loud and clear, and he knows that he'd better not let you out of his sight.'

David assured Sanders that he had no intention of allowing Miss Lloyd to get much further than arm's distance, much less out of sight.

'Oh yes, cherchez la femme and all that, and very nice too. But I'm bloody serious, and I'm talking to both of you. You're going down to do a job of work and no hanky-panky. Furthermore, I've tried to get hold of Bridgeman, and he's out, following up some clues on what his department calls related matters. He's taken most of his staff with him, by all accounts, probably has a conscience about the other fires he never bothered about. But, Miss Lloyd, you may be able to help. I was extremely dubious about your presence two days ago, but you did give us the first glimmer of at least an idea for a motive; although I'm damned if I can see how much farther along we are in that respect.'

Elizabeth thanked Guy Sanders warmly for his encouragement and gave him her best smile. He nodded and thought to himself that if he was in Thomas's shoes, he might not have heard the instruction about no hanky-panky. 'Do you think…' she said, 'that Jim Marshall, I'm sorry, Detective Chief Superintendent Marshall, at Scotland Yard, might be informed? I'd like him to know that I'm still on the case and that his faith in me is justified.'

'Already in hand, Miss. Neither of you need me to tell you that we only have to find one incendiary device of similar design to link the two arson incidents – and perhaps more if Bridgeman finds anything – without any shadow of doubt. If we do find one, the Yard has to be in, as they have to coordinate if the crimes are in different parts of the country; and of course, in a serious case, their presence is essential.

'Before you came in, by the way, I relayed to the Dorset police a description of what they should look for. Down there, arson is most unusual, and I don't think they would search very hard, unless we encourage them. Even if they found a piece of pipe, they might not attach too much significance to it. So that's in hand, and the Army will be asked to co-operate too. With any sort of luck, they may have found something by the time you get there. They will want to keep the evidence for the time being, naturally, but it will be enough at this stage for you to identify it to your own satisfaction.

'And if there is something, inform me immediately. Our four birds have certainly pulled a fast one on us. I'll chase up their records. All we have so far is that Big Jim was fined for doing a ton-up on the A1, and Eastwick is an honest bookie. I didn't expect Eastwick and Dudman to have left London; and you, Miss Lloyd, thought Castleman was in Paris, while you, Thomas, were sure Big Jim was up north. Of course, right now, we can't be sure of anything, and we have no evidence whatsoever even to connect the four of them in anything more than casual friendship.'

'What about the coincidence of the song and those notes on the back of the beer-mat? And isn't there a vague indication of a common interest, admittedly for different reasons, with Japan?'

'All coincidence. That's not evidence. Now, off you go, I'll take care of the staff work at this end, and try to locate at least a couple of our alleged arsonists. Let me hear from you soon.'

* * *

57

They headed for the West Country, across Chiswick Bridge, through Richmond, to hit the new M3 Motorway at Sunbury, quickly leaving behind the red bricks and chimney pots of the Middlesex suburbs. They enjoyed the freshness of an exhilarating March morning, and the trunk highway provided much rural scenery, often with a grandstand view. Early flowers graced the embankments, patches of primroses, celandines, and dandelions formed patchworks of yellow against the spring green of the grass verges.

Nature had quickly come to terms with the new problem that had been thrust upon her. The scars of exposed excavations had disappeared, the new road was becoming as much a part of the English scene as the fields and hedges of the Enclosures had once obliterated the open heaths and common lands. They passed the occasional kestrel hovering over the landscaped borders and ditches that had regenerated populations of tasty vermin.

'I remember,' David began, 'when it took three to four hours, at least, to drive up from Blandford, depending how often you broke the speed limits on the old A30. Now it only takes two or maybe half an hour more. And that's something to remember if we have to check any alibis. If our Gang of Four did set the Ashmore fire, and made sure it was well alight, they could have been back in London before the Shaftesbury fire brigade was on the site. Eastman and Dudman could have arrived home late with a plausible story for their respective ladies – drinks with the boys, etcetera, and covering for each other; and Big Jim could have been their wheel man, back to London, and on up north. Castleman has already made up his own story.'

Elizabeth emerged from a bucolic reverie. 'Let us apply some grey matter. This fresh air should clear our heads, and try to think of a motive, or the absence thereof. Let us assume that we have not one, but at least two, unexplained fires, carefully planned, and –

if my experiment theory is correct – to provide our arsonists with some practice. Two things strike me as significant: to come all this way: first, the ultimate target must be important; second, it won't necessarily be in London.'

'So where would this target, as you call it, be? Why should our four men, who so far seem not to have the slightest suspicion of criminal records, wish to commit first degree arson, and against whom?'

'If I knew that, we would not be wasting our time going to Dorset. Think! What do we know about our four suspects? Other than a common dislike of Japan, what could be the binding link between them apart from the nostalgia of misspent time in the army?'

David negotiated the branch off the M3 to the old A30. 'I've thought of one link, but it's not much. The finances of three of them have taken a beating lately; and Eastwick's bookie business might not be all that cheerful. We do know that Big Jim's business has declined badly; Castleman's tourist trade has fallen off, and Dudman's repair business is not too bright. All hearsay, of course, and we could be wrong. But they could all use insurance money.'

'At least Walter's wife did not seem to indicate desperation. She just complained, mildly, without malice, that Walter spent more time these days with his bows and arrows than was good for running his business, and all she could do was sell things, not repair them. His heart didn't seem to be in the business as it used to be. But nothing definite.'

'Come to think of it, Castleman's jaunt to the Continent doesn't look like the action of a man who is hard up.'

'That's irrelevant. In the travel business, agents get discounts, even free travel. I doubt if it costs him more to spend the weekend in Paris with a girlfriend than it would to stay home.'

'Changing the subject, did you notice that Sanders referred to you as an insurance investigator when he was on the phone to Dorset?

That was decent of him. I think he's taken a liking to you; after a shaky start.'

'Yes, wasn't he a dear? Matter of fact, I've taken a liking to him too.'

'Steady on, old girl; you hardly know him, and he swears like a trooper – which, I think, he once was.'

'Oh, I don't mind salty language. Billy Graham said it was all right for President Nixon, so Guy Sanders can be forgiven. It's probably only a cover. He's a lot softer than he would like you to think. And one thing's for sure: by his action this morning, he is on top of his job. Would you like to hear me swear?'

'No, I would not.'

'Don't be stuffy. Keep your eyes on the road.'

'You're right about Sanders. He's a good sort; he wouldn't be where he is now if he was just a flat-footed copper. Listen, let me try a wild one on you. We're looking for a common denominator. Let me get back to the Japanese coincidence. Frank Eastwick had a reputation as a Jap-hater, dating back to his prisoner-of-war days in Malaysia or Thailand? Bill Castleman was in the same camp. Now take Big Jim. If you were in his shoes, which foreign cars would irritate you most? Toyota and Datsun, flooding the British market. That Datsun sports car could have ruined his British sports car business. Dudman could have suffered in the same way with the competition from Japanese television sales from competitors because his customers rushed to buy them instead of having their old ones repaired.'

David waited for the verdict, as he manoeuvred his MGB carefully around the centre of Salisbury, to hit the road to Blandford. He explained that this was a more scenic approach to Ashmore than the direct A30 via Shaftesbury.

'I wouldn't dismiss that as an impossibility, but it does seem like a bit of special pleading. But I can't think of anything better. Supposing they do turn out to be a bunch of anti-Japanese psychopaths, where does that get us?'

'They could be practising to destroy the Datsun container terminal at Liverpool or wherever the shipments arrive in the country. That would give some satisfaction to Big Jim. But the same argument could apply to Walter Dudman, except that in his case, it would be a warehouse full of Sonys and Panasonics.'

'But what about Bill Castleman?'

'We could assume, for the sake of argument, that the decline in his Far East tour business was directly responsible for the fall in his earnings; and this re-kindled an old hatred.'

'Sounds rather far-fetched. The same applies to Frank Eastwick, but his business is unconnected with Japan. Those foreign visitors that Mrs Perkins mentioned – they weren't Oriental. Even if she didn't see them in the light, she would know "Ja" from "Hai".

'How did you know the Japanese for "Yes?" '

'I knew one or two Japanese girls at college. One of them taught me a few words, but I never troubled to learn the language properly. Her English was too good. May I ask how you learned to say "Hai"?'

'We used to hold geisha parties in Piddletrenthide.'

David had the satisfaction of at last producing a genuine chuckle from Elizabeth, and they were in good spirits as, on the last leg of the journey, they turned up the B3081, negotiated the village of Sixpenny Handley, skimmed through Tollard Royal, and approached the village of Ashmore, 800 feet up on a little peninsula of rolling downs just inside the Dorset county boundary, and where the former War Office had once decided to build an army training camp.

David rounded the Ashmore Pond, passed the White Hart Inn, and followed the road signposted Fontmell Magna. Soon, on a small plateau of downland, there came into view what was left of Ashmore Training Camp, now – like a certain warehouse in west

London – consisting of only a few ashes, with a few fingers of smoke still rising, as if someone had dropped a few gigantic cigarette butts. Yesterday's rain had stopped, but everything was still wet. Silhouetted as it was against the soft dull greens of the woodlands and open fields of the Cranborne Chase countryside, it made a grim sight.

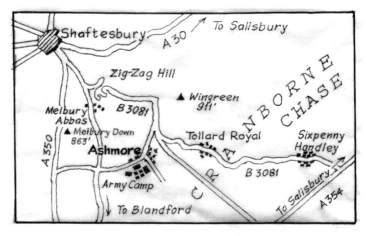

One of the highest villages in Southern England.
Ashmore is unusually isolated even from its surrounding neighbours.

Standing by the main gate was a small cluster of uniformed men, some in khaki, others in the dark navy blue of the local fire brigade. Their vehicles were parked along the lane, the army's two jeeps, the firemen's bright red fire engine which stood out in stark contrast with the grey dullness of the background. A few villagers completed the discussion group. One of them was addressing the army officer, a captain, who looked around the scene somewhat vacantly, as this had been the first assignment that had taken him out of his Admin. Office for the last two years.

'P'raps theese'll give us back theese vields, now thick camp be burned down. B'aint no use to ee now. Bloody scandal buildin' on good grazin' land when Blandford Camp be only vive mile away. Thee 'asn't got nar excuse now.'

The captain did his best to ignore the comment, half of which he could not understand, and was relieved to see David and Elizabeth, providing him with an excuse not to answer difficult questions. 'I'm afraid there's been a fire,' he declared. (Laughs from the rural chorus.) 'This is, correction, was No. 748 Army Training Camp, and some imbecile set fire to it last night. Your colleagues have gone. As soon as they established it was arson, they left me in charge, and went off with the spoils to – I think – Shaftesbury Police Station.'

'The spoils? What exactly do you mean?' David asked, trying not to appear excited.

'Just inside the gate, the police found what they alleged to be an incendiary device. Just a piece of pipe. They were under instructions to look for something of the kind, as they didn't waste time examining it closely.'

David checked with the locals as to the shortest way to Shaftesbury. 'Down through Washers Pit, then turn right. But don't go that way,' the unofficial spokesman declared.

'Why not?' David enquired, mystified at the apparent contradiction.

''Cause t'other way be quicker then the short road, go down Zig-Zag Hill.'

David grabbed Elizabeth's arm. She had been an amused witness to rural logic as well as the dialect. They set off to the police station in Shaftesbury, where they were told that, under instructions from the Chief Constable of Dorset, the device had been passed straight on to Dorchester for forensic testing.

David explained to the local Inspector that it was vital for the C.I.D. Arson Squad to be able to compare, as soon as possible, the devices from both fires, to establish beyond doubt that they were by the same hand.

'Dunno what the hurry is. You're not expecting another bit of arson immediately are you?'

'Well no. But I'm extremely worried. The next fire could be worse, and could happen any time, and because of this particular incident, apparently anywhere. I'd be grateful if you would pass on our concern to your Chief Constable, and impress upon him that there would be considerable advantages to us all if we could coordinate our efforts. Not...' David hastened to add, ...'that we doubt the efficiency of your forensic people, it's just that we feel that some duplication could be avoided.'

'I understand, Inspector. It seems that you know what it looks like, but we do have a rough sketch.' He produced a small file, with typewritten notes. The sketch was far from rough and something caught David's eye. Unlike the incendiary devices found in west London, the Ashmore tube had stamped into the metal, quite clearly, the inscription "Made in England".

Chapter 8

Nightingales?

Elizabeth reminded David that, English-made pipe-bombs notwithstanding, it was past lunch-time, and gladly taking the hint, he steered down the back lanes below Shaftesbury to Ye Olde Two Brewers at the bottom of the famous Gold Hill, where they serve a fair pub lunch, Eldridge Pope's beer, and in the summer, from its garden, is a near-perfect view of Melbury Hill and the Blackmore Vale, a fair sample of England's lush greenery at its best. He took the opportunity, as soon as Elizabeth was suitably equipped with a gin and tonic, of telephoning Sanders to report on the irritating habits of the Dorset Constabulary.

Sanders was less concerned than he expected. 'Don't worry about the delay,' he said. 'While you've been touring the West Country, we've been doing some police work. Not half as romantic as what you've been doing, but effective.'

David murmured encouragement. The Chief Inspector must be on to something.

'We've checked on all four suspects. Smith is, as far as we know, somewhere up north; Castleman went to Paris yesterday; and as soon as you left this morning, I found an excuse to telephone both Dudman and Eastwick. Both of them came in late, after midnight last night, later than their usual arrival home. Tried again this morning to find that Dudman caught the S.A.S. flight to Copenhagen this morning.'

David observed, respectfully, that in all four cases, the gentlemen in question could have still been in Dorset as late as 9.30 or so the previous evening. Sanders was sceptical. 'It would be stretching things a bit. Also, they've found some bits of pipe at St Albans and Wandsworth, and although a month's neglect hasn't helped, they think they can establish that the same tools were used to make those pipes and the Wood Lane ones too. Coincidentally, there is a proximity to the homes of our suspects.'

Interestingly, the unexplained fires were located near the homes of the four suspects.

'Before I come back, would you permit me to make some cursory enquiries to see if I can establish a closer connection, other than the similarity of the incendiary devices? Oh, and another thing, would you ask your forensic people if they can discern an inscription "Made in England" on any of the pipes?'

'All right, but you'd better be back at H Division first thing in the morning. I take it that Miss Lloyd is still with you. I hope she's insured against all risks.' Sanders chuckled as he put down the phone, pleased with his parting innuendo.

Over generous portions of steak-and-kidney pud., voted at least on a par with cannelloni and pasta, Elizabeth had drifted into some deep thinking, and finally plunged. 'You were theorizing that our four men just might have been down here, instead of where they all claim they were. Isn't it possible that they could all have travelled to Dorset together? Big Jim only said he was going north. We were only told that Castleman was going to Paris. Smith could have picked up Castleman, and, for that matter, Eastwick, even in the Rover that was supposed to be sold, then headed west, picked up Dudman at his archery place – Virginia Water is on the A30 – we passed through it. Then after setting fire to the camp, which would not have taken long, they could have returned as quickly as they came. We've already proved ourselves that two hours' fast driving is all that it needs.'

David was impressed, and said so. 'I wonder if we could prove it…?'

'We could start by trying to find out if there was a red Rover 3500 around Ashmore last night – remember that was the car that Big Jim took from his showroom for his alleged expedition up north.'

'Sounds like a wild goose chase, but worth a try.' David called Sanders again, and was gratified that his chief took him seriously. He promised to check the number plate of the car that Big Jim "went north" with; and put out an all-stations call to trace its current whereabouts.

* * *

The group outside the former Ashmore Training Camp had dwindled to six: two private soldiers, one village policeman, and three local worthies. The fire brigade had gone home, as had the senior representatives of the law and the army.

'They put me in charge,' said the constable, 'and if I have my way, we'll get this land back for Ashmore.'

David expressed sympathy. 'Good riddance, I'd say. Blot on a beautiful landscape. Did anyone, by chance, see anything unusual last night, anything that might point to somebody being up to no good, or any strangers, perhaps? Did anyone see a car that they did not recognize as being local?'

One of the locals spoke up. 'Oi zaw a red car, sporty-ish, outside the White Hart last night.'

The constable was annoyed. 'Whoi dissn't thee tell oi?' he demanded, dropping his official diction into the dialect.

'Theese didn't axe about a'r car, theese only axed about strangers.'

'If 'twere a ztrange car, 'twould be ztrangers, 'ouldn't it?'

'Ah. Oi zpose 'twould.'

David broke up the debate in basic logic. 'What happened to the car? Did you see any men? What time was it?'

The villager digested this flurry of questions. 'Cain't zwear to't. Just stopped vor a few minutes, round about zix o'clock. Pub weren't open. They turned around and went back to Sha'sb'ry.'

'How do you know they went there?'

''Cause they took the Sha'sb'ry road.' With which further indisputable example of basic logic, this line of enquiry appeared to be closed.

* * *

As they drove back down the Zig-Zag Hill, Elizabeth voiced her thoughts: 'These fire-raisers apparently had about three hours to kill. Let's assume that they arrived in the area early in the afternoon, inspected the premises, as it were, then returned after it got dark, early evening, set off their incendiaries, and then beat it back to London. The timetable would fit.'

'I see where you're going. What did they do between, say, about six and nine in the evening? Probably did what they usually did on a Thursday. Had a few beers together, but not at the local White Hart. Elizabeth, we're going on a pub crawl.'

She consulted the map. 'They would probably have turned off the A30 at Ludwell. No need to go right into Shaftesbury. So let's try there, and then all the pubs in the town.'

By nine o'clock, they had visited the three pubs in Ludwell, the eight in Shaftesbury, and even the Rising Sun on the A30 Salisbury Road. The consumption of fruit juice and gin and tonic was considerable but enquiries about a red Rover of four out-of-town customers drew a blank. They finished up at the Half Moon Inn, seeking mutual inspiration.

Elizabeth looked up suddenly. 'David, why did you take the Blandford Road, and not the quicker A30? It wasn't all that scenic.'

David smiled complacently. 'It may have looked quicker on the map, but it wasn't necessarily the quickest. The A30 goes through Wilton and a few villages, where you have to slow down, whereas the Blandford Road is straighter, with fewer villages. But I probably took it from habit – the way I used to come from Piddletrenthide to London and back. It's more scenic and there's a good pub at Tollard Royal to break the journey.'

'Could our four have thought like you did?'

David made an effort to think clearly. It wasn't the fruit juice. It had been a long day. 'You could have something. One or more of our stalwarts might have done his basic army training at Blandford – my God, maybe even at Ashmore – and may have been familiar with the route that I took. It would be worth a try.'

'We'll have to be quick. Let's start with Tollard Royal.'

* * *

Tollard Royal is a tiny Wiltshire village, just across the Dorset border, nestling amongst leafy glades of oak, beech, and chestnut in a shallow valley within the folds of downland that make up what is left of Cranborne Chase. Many centuries ago, the region was one of the best stretches of hunting country in the land, rivalling the contiguous New Forest. In the days of the Conqueror, or before, the hunt must have been exciting, as the more open chalk downs interspersing the wooded valleys offered the prospect of many a thrilling chase for the deer. At one time they roamed in abundance, but could now be seen only rarely, and seldom by day. Tollard had acquired its royal status as an honour conferred by King John, whose name is commemorated by the ancient hostelry.

David turned into the inn's car-park, with a full half-hour left before closing time. He noticed that the King John also claimed to be a hotel, and thought that this information could be put to good use. The prospect of driving back to London in the dark, after a long day on the job, did not fill him with enthusiasm.

He seated Elizabeth on a well-worn settle, close to a roaring log fire whose welcome warmth contrasted with the chilly and damp night outside. A small group of regulars, plus an intelligent-looking dog of questionable ancestry, were around the bar. The atmosphere was comforting, the surroundings were full of character, walls lined with trophies of the chase, mantelpieces and shelves filled with the bric-a-brac of indoor sports: darts, skittles, and shove-ha'penny. Behind the bar, pewter tankards hung on hooks, and two old-fashioned beer barrels were positioned neatly on trestles.

Not intending to drive any more that night, David ordered a pint and a gin and tonic. More in hope than in expectation, he asked the same question that he had repeated a dozen times that evening. He almost dropped his tankard when the barman replied, 'Why yes, there were four men here last night. Never see'd 'em before. Reckon they came from London; by the sound of their voices.'

'Did they come in a red Rover?' David could hardly hide his excitement.

'That I don't know, Sir. I never looked outside. But there were four in here all right. Came in just after seven and stayed about two hours. Good company too. But they must have had a car. Come to think of it, the big fellow was dangling his car keys as they came in. Jim, I think they called him.'

David made several decisions simultaneously, and put them into words. 'I am a police officer. I would appreciate discussing these men's visit in more detail, as they are suspected of a crime. And my friend and I would like to stay the night, if there are rooms available.'

Grinning a little, the barman reacted with commendable speed. 'So that's why you were so interested. Hang on for a few minutes, while I close up the bar and then we can talk. Yes, we can put you up for the night, and I can fix you up with a bit of supper if you wish. My name's George Allford, by the way. Time, Gentlemen, Please.' He raised his voice with authority, and dealt courteously but firmly with old Tom, who claimed that George had not followed pub protocol by calling for Last Orders.

The landlord closed the heavy oak door, and slid four enormous bolts into place, as if to barricade the King John against the onslaught of an attacking army – as it may well have done in Cromwell's time. He pulled a chair up close to the fire and motioned Elizabeth and David to share the dying embers. 'My wife's got some cold chicken and she's frying up a few vegetables to go with it. Hope you like bubble-and-squeak. And we have a nice room upstairs. She'll put a hot water bottle in the bed – no central heating here, I'm afraid.'

David glanced at Elizabeth hastily. 'I think you must have misunderstood me. I asked for rooms, in the plural. The lady is a friend of mine, but we are not married, and she is not that friendly, at least not yet. I was assuming that you had two singles.' He turned in silent appeal to Elizabeth. 'In the name of Owen Glendower, I really did ask for rooms, I swear it.'

George chuckled. 'That makes a change. I get more of the opposite. This is a nice hideaway, off the beaten track, you might say.'

Elizabeth took up the conversation, turning pointedly to George. 'I do hope you have adequate accommodation, because we are both very tired, but…' she savoured the words, '…we are definitely not that friendly, whatever he means by that, and I'm not sure where my companion cooked up the "at least not yet" bit. I shall welcome the hot water bottle.'

David groaned inwardly, and changed the subject. 'George, I'd like to ask you what you meant about those four men being good company.'

'Friendly types, all of 'em. Made themselves at home, challenged the locals to a game of darts, and bought drinks all round when they lost. They were singing part of the time, and one or two of our lads remembered some of the army songs they were singing. No ladies present, thankfully, they only come in on Saturdays and Sundays.'

David decided to go for broke. 'If I were to hum a tune, would you recognize it as one they were singing, amongst the other songs?'

'I might. Try me.'

After a couple of false starts, and a smile suggesting a slight thaw from Elizabeth, David managed a passable rendering of the chorus of *There'll Be a Hot Time in the Old Town Tonight*. He was rewarded by a sign of recognition from the landlord.

'That's it! How did you guess?'

'Never mind. Did you hear the words?'

'Not really. Let me think, how does it go? Dum dee dum, de dum… I never did know all the words, except the last line about the Hot Time. I think there was something about nightingales.'

'Nightingales!' Remembering Charlie Woodhouse's memory, David could hardly wait to go on.

'Yes, that's what it sounded like. Something about nightingales not singing any more. The words didn't seem to make sense.' George thought hard, and hummed some more under his breath. 'I can't swear to it, but I'm pretty sure that the word "palace" came in somewhere.'

David digested this information doubtfully and tried another tack.

'Can you tell me anything else about these characters? Did they talk about anything particular?'

'One of them, the tubby one, was very interested in those.' George pointed to an old painting at the other end of the bar of mediaeval archers drawing longbows. 'He seemed to know a lot about them. I got the impression that he might have been an archer, perhaps down here to visit the Chase Archery Club at Cranborne.'

'Did one of them wear glasses?'

'Yes, the blondish bloke. He seemed to be leading the sing-song, especially the Hot Time one.'

David put in an urgent call to Roy Sanders, who was not exactly pleased at being awakened just as he had fallen asleep; but became quickly alert when he heard the news. His reaction was predictable. 'Meet me at 10 a.m. Sharp, H Division, tomorrow morning.'

David looked round for Elizabeth. She had gone to bed.

Chapter 9

Turn Out the Guard

The journey back to London on Saturday morning was an anti-climax. The two sleuths had slept soundly, breakfasted early, and had set off just after 6.30, both very subdued. They said very little until well past Salisbury. David kept his mind on his driving while Elizabeth fidgeted nervously. David finally broke the silence.

'Look here, I hope you're not still sulking over that room business last night. You really don't think I asked for one room, do you?'

'No, I don't think you did.'

'You can be damned sure I didn't. So what's eating you?'

'I didn't like your "at least not yet". It sounds as though you were presuming a great deal more than our short acquaintanceship justified.'

'I was tired last night. One or two words slipped out. I was being flippant, and honestly didn't mean to offend. Would you feel better if I said that I need your professional help on this case? In spite of my lapses, I hope you will stay on it with me. Straight up, strictly professional. When this is settled, one way or another, we'll just go our separate ways. Shake hands?'

Elizabeth thawed slightly, permitting herself a self-conscious smile. David smiled back and gently touched her hand for a brief moment. She did not snatch it away, as he had half expected. But he was careful not to prolong the armistice negotiations, and changed the subject.

'Let's talk about our four arsonists. We're well on the way, and Guy Sanders will be right behind us. He's a hard man to convince, but once he backs you, he's a tower of strength. And I have a sneaking suspicion we shall need all the power we can muster before we're through.'

'Do you think these men are dangerous?'

'Hard to say. Arsonists are a funny breed. They have to be motivated, as a rule, nothing spontaneous. There are the occasional idiots who think a small fire might be a bit of a joke, and finish up with a blaze that frightens them as much as it does the victims. Revenge is a common motive, and planned destruction for political and sometimes, sadly, for religious ends, occurs only too frequently. But you referred, I think, to physical violence. In my experience – which, I hasten to say, is not extensive – this is seldom the case. People often die as the result of arson, but this is invariably accidental.

'It's the same with burglars, including the real professionals who specialize in the high-value stuff. They are seldom violent, and most of them take pride in their skills. Most self-respecting burglars take a dim view of the amateur thugs who do occasionally carry guns, and even more occasionally use them. The days of the armed bank-robbers are almost behind us.'

'You don't think that Frank and his team are dangerous, then?'

'No. I'm almost certain that we have stumbled upon an expert gang of arsonists who have gone to great pains to achieve a perfect way of doing it, and are systematically pursuing a single goal. But that goal is simply arson, first-degree arson, if I could coin a phrase. As you so rightly deducted, they have been practising, with increased effectiveness with each successive fire. And if the progression continues, and unless we can stop it, what we have witnessed so far may be a mere nightlight compared to the conflagration that is to come.'

Elizabeth summed up David's analysis. 'The Hammersmith fires, and the other ones near London, and now Ashmore, they were just dress rehearsals for the big night? Any doubts?'

'None. Right now, Bridgeman is sure to be trying to prove a connection between all the fires that led up to Ashmore. You can't fault this gang for thoroughness. Now, I've said this before. It was your inspiration to work out the motive. The police owe you for that, and look where we are now. If we can prove that our four criminals were at the scene of Hammersmith and Ashmore, they are going to be in the hot seat.'

'We can prove it? Isn't it all less circumstantial now?'

'Oh yes. Constable Michelmore recognized the two men, and would go into the witness box. Cheeseman's evidence is a little weak, but would put Big Jim on the spot, because of the positive identification of the red Rover. But our star witness is George Allford. He's an observant and intelligent chap, and would pick the four out in an identification parade. They would be hard pressed to explain away their movements on Thursday night. Circumstantial evidence is not always incriminating, but the chain of events the night before last, coupled with the precise timing of their itinerary, would make an extremely strong case. Also, suspects often incriminate each other, with conflicting stories.'

Elizabeth pursed her lips. 'That's all very well; but we still have to find them.'

David was more confident. 'Oh, we'll find them. They were in Dorset 24 hours ago; two of them were at home yesterday morning; and I'll bet Big Jim hasn't gone north, and Bill Castleman hasn't gone to Paris.'

Elizabeth was equally confident. 'I think you're wrong. The birds have flown.'

'I'll wager that all four have disappeared. Big Jim somewhere up north, to create an alibi; Castleman to Paris, Walter Dudman to Copenhagen for his archery meeting; and Frank Eastwick lost in the crowd at his dog-track.'

'It's a bet. What are the stakes?'

'What if I win? You need taking down a peg.'

* * *

David's chances were dashed when they learned on arrival at H Division that he had already lost his bet. Sanders was in high dudgeon, rampaging around the station, berating anybody within earshot of the simple-mindedness of the entire Metropolitan Police force, especially H Division, and particularly himself.

'To think,' he bellowed, 'that I spoke to two of the bastards myself only yesterday morning. "Is that Bert Eastwick?" I said. "No, this is Frank Eastwick," he said. "Sorry, wrong number," I said, all bloody smart-arse. And that's the only contact we're likely to have with the chief torch for the next fortnight. As for Walter fucking Dudman, I practically waved him goodbye. S. A. bleeding S. to Copenhagen, off to shoot his bloody bows and arrows. Arrows! Bloody excuse to visit the porno shops more likely.'

David was all innocence. 'Sounds as though our friends were not at home, Sir?'

'All right, all right, don't rub it in. You were right and I was wrong. But we're not getting anywhere. Now I've got one for you. Do you know where they found the Rover?'

'Leicester? Manchester? Derby? Trace it through the auctions did you?'

It was Sanders's turn to savour the moment. 'They found it in a car sales lot at Dover. Local dealer bought it yesterday for cash. Sold by two men who fit Big Jim's and Frank Eastwick's descriptions to a

Tee. They took a taxi to the Cross-Channel Ferry.'

Elizabeth finally broke the pungent silence that greeted this news. 'Perhaps they have just gone on holiday, to celebrate their success. But at least it gives us a breathing space. They seem to have taken careful precautions, but I don't think it's because they suspect that we're on to them. Unless your telephone calls roused their suspicions.'

Sanders was coldly sarcastic. 'I can assure you, Miss Lloyd, that although I may look like a copper, I can on occasion contrive not to sound like one.'

Elizabeth was about to say something about understating the case, but decided that, if she wished to stay in it, she had better hold her tongue.

David came to her rescue.

'Miss Lloyd may be right, Sir. They will probably spend the weekend on the Continent, which will give us some time to do a bit of thinking, and a bit of sleuthing. By the time they get back, we shall know a great deal more about their businesses, lives, and habits. We can be ready for them and at least put an abrupt end to their particular line of arson.'

'Already in hand. We've put a check on the ports and airports, asking especially to watch for the four names, travelling back either from Paris or Copenhagen. If we miss them at the ports, we'll wait for them at their front doors. We can question their relatives and associates, and with a bit of luck latch on to some kind of motive. I'm waiting for a call from Bridgeman now. I have also approached Interpol with descriptions of the suspects.'

Elizabeth gave Guy Sanders one of her most inviting smiles, and asked if she could dare to ask a question. The Chief Superintendent softened. 'Go ahead. We would all like to fathom out the motive. Your idea of rehearsing for the big event is sound. But why? This isn't a Whodunit, and we are pretty sure we know Howdunit. This is a Whydunit.'

'We have been discussing their being across the Channel, possibly just for a few days' break; but we have been assuming that this would only be for a few days. But why did Big Jim sell the car? Remember, he doesn't suspect that we are on to him, so that could not be the reason, just to cover his tracks. He sold the Rover 3500, the best car he had in his showroom, and certainly not up north, where he knew all the dealers and could have got the best price. If he intended to come back in a few days, or a week even, he could have parked it, picked it up on his way back, driven it to London, and sold it at a much better profit than the quick sale he made in Dover.'

Sanders sniffed. 'Can't draw any firm conclusions from that.'

'I agree. But why Dover? It's an unnecessary complication, just as inexplicable as George Allford's Nightingales and Palaces.'

'What the hell's that? Why didn't you tell me about this?'

'We couldn't get around to it, with all this talk about Dover.'

David did his best to explain and to corroborate the reasonableness of Elizabeth's question, and emphasized that George Allford was a solid character, unlikely to imagine words that were never uttered. 'I don't think you gave much credence to the song title,' he said defensively.

At that moment they were joined by Inspector Mike Bridgeman, who had returned home from walking his dog. On being told that Sanders wished to speak to him, he had put two and two together, having been alerted to the news of the Dorset fire. There was a secondary motive that persuaded him to leave home halfway through a Saturday morning. Chelsea were playing at home that afternoon, and he could kill two birds with one stone, as Stamford Bridge was on the way back from H Division. He could be back in time for a late tea, and an evening's homework on Japanese police methods, in preparation for the visiting delegation. Such hopes were quickly dashed.

'What's all this about nightingales and palaces?' he demanded, coming in at the tail end of the discussion. David again recounted the puzzling evidence of George Allford, and filled him in on the events of the past couple of days.

Bridgeman was silent for a few moments and then started to whistle quietly. Sanders suddenly sat bolt upright. The whistle became recognizable as a tune, and to David's and Elizabeth's astonishment, Sanders started to hum in tune with the whistle; and to their further amazement, the two older men broke into song as they reached the end of the verse '...And the Nightingale Sang in Berkeley Square.'

Elizabeth suppressed a giggle. Suspecting some kind of joke, David asked what this musical performance was all about.

Mike Bridgeman was unexpectedly serious. 'A little before your time, lad. Old wartime song. Vera Lynn used to sing it for the forces. Do you see a connection? Four men of the wartime generation, paraphrasing words to imply that the said nightingales might not be singing any more in Berkeley Square, of all the unlikely places.'

'Well...?'

'Now associate that with a reference to a palace or palaces.'

Light dawned. 'You mean that our four torchers have been rehearsing to set fire to a palace near Berkeley Square!'

'It's a plausible explanation.'

'I suppose it is. But with respect, Sir, it does seem rather fanciful.'

David toyed with the idea of casting doubt on the reliability of the evidence, but quickly recalled that he himself had stressed the integrity of George Allford's word. 'Here's a thought. Why Ashmore? Was that site chosen because of a perverted sense of humour? You know, more Ash?'

'So what?' demanded Sanders, irritably, and David was forced to admit that this startling revelation did not amount to very much.

Elizabeth ventured to offer another suggestion. 'Do you remember that Bill Catleman's secretary said he liked poetry, and that Charlie Woodhouse thought he saw him scribbling a verse on the table-mat at the club, and that he seemed to be sharing a private joke? Perhaps Bill altered the words of *There'll be a Hot Time in the Old Town Tonight* to fit their private joke – if you can call arson a joke. Perhaps the nightingale was in the woods near Ashmore. Let us ask George if he can remember anything else.'

Sanders grunted, picked up the telephone, and put it on the speaker. George Allford came on the line. He confirmed "nightingales" and "palaces" and thought he heard the word "timber". And one of his regulars who heard them singing thought it was a song about his own pub because he swore he heard the words "King John" and a reference to someone named "Eric". Yes, he remembered Vera Lynn singing about the nightingales in Berkeley Square but he only heard "palaces" not "squares" and it was the wrong tune anyway. But he was absolutely sure about the palaces.

Mike Bridgeman took up the discussion. 'Quite frankly, I'm worried. That emphasis on a palace or palaces. Let me fill you in on what we have found out here.' He brought them up-to-date with the intensive work that he and several of his men had put in during the past 48 hours on the three unexplained fires at St Albans, Wandsworth, and Uxbridge. Nobody had put much thought to connecting them, but now there was the coincidence that they had all occurred late on Thursday evenings. All had resulted in the destruction of an assortment of disused, derelict huts or sheds. The fire brigades in each case had decided that they were simply caused by petty vandalism, because of the valueless nature of the damage. Some youths had been questioned, but no further action had been taken. But now the remnants of a pipe-bomb had been found at St Albans, two had been found at Uxbridge, and at Wandsworth pieces had been found that were being examined in the forensic lab.

Having summed up, Mike telephoned Detective Chief Superintendent Jim Marshall, who was relaxing at home with his favourite pipe and the *Times* weekend crossword. After listening carefully, his instructions were succinct and strict. He was taking no chances.

Mike conveyed the message. 'I was right to be worried. Jim Marshall is even more worried than I am. He wants these men picked up and questioned before they do any further damage. He was alarmed at the mention of palaces. If anything else goes up in flames, we would have to face serious questions from the gutter press – and suppose that is a palace. Think of what palaces spring to mind! I think he's scared.

'It's all so uncannily innocent. This is becoming a complex case. These four men have no record. They have led blameless lives. No connection between them except memories of wartime years. Yet here we are, apprehensive that they are planning – very systematically I might add – some kind of arson in an apparently grand manner. Could be an inferno in a public building such as a museum. The reference to palaces is disturbingly ominous. In addition to locating them, whatever it takes, he wants material evidence from Dorset on his desk by Monday morning. He wants detailed reports on the life history, backgrounds, characters, habits, who else they associate with, of all four. And he wants all that tomorrow.'

'On a Sunday…?' Elizabeth asked. 'Does he think our men will return before the weekend is over?'

'As I said, he's taking no chances. We are going to be busy. They have eluded us so far by doing the unexpected. We'll have extra security guards at the Channel ports, and at London Airport and Gatwick. And we'll make the rounds to their homes again.'

'We were discussing the behaviour of arsonists,' David observed, 'and agreed that they are not normally aggressive or violent. But they sometimes kill by accident. Do you remember the dance-hall fire in the Isle of Man? They were just careless and irresponsible teenagers, but dozens of people were killed because they could not get out because it was a big building. So is a palace.'

The full significance of the word crept insidiously into their minds. They were all aware of the relative proximity of Berkeley Square to the Palaces of St James's, Kensington, and – perish the thought – Buckingham.

'Plenty of palaces,' Sanders remarked, 'if they are rabid anti-monarchists, but no sign of that. Come to that, if they are anarchists they could be going for the Palace of Westminster – modern-day Guy Fawkes. And what about religious fanatics? That would bring Lambeth Palace into the reckoning and a threat to the Archbishop. But this gang have no record of any prejudices whatsoever.'

He looked round, to invite any other theories.

'What about the Palace Theatre?' David suggested.

Sanders snorted at what he felt was unwarranted flippancy. 'Listen! We don't have time to speculate, we have to do what Marshall wants: find out about all these men, even what they have for breakfast. We can get the highest authority, including search warrants. Right Inspector?'

The last remark was directed at Mike Bridgeman. 'Yes, right down the line. It's a tight assignment, but we all know the suspects and we can share the chores. Most of my chaps are still tying up the loose ends of the earlier fires, so it is up to us. I'll go to Finchley Road and see what I can find out about Big Jim. You, Guy, are local, so you can take Frank Eastwick. And Thomas, would you take a close look at Dudman, and if you have time, as it is in the general area, call in at Castleman's place? I'll see that you get the warrants. Otherwise, do it tomorrow.

We sometimes work on Sundays,' he concluded, smiling at Elizabeth.

'May I stay?' she asked meekly. 'I have actually met Mrs Dudman. The continuity might ease her suspicions, if she has any. You know… woman-to-woman talk.'

Mike paused before giving his assent. 'We do have to thank you for alerting us to the arson in the first place; and your insurance connections are relevant, at least to the Hammersmith blaze. Also, in your special case, I don't think Jim Marshall would object. In fact, he might be pleased to learn that his old friend's daughter is following in his footsteps. But I must impress upon you that you are only assisting Inspector Thomas, and you must carry out his instructions precisely.

'And a final word. Any information that might make it easier for any of the four to be apprehended must be relayed immediately to me. Until Monday, we can use H Division as the focal point for coordination. We may pick them up at the ports. I don't think they know we are on their trail, so we may be lucky. So far, except for last night's meeting at the pub, we have no further indication that they have been together.'

Keen observers that Saturday afternoon may have noticed that there were rather more guards than usual on duty around St James's Palace. A number of plainclothes men mingled unobtrusively among the sightseers at Buckingham Palace, where the Royal Standard indicated that the Queen was at home. The Houses of Parliament and Lambeth Palace received more than their usual attention from the uniformed constabulary. Even the cloakroom of the Palace Theatre was watched for any unusually-shaped packages among the audience.

Guy Sanders may have thought David Thomas's suggestion to be frivolous; but Detective Superintendent Jim Marshall did not.

Chapter 10

The Trouble with Walter

Mike Bridgeman telephoned the Chief Constable of Dorset. He asked for the urgent despatch of anything looking suspiciously like an incendiary device that could be found in the ashes of the Ashmore Training Camp, other than the one that had already been taken to Dorchester for inspection. He then drove off in the direction of Finchley Road and Big Jim's Car Mart. Guy Sanders called for his Jag and gave instructions to the driver to get him to Frank Eastwick's place and look sharp about it. David escorted Elizabeth to his MGB.

'Fate has thrown us together again,' he remarked cheerfully, 'let us renew our acquaintance with Mrs Dudman – Gladys, didn't you say her name was?'

'Yes, but now it's the official approach, a great deal more ominous than our friendly little gossip last Thursday. She will recognize me, and think I'm a bastard.'

'Don't worry. I shall take full responsibility, and say that you were acting under orders, and she will assume that you are a plainclothes policewoman. We need not enlighten her. I shall explain that we were anxious not to alarm her unduly until we were more certain of our ground, but that now we are worried.'

They entered the shop, where a young man was assisting Gladys

Dudman during Walter's absence. David drew her aside, discreetly, and said, softly, 'Mrs Dudman, I am a police officer, and this young lady, whom you have met already, is assisting me in making some enquiries about your husband. Can we have a few private words?'

Gladys looked alarmed, and if she took offence at Elizabeth's presence or previous encounter, she showed no sign. 'Good heavens, what is the matter? Has Walt had an accident? Is he all right? Is he in any trouble? Where is he?' She opened a door at the back of the shop and ushered them into a small parlour, which in turn led into what obviously was Walter's workshop for radio and television repairs.

'One thing at a time, Mrs Dudman. First, as far as we know, your Walter is all right – physically, that is – and we assume that he is in Copenhagen. But I am sorry to have to tell you that he may be able to help us in our enquiries about a possible crime. Not, I hasten to add, a violent one, nor, as far as we know, a vicious one, but one that is unfortunately in the book all the same. I must inform you that it is in both your interests – and I mean this in the kindliest way – to answer our questions. You may be able to save yourself a great deal of anguish, and even more important, to save your husband from getting into deeper water than he is in already.'

'You mean that he is in trouble with the police?' Gladys's mouth dropped. She was plainly agitated.

'Not yet. But we must find him, and quickly, to try to prevent that situation. Can you tell us please exactly where he went over the weekend?'

Fidgeting nervously with her fingers, Gladys looked from David to Elizabeth and back several times, and moistened her lips. She looked alarmed, as well she might be. But a life of hard work with Walter and her family had equipped her with some resilience which stopped the flow of tears that David had half expected. She did not answer the question but blurted out, 'Oh, I do wish you would tell me what is wrong. I am sure there has been some mistake. Walter is not the sort of man to harm anybody.'

'Quite. But that is irrelevant at the moment. We suspect that he may have been less than honest with you in one or two small matters.' David thought that to be a masterpiece of understatement, if they were, indeed, dealing with a man who might be conspiring to set fire to the Houses of Parliament or Buckingham Palace. His wording struck a chord.

'Is it about money?'

'I have no idea. But if Walter had any money problems, then we would like to hear about them – in strictest confidence, of course. It may be significant to our investigation.'

Gladys nodded towards Elizabeth. 'I told this young lady that Walter is not so well off as he used to be after he came out of the Army. But he has been out of sorts lately. He tells me not to worry, but I do. I don't like to pry, but I have been worried, so when I saw an envelope from the bank a few weeks ago, marked private, I just had to look at it without his knowing. You know how it is?' She looked appealingly at Elizabeth, who reacted appropriately.

'Yes, of course, I understand. You must have been terribly upset. Men don't realize that by keeping their worries from the weaker sex, as they think of us women, they actually worry us a great deal more. After all, what is marriage all about, if you can't share the burdens as well as the benefits?'

Mrs Dudman felt that she had an ally. 'Oh, you're so right. Can you imagine how I felt when I discovered that Walter was more than £315,000 overdrawn? But I felt better after I'd thought about it a bit—'

David interrupted. 'But surely £315,000 is enough to worry about?'

'Well, not if you see it my way. You see, our house in East Cheam is paid for, and what with inflation and all that, it must be worth at least £350,000 on the market today. We could sell the business, move to a smaller and cheaper place in the country, pay off that debt, and we could manage – especially with our social security in a few years' time.'

'As a matter of interest, how was it, exactly, that Walter's business fell off, after such a good start after the War? I thought television repair business couldn't miss.'

'It was his principles, which in the end turned out to be his downfall. You see, he never forgot the treatment that his pals had from the Japanese in the prison camp in Malaya, although he wasn't a victim personally. But he held a grudge against them, and swore he would never do any business with Japanese-made goods. The trouble was that it was all good stuff and all the big dealerships in the High Street went for Sony, and Panasonic, and all the others. Much of Walt's business dried up, and it was years before he would touch anything Japanese. But when he did, the market was different. The sets were much more reliable than before and the repair business dropped off. But Walter would never steal. But I'm afraid he can never raise £315,000, so that's that.' Mrs Dudman was clearly resigned to a cottage in the country.

David spoke gently. 'We cannot be definite, Madam. I respect your faith in your husband. But we really must get in touch with him before this thing gets any deeper.'

'What thing? How can I help?' Gladys looked earnestly at her ally; Elizabeth could hardly believe the unemotional tone in her own voice. 'You must help by telling us where he is. If you withhold evidence now, you would not only damage Walter's position, you would put yourself in an extremely delicate situation.'

David nodded. 'I don't want to be unfair, or unkind, but that is the truth of the matter.'

'Very well, then.' Gladys reached for her voluminous handbag, big enough to hold half a dozen transistor radios, and after fishing down the depths, extracted a piece of crumpled paper. 'He didn't say which hotel he was staying in at Copenhagen. He said it had all been arranged at the archery club. But he did leave an address, in case anything happened – although I can't for the life of me think why anything should happen.'

She proffered the page torn out of a notepad. On it were the words "Gerhard Heinemann, Deutsch-Danische Nordsee Petroleum Erforschungs A.G., Vesterbrogade, 89, Kopenhavn." Elizabeth translated that this was the German-Danish North Sea Oil Exploration Corporation.

David became more intense. 'Any idea who this Heinemann is? Has Walter any connection with any oil company?'

'Not that I know of. But it wouldn't be unusual for somebody in that business to be involved in sponsoring the archery meetings. They do that at his club here.'

Mrs Dudman grasped Elizabeth's arm, and looked imploringly at David. 'Please find him quickly. I believe you when you tell me that he is in some kind of trouble. He hasn't been himself lately, not the Walter that I used to know only a few months back. But he would never do anyone any harm. Please, please, help him.'

David spoke very gently. 'Mrs Dudman, I can assure you that the police are far more anxious to prevent crime than they are to punish wrongdoers. If your husband has done no wrong – and we have no proof that he has – the sooner he is apprehended, the less further harm he can do to himself, if he is in the wrong company. We shall do our very best to avoid giving you any further distress.'

'Thank you, er... Inspector, is it? I would be grateful if you could let me know what happens. And do tell me if there is anything more that I can do. Walter must have been out of his mind to get mixed up in anything wrong at his age. We must all do our best for him, silly damned fool. I shall have to take some sleeping pills tonight.'

'I thank you, Mrs Dudman. You have been wise to give us this information. I have to ask you to be available at any time. I have your telephone number here at the shop, but perhaps you would write your home number on the back of my business card.'

* * *

On the way back to H Division, Elizabeth felt pleased with herself, especially when David remarked, 'I think you struck just the right tone in dealing with Mrs Dudman. I thought you would be too sympathetic, and that would have been counter-productive. But you broke the ice and released the tension.'

For once, her reply was not studied or defensive. 'I did feel sorry for her, but I did remember his recent record of doubtful integrity. I thought you were kind to her too; no strong-arm stuff. My opinion of the plainclothes police force has improved considerably during the past hour.' Elizabeth made the last remark with a disarming grin.

'We're not tyrants, you know. We do sometimes do a bit of play-acting to put people off their guard, but this was not one of those cases. By the way, when you saw Mrs D. the other day, you did not tell me that her hair was the same colour as yours, a sort of rich auburn, tinged with chestnut.'

'For one thing, it did not occur to me; and I would probably have refrained, for fear of some Welsh witticism. Also, I hadn't realized that you had paid all that much attention to such details, as I am not a suspect.'

'I must disillusion you. I could describe you very accurately. We detectives are trained to observe everything. I could draw an identikit by which any of my colleagues could pick you out on an identity parade.'

'Could you now? So you have a little dossier on me?'

'Certainly... but it's not yet complete.'

* * *

It was past tea-time when David and Elizabeth arrived back at H Division to report to Guy Sanders. 'What have you got?' he demanded sharply. The prospect of a long weekend's routine work did not make him particularly receptive.

'We have made modest progress,' David said, 'to start with, we have a contacting address for Walter Dudman in Copenhagen, and we have also confirmed that he is in debt up to his eyebrows. Further, the idea about what may be termed "The Japanese Connection" is quite evident. Remember that we thought that the four might have a mutual grudge against the Japanese, and might be planning to set fire to a Japanese car dealership? Well, Walter Dudman fits that theory, except that his target would be a big television or electronics importer, or someone in trade with Japan.'

Sanders got his priorities right. He glanced at Mrs Dudman's piece of paper, called Scotland Yard, and requested Interpol's cooperation to persuade the Copenhagen Police to apprehend Walter Dudman, if he could be found by reference to the address of Herr Heinemann. He also demanded to know why David had not relayed the information by radio sooner.

'Do you know if he stayed in a hotel?'

'He may well have done, but he may have stayed with this Heinemann chap. This address is all we have. It's a bit rum, though. Nothing to do with bows and arrows, except Mrs Dudman's idea of sponsorship, which is unlikely.'

'Nothing to do with Japan, either. Or bloody palaces.'

With which perceptive statement, silence fell on the assembled trio.

Sanders finally broke it himself. 'Would you like to hear about our alleged affluent bookmaker? Same story. He owes money right, left, and centre. He lost his touch about two years ago, started to drink too much, and has lived from hand to mouth for several months, according to some of his fellow bookies. As to the Japanese thing, he did have a very tough time indeed. But tell me this. What the hell do money shortages and a common dislike of the Japanese have to do with setting fire to palaces in London?'

'Putting it like that, Sir, there's no sense to it, is there? Someone could be hiring their services as arsonists. They could be anti-monarchists, rabid religious nutcases, or just plain terrorists. What about the Wessex Nationalist Party? Ashmore's in Wessex.' David spread his hands in a gesture suggestive of complete bafflement.

Elizabeth felt that it was time that she justified her presence. 'Don't you think it worth pursuing the one common denominator we have, other than that all four men seem to be short of money? If Inspector Bridgeman confirms a special emphasis on Jim Smith's business failing because of Japanese competition, this would seem more than a coincidence. Remember that Castleman was in the prisoner-of-war camp with Eastwick, and his travel agency may be suffering from Japanese competition too.'

Sanders demurred. 'I rule out revenge. If they all bore a strong grudge, they would have acted years ago. Time may not be a great healer in their cases, but the memories would have faded by now.'

Elizabeth pressed her case. 'But they weren't such close friends until recently. The embers of hatred may have glowed again during their beer-drinking sessions, as they realized their respective motives for getting their own back: Walter's television competitors, Big Jim's car rivals, Castleman's declining tour business; and according to Charlie Woodhouse, Frank Eastwick has borne the scars physically as well as mentally all his life.'

Sanders nodded. 'Nevertheless, that's not enough. That is why I think Jim Marshall is concentrating on the money angle. For such an elaborate operation, there just has to be a pay-off somewhere. These four are broke. Therefore, there must be an outside sponsor. Someone else may want revenge on Japanese exporters, and found this team to form a "This Torch for Hire" gang. Ah, here comes Bridgeman now.'

Mike Bridgeman confirmed their suspicions. The experience of English sports car enthusiasts looking at Big Jim's MGBs, then walking across the road and choosing the 290Z had hit his pocket as well as his pride.

'Big Jim…' he said, '…may not be very big much longer. He is in the hole for something like £330,000, and the bank could foreclose on him any time.'

Elizabeth made her point. 'That corroborates my two common denominators. They are all broke, and they all hate Japan.'

Mike smiled, with an air of satisfaction, almost triumph. 'I'll give you a denominator which may not be common, but we had better think about it. Jim has a workshop behind his showroom, where the old bangers are given a face-lift, along with adjustments to odometers, I don't doubt. Underneath one of the benches is a considerable store of metal piping, in odd lengths, odd diameters, and of different metals, none of which have anything to do with motor-cars. Several pieces have been sawn up recently – the saw marks are still fresh. Also, there are marks where the pipes have been clamped in the vice, and I'll wager that forensics can prove that some of the pipes that we've picked up so far have similar marks – we never thought to look for them before. Any news from Dorchester, by the way?'

The telephone rang, but it was from Tollard Royal, not Dorchester.

'George Allford here. I've been thinking about that song those visitors were singing, the one about a Hot Time in the Old Town. I can't think of the exact words, but there was something about drinking in pubs. And one of my regulars swears that he heard a reference to Ashmore. I told him that Ashmore is not a town, but he insisted.'

David picked up the receiver. 'George, this may not be important, but you told me that one of the men took a big interest in that archery picture you had on the wall. Did you receive an impression that he might have been visiting your district because of that?'

'Why yes. There is an archery club in Cranborne. He might have been down for a practice shoot.' George rang off, leaving much food for thought.

Mike Bridgeman got up to go. 'Guy,' he said, 'I'm taking no chances. I'm putting extra men on every establishment in the centre of London that's anywhere near a palace or similar structure and is prominent in promoting Japanese manufactures, radios, televisions, cars, you name it. There are probably specialized Japanese Trade Centres. Also, any sign yet for a search warrant for Castleman's flat? And twist Dorchester's arm for dragging their feet.'

* * *

For once, Mike had underestimated his country cousins. As his car disappeared, another arrived. A heavily-built plainclothes Detective Inspector, Jack Hillier by name, entered the portals of H Division, bearing gifts. He spoke in the broad accents of the West, though not in the dialect. 'We searched the ashes at Ashmore, and came up with these.' He opened a package and produced two devices that they all recognized as almost exactly the same as those found at Hammersmith. 'You'll be intrigued by this little bundle – he opened a second package – these little blighters were all over the place.'

Intrigued was an understatement. Jack Hillier had produced about a dozen thin tubes, approximately an inch or a little more in diameter, pointed at one end, and now quite empty, though charred black for the most part. Some were damaged, by being burst open. But one was undamaged, and Jack Hillier handled it with great care.

'This one didn't go off,' he said, with some satisfaction.

The manufacturing process was now revealed in all its detail. With minor differences in diameter and metallic content, they were all of common design. Sure enough, there were marks that suggested the use of a vice. But one distinguishing feature riveted the attention of the assembled sleuths. At the blunt end of the tube or pipe, a neat groove had been filed across; and there were signs of the same refinement on the others from Ashmore.

Exhibit A was passed around, and then Guy Sanders erupted.

'Bows and bloody arrows,' he ejaculated. 'Walter Bloody Dudman.'

'Explains automatic built-in ignition,' said David.

'Poor Gladys,' murmured Elizabeth.

Chapter 11

Robin Hood

A further talk with Gladys Dudman was agreed upon to be essential. As the search warrants for Bill Castleman and Frank Eastwick had still not arrived at H Division, Guy Sanders suggested that David should pay her a visit first thing in the morning. 'I'd like you to report to me and Bridgeman as soon as possible. Take your car. One of ours would disturb the Sabbath calm of East Cheam, and wouldn't make Mrs Dudman too happy either. Take Miss Lloyd if you like, if you think she can help – and if you have no objection.'

Elizabeth ignored the sarcasm. 'I think I may be able to contribute. Mrs Dudman seems to be more at ease with me. Not that Da… Inspector Thomas hasn't been the soul of discretion.'

David took Elizabeth back to her flat, calling in at the local pub for a nightcap and a sandwich en route. It had been a long day.

The next morning, as they approached the tidy detached house in Garden Road, East Cheam, David remarked that at least the two of them together would relieve Mrs Dudman of possible gossip among the neighbours. 'We could be mistaken for members of the local church choir, coming to discuss the selection of hymns.'

'Not if we break into "There'll be a Hot Time",' Elizabeth grinned. She was in good spirits, as she felt that she was now a member of the investigating team, especially after the startling news of the evidence that Walter seemed to be firmly implicated.

She had resisted the idea of inviting David in for an extra nightcap, but had been glad of a good night's rest. She was up early and ready when David called for her at 8.30 on a brisk, windy March Sunday morning.

Less than an hour later, Garden Road was almost deserted as the MGB drew up outside No.63. Only empty milk bottles and lines of cars parked nose to tail betrayed the presence of human habitation. Hard-working suburbanites had acquired these houses when they were built close together in an age when bicycles were assumed to be the maximum vehicle requirement for a family of six.

Mrs Dudman opened the door about three inches, and said 'Oh' about four times, with four shades of meaning, the last clearly an abbreviation for 'please wait a few minutes while I put something on.' In due course, they were seated in the front parlour, gracefully accepting the offer of a morning cup of tea. 'I didn't expect to see you so soon as this,' she exclaimed, still adjusting a square of unidentifiable material around her hair to hide the overnight clips. 'Is Walter all right?'

David had to be stern, but he tried not to sound harsh. 'The fact is, Mrs Dudman, we already suspected that your husband was mixed up in something that could not be classed as vicious or violent, but nevertheless is unpardonable. We have to see you again – and I apologise for coming at this inconvenient time – because further evidence has come to light which confirms our suspicions. We must all work together to prevent a possibly serious situation from becoming a disaster. I cannot tell you the details, but I must ask you some questions. I want you to trust us. We are trying to act in your husband's best interests, and your cooperation would be most appreciated.'

Mrs Dudman must have been half-expecting some further development. She clasped her hands and made an admirable effort to remain composed. 'I'll do anything to help Walter, whatever he's done,' she said quietly. 'Tell me what you wish to know.'

'To start with, can you tell us about his archery club? It's not everybody's hobby, like football or golf.'

'Oh, he's been doing that for years, and he is really quite good – he is much stronger than he looks. I used to go with him, but I haven't been lately. He used to call me Maid Marion, and I called him Robin Hood.' She managed a weak smile. 'But that was long ago. I began to lose interest, and preferred to go to the pictures with a friend. I think he liked that too, so that he could have a few drinks with the boys.'

She rummaged in a pigeon-hole in Walter's desk, and produced a folder of papers. David found a representative account of Walter's archery activity: letters from the secretary of the Virginia Archery Club at Sunningdale, reminders of overdue subscriptions, notification of archery fixtures with other clubs. David noticed the Chase Archery Club of Cranborne on the programme, but no sign of any date or meeting in Copenhagen.

Mrs Dudman, meanwhile, had gone to another room and returned with a photograph album, in which there were several pictures of Walter proudly holding his bow, and in some instances holding a trophy.

'That's a dangerous-looking weapon,' David remarked. 'I'll bet Robin Hood could have used one of those to advantage.'

He regretted this turn of phrase immediately. Gladys gripped his arm. 'Don't tell me he's shot somebody,' she implored. 'He was always saying what a deadly weapon it was. But Walter wouldn't – he just couldn't – actually shoot somebody.'

'I'm sorry, Mrs Dudman, I didn't mean to frighten you. No, of course we don't suspect Walter of anything so callous. But you will agree, I think, that one of these bows could be misused?'

'Oh yes, Walter often mentioned that. Would you like to see one? He bought a new one recently, but one of his old ones is upstairs.' Mrs Dudman returned with a long black case, which might have contained a large musical instrument. Sure enough, the bow did look extremely lethal. David picked it up, very carefully. The string, actually a nylon cord, hung limply. 'Walter had a special way of putting the string on properly,' Gladys volunteered. The wooden part of the bow itself was made of many laminations, beautifully crafted, elegantly curved in the classical cupid's bow shape, with a carved section in the middle, made-to-measure for the human hand. There were several metal inserts in the middle of the bow. Gladys pointed to some compartment in the case. 'They use special sights,' she said, 'which clip on to the bow.'

David inspected the sight. It seemed to cover every eventuality of crosswind, headwind, or combination of both, and was marked for different ranges. There was little doubt that such a bow, in the right hands, could be used with deadly accuracy. He was mightily impressed, as Robin Hood himself would have been.

Mrs Dudman felt she could stand up for Walter's prowess. 'I suppose I shouldn't say this to a policeman, but Walter always claimed that with this kind of bow, he could kill a man at 300 yards. I know one thing, because I've seen him do it – he could put a whole bunch of arrows on a target at 100 yards. And those bows are strong. I couldn't even pull the string back.'

Elizabeth felt that she could add the feminine touch to David's approach, which, she felt, had been decently done.

'This is absolutely fascinating,' she said. 'I hadn't realized that archery was so specialized. Why, your husband must possess all kinds of qualities – strength, steady hand, calm temperament, and everything.' She hoped that a reference to everything might expand the scope of information-gathering.

David picked up the flow. 'I assume…' he said gently, '… that Walter doesn't meet with quite as much success as he used to. These photographs, I see, were taken about eight years ago.'

'Well no.' Gladys was now quite relaxed. 'Walter isn't the same old Robin Hood, at least not with his bow and arrow. He still goes to his archery club, but doesn't compete so much these days. But he is a popular member and they like him to go along with them on competitions, because he's good company.'

'Was this the case with his visit to Copenhagen?'

'I suppose so. The main thing, he enjoys the break, away from his workshop. He needs to get away from his bench. His customers make me sick. They buy their cheap televisions up the road but don't provide the service. They expect Walter to repair them if they can't get a good picture.'

'Mrs Dudman, I've just had a thought. Would you mind if I telephoned the Virginia Club?' David had been reading a small folded card, with a calendar of events, and explicit instructions spelled out concerning penalties for non-appearance, or failure to notify the secretary of any illness within 48 hours of a fixture. Archery, it seemed, was very demanding on fitness, and any illness was not to be indulged in at the weekends.

Meanwhile, Elizabeth chatted to Gladys, with whom she felt almost on Christian-name terms. She was touched by the wifely concern for an errant husband. It was hard to imagine that such an ordinary family could find itself enmeshed in – to use David's phrase – first degree arson. But all the evidence pointed to the probability that not only was Walter Dudman involved in such an escapade, but also he was almost certainly taking a leading role.

'What lovely hair you have, Miss,' said Gladys Dudman suddenly. 'Mine used to be very similar to yours, but I can't do a thing with it now, and there's more than a touch of grey, I'm afraid.' She lowered her voice. 'Actually, I use a little dye, but this is the colour it always was. Walter fell in love with it at the start. I hope your Inspector has noticed yours too.'

Elizabeth was glad that David hadn't heard that remark, although she was inclined to share Gladys's thought. She wanted to console this lady who was in an unfortunate situation. 'I hope you won't mind me saying this, but you and Walter must have had a happy life together.'

Mrs Dudman took Elizabeth's hand and gripped it firmly. 'We have been very happy. We've had our rows, of course; who hasn't? But never anything serious. He's a good loyal husband, and great fun always to be with. And...' she looked Elizabeth straight in the eye, '...I shall stick by him now, whatever he's done or hasn't done.'

Elizabeth had to say something to avoid revealing the emotion that she felt for Mrs D. 'Is there anything I can do? I cannot interfere with the law, naturally, but there may be some personal message or something...?'

Gladys thought for a moment. 'You are very kind. Let me think. Oh yes, I have the very thing. I am sure that it will not interfere with your work and the law.' She disappeared upstairs again, and reappeared with a voluminous green sweater. 'Give this to him, if you can, with my love. It's one line that I knitted myself, when he used to go to some chilly ranges, and he would put it on under his windbreaker.'

She held the sweater up. The reason why Walter wore it out of sight was evident. Mrs Dudman had knitted into the green background, in vivid yellow, two facing stags, with a caricature of Robin Hood brandishing a bow and arrow in the middle.

'He'll know from this that nothing has changed between us. This sweater has been the subject of a lot of laughs – which I won't elaborate on. But it might keep him warm, and will symbolize the bond between us. You see, I love him very much.'

If David had not come off the telephone at that moment, Elizabeth would have had her hankie out and gravely endangered her continued value in Mrs Dudman's eyes as a representative of the law. Instead, she took the sweater, reassured Mrs Dudman that whatever else he might be, he would not be cold. Reminding Gladys that she must not discuss the subject of Walter's travels with anyone, repeat anyone, she hastily made tracks towards the door, as she could see that David was about to do likewise.

After they had driven off, David was curious. 'What on earth have you got there, and furthermore what have you been getting up to with Mrs Dudman?'

'Oh, David, I just couldn't refuse. She asked me if I would give Walter this hand-knitted sweater, if I saw him, as a symbol of their love. What could I do?'

'I believe you are genuinely sorry for Mrs Dudman, and to be honest, so am I. I cannot believe that she knows anything about Walter's odd behaviour; but I certainly reserve judgement on him. I just spoke to the secretary of his archery club. He confirmed that Walter used to be a top-class marksman, but he's older now and not in competition class any more. But here is something else, and this is why I had to wrap things up quickly. Walter Dudman was not picked for a team to go to Copenhagen, for the simple reason that they don't know of any club there. The match is in Brussels.'

* * *

The news did not raise Sanders's eyebrows as much as David expected. 'Makes no difference,' he said. 'We've heard from Copenhagen. They've tried this Heinemann's address, but there's no-one in, although that may not be surprising at the weekend. We'll keep trying. So why don't we try the others? Here's the warrant for Castleman's place, but I can't authorize Miss Lloyd going along with you this time.'

Elizabeth smiled sweetly. 'I don't need to go anyway, but I think I helped to break the ice with Mrs Dudman. We have the same hair, and she has trusted me with Walter Dudman's sweater. Look.'

Guy Sanders stared at Robin Hood and the two stags. For once, his flow of expletives deserted him. But his stare took the smile off Elizabeth's face.

'You may think this too sentimental,' she asserted, 'but I am going to ask permission to stay with this case. I have already contributed to it. If I hadn't followed up my conviction in the first place, we wouldn't all be here now, and who knows what might happen next? I feel that I have a proprietary interest and a right to be part of the team. I've paid my dues and in any case this whole thing started with insurance.'

Sanders was poker-faced. 'As you are a private citizen, I am not sure that we can give you specific orders or instructions, but you had better not interfere with our procedures, and must keep out of the way unless we need you. I suppose Inspector Thomas has no objection?' Sanders's glance in David's direction held no subtleties. David assured him that Elizabeth would not be in his way, and his own glance at Elizabeth suggested that a way would be found.

The Detective Superintendent had the last word. 'And you can keep that bloody sweater. It's not evidence.'

Chapter 12
Poet Laureate

David felt strangely alone as, armed with a search warrant, he drove up to William Castleman's flat in Scarsdale Villas, West Kensington. He had deposited Elizabeth on the way, and left Guy Sanders telephoning Mike Bridgeman, as promised, before going over to King Street to take a look at Frank Eastman's place. He realized that he had become used to having her around, especially as she was a dazzling exception to Thomas's Law, which stated that women were either beautiful or smart, but seldom both. She was charming, albeit with spirit; and her intuition was right on the mark, in addition to a sharp intellect. In short, she added up to the most wonderful girl he had ever met. He found himself devising how to keep her on the case.

His daydreaming was cut short by his arrival at Scarsdale Villas, where predictably there was no place to park, even for a police car. Castleman's flat was on the second floor, completely self-contained. He let himself in with his skeleton key, and surveyed the scene. There was nothing remarkable or unusual. The furniture was modern but not ostentatious. The stereo-player took precedence over the television as the focal point in the living room. Pictures of faraway places, mostly oriental, a Swissair calendar, and a plastics model of a Douglas DC-3 bore witness to his evident participation in the travel business. Timetables, maps, and brochures, the kind beloved of Charlie Woodhouse, were scattered over the coffee-table. A cabinet contained a neat collection of jade and ivory statuettes, and a traditionally-costumed Japanese doll. The bookshelves displayed a mixture of good literature, with an accent on poetry, books on jazz, and several expensively produced tourist guides. Several were about Japan, including one or two dealing with the wartime atrocities.

David's attention was drawn to the roll-top desk, as he rummaged through the piles of papers. Obviously, Bill did much of his work at home. Near the top of the pile was a file that seemed to have been used quite a lot, as it was dog-eared and well-thumbed more than the others. It was marked "Yokohama European Tour Agency". Apparently Y.E.T.A. had been switching several of their expensive tours from Castleman's to various other agencies. The letters from Japan were courteous and the negotiations had been long-drawn-out. But the last letter, dated only a few months back, was final. Bill Castleman was out.

The next thing that caught David's eye was a bundle of airline tickets, and running through them, he was astonished to find that one was still current. It was an Air France ticket to Paris, open-dated to Rome, then back to London. Although the departure date was Thursday, 23rd March 1975, the ticket was indisputably unused. Wherever Bill Castleman had implied he was going to, the odds against Paris for his weekend tryst had suddenly lengthened considerably.

The desk revealed nothing further, except that Bill seemed to like travel as a vocation, not simply as a means of support. He seemed to be an interesting cove, and David turned his attention again to the bookshelves, remembering some advice that had been given him that you could judge a man from the selection of books in his home library. It was interesting. They ranged from paper-backs to a few collectors' items, including beautiful leather-bound first editions of Spenser's *Faerie Queene* and Milton's Poetical Works. Oddly, next to the vintage volumes, and seemingly out-of-place in its context, was a new ring-binder, which, on closer perusal, revealed one or two catalogues of traditional jazz LP records and some notes on them, presumably written by Bill Castleman himself. They were mostly verse, competent and sometimes amusing. There was one about a jazz band's series of one-night stands, written in the style of Pope; and some attempts at contemporary lyrics for twelve-bar blues. There was even a requiem for Louis Armstrong.

He was about to return the binder to the shelf when a loose sheet, which had not yet been three-hole-punched, dropped out. He read the typewritten doggerel, eyes boggling with each successive verse:

When you hear the fire bells tingaling
On ten wood huts, the ten fire bombs will cling
In Charlie's Club, the Hammersmithians sing
There'll be a Hot Time in the Old Town Tonight

Near the old hill town the fire bells start to ring
To Ashmore Camp their hoses they will bring
And in the King John Inn the Four Just Men will sing
There'll be a Hot Time in the Old Town Tonight

The nightingales no more will sweetly sing
The Palace's old timbers will all be smoldering
In Eri's Cabin bar we'll have our final fling
There'll be a Hot Time in the Old Town Tonight

Chapter 13

Porno and Palaces

David Thomas, Guy Sanders, and Mike Bridgeman were gathered at H Division headquarters, which was quickly becoming the centre of operations. Sanders was enjoying the privilege of being on his home territory, and having the head of the Arson Squad as visiting guests. He kept his intercom going at frequent intervals, and fired various instructions to a small band of constables who performed various minor chores, including making the tea. He dealt peremptorily with Constable Marsh who wanted to be reimbursed for three weeks' overdue tea-club money, and was positively rude to Constable Michelmore, who had only observed that it looked like being a nice sunny day, considering the time of the year.

Sanders had stared at Bill Castleman's poetic masterpiece for fully five minutes before swearing eloquently for a further three. He came to the end of his impressive vocabulary, carefully compiled during many years of frustration with the flower of the British Army on parade grounds at Aldershot. 'If it's not bloody psychologists, it's fucking poets. What do you make of this?'

Mike Bridgeman tried to improve the tone of the discussion by mildly observing that, while the poetry might not be first-class, the information contained therein could be extremely useful, provided that the combined intellects of the assembled company could decipher the implied message, if there was one.

David agreed. 'Let us start with – as my Euclid master used to say at school – what are we given? Three verses, the first two of which refer to the most recent occurrences of arson that we all know about. It follows that the third verse refers to a further occurrence which has yet to happen. It confirms both Charlie Woodhouse's and George Allford's recollections of the strange words, in particular George's nightingales, palaces – not just places, you notice – and his timbers. They all follow the same format, references to the site of the fire-raising, then to where the "Four Just Men", as he calls them, will be celebrating the escapade. Why "Four Just Men"?'

Mike knew the answer. 'That refers to a book by Edgar Wallace, a well-known detective story-writer of the Twenties and Thirties. He invented these characters who executed revenge on various criminals who, for one reason or another, had placed themselves beyond the reaches of the Law. Kind of Twentieth Century Robin Hoods. The reference here suggests that our arsonists appear to think that theirs is a just cause, and that they are the self-appointed executors of a morally-justified trust.'

'It all points to London,' said Guy Sanders. 'As soon as Thomas read that last verse over the blower, I got on to the Yard and they've circulated all stations to find a Bar with the name of a Cabin and for a barman named Eric. Castleman may not be much of a poet, but he's either bad at spelling or a bad typist. Can't even spell smouldering.'

'Oh, I think that's just his typing. Missing a letter in "smouldering" – and in "Eric" too, you notice – were just the sort of slips that we all make, especially when we punch the machine with two fingers.'

'But do you agree on London?'

Mike Bridgeman agreed. 'Certainly. The nightingale reference seems just about right. These men are of an age to remember the wartime song *A Nightingale Sang in Berkeley Square*, especially when it was sung by the Forces Sweetheart, Vera Lynn. Reminiscing played a large part in the four men's friendship; and while it could be argued that there are other towns with palaces, I think the nightingales refer to London, and perhaps in the vicinity of the West End at that.'

'But what about the timbers?' Sanders was acting as a devil's advocate.

'A figure of speech, no doubt. I don't think that actual timbers were meant. The quotation "stone walls do not a prison make" does not necessarily imply that all our prisons are made of stone.'

'But Allford had a point, didn't he? The timbers could be a reference to a wood, and nightingales sing in woods. But he didn't catch any direct link with palaces, the word he seemed sure about.'

David Thomas posed a question to Sanders: 'Have you confined your search for Eric and his Bar only to the West End, or have you spread the net wider?'

'I'm playing safe, and extending it to the entire metropolitan area. It could be anywhere, for example, nearer to Big Jim, who is not far from Alexandra Palace, which is in north London – but I would bank on it being nearer to the centre, to be convenient for all four of our bloody just men.'

Mike Bridgeman summarised the consensus: 'It's agreed, then. We'll try to identify Eric's Bar, where these characters might possibly assemble for a carousal before what they call their final fling, in the unlikely event that they all manage to return home through the ports. We have every possible route covered, not just Dover, but Newhaven, Harwich, Folkestone, Southampton, and even Weymouth; and we are notifying Southend and Southampton Airports, as well as London and Gatwick. Of course, we don't know for sure that Castleman even went across the Channel. We know the ticket to Paris was a blind, so he may still be in London, setting the whole thing up. Quite a bit of irony about the situation. We don't know where they all are; and they have no idea that we are on their tails.'

David took up this last theme. 'That's an interesting aspect of this case. The four men have organized themselves in such a calm neat way, and their backgrounds are all so innocent. They are just ordinary people. They probably never gave a second thought to the fact that a constable on his beat might have noticed them. And only Miss Lloyd's obstinate persistence, and our willingness to explore her theory, gave rise to any suspicions on our part. So in one sense, we have the advantage. They are unlikely to be taking any special steps to avoid detection, and will return to England by the same route that they took going out, and they might even lead us to Eric's Bar. So should we not pick them up at the ports, but follow them to their homes or to their destination?'

'That sums it up pretty well, I think,' said Mike Bridgeman. 'And that's a good thought. By the way, Guy, what did you find at Frank Eastwick's?'

'Thought you would never ask,' grumbled Sanders, now in better humour. 'What I've discovered is of no small consequence. Our honest Frank had a nice little side-line in Scandinavian pornography, which presumably he was able to circulate at the dog-track. This isn't a top-line case for the Vice Squad, but I'm glad that Miss Lloyd wasn't with me. Luckily she was your responsibility, eh, Thomas?'

David ignored Sanders's raised eyebrows and knowing look. 'Oh, I think she's fairly well emancipated. These days it would be hard to shock anyone over the age of twelve. But was there anything to relate Eastwick to anyone or anything connected with our case? We are still mystified as to the reason why they have concocted this elaborate scheme at all, not to mention the mechanism for doing it.'

It was Sanders's turn for a mild triumph. 'I hoped you might say that. I found Gerhard Heinemann's business card. The address is the same as Walter Dudman's contact address in Copenhagen. I found it just lying around, on his bedside table, with the typical assortment of odds and ends that collects when you turn out your pockets. Remember that Mrs Perkins thought Frank had some German visitors? They could easily have been Danish.'

Mike Bridgeman stood up pointedly and made an announcement. 'It's time we told Jim Marshall. There's something sinister about all this. I don't know what, but whatever it is, I don't like it. Call it an old policeman's gut feel, if you like, or Miss Lloyd might admit to it being intuition. So, Guy, telephone Jim and summarize where we stand.'

Sanders did so, and then dropped the receiver abruptly. He turned to his colleagues. 'We're being honoured. Detective Chief Superintendent James Marshall is coming to H Division. Right now. Can't understand why. His coming here won't get us any nearer to watching them at the ports.'

They filled in the time by sampling Constable Marsh's tea, which that worthy grudgingly supplied after extracting overdue contributions from his irritated Chief.

* * *

At almost exactly 3.00 p.m. a menacing-looking pipe, closely followed by Jim Marshall, breezed into H Division, bringing a strange aroma suggestive of burning incense mixed with farmyard hayricks. He greeted the three policemen with 'A fine ants' nest you've turned up here, I must say. If you don't mind, I'd like to hear it all through from the beginning, and I'd like to see the exhibits.'

Mike Bridgeman expressed their opinion that, with the clue of Eric's Bar, and with the ports covered, the net was closing in, so that the question of the exact location of the next instalment of planned arson was not critical. Guy Sanders and David Thomas nodded their concurrence.

111

Marshall smiled grimly. 'I'm afraid that this may be more complex than you think. That's why I've come over, because I could not talk about it on the telephone. I want you to listen carefully.' He need not have bothered with this last instruction. Not often did a C.I.D. Chief Superintendent bother to visit a Division , and even less often on a Sunday afternoon. He had an attentive audience.

'I have some information which is a closed secret, and you must understand that what I am about to tell you is privileged information. Indeed, I could hardly put it more strongly if I suggested that any disclosure would amount to a crime closely resembling, if not actually, High Treason. You are privileged because of the coincidence of names that Sanders mentioned. One is a place, Copenhagen. The other is a name, Heinemann, a connection, which I will explain.'

If a pin could have been heard to drop before, the silence in Guy Sanders's office was now absolute. Watches could be heard ticking. Marshall was speaking in a low, almost conspiratorial, voice.

'I have been involved on and off recently with arrangements for a high-level Japanese Trade Delegation which is visiting London next week. They arrive tonight in fact. We in the C.I.D. are not responsible for their safety, that's the job of Special Branch. But the Japanese have brought with them some senior members of their police department to confer with us on matters of mutual interest in security, and to exchange ideas on crime detection and other police ideas generally.

'This would have been fairly routine, with the Home Office coordinating the various agencies responsible for the Trade Delegation's welfare, safety, entertainment, you name it. But the routine curriculum of trade subjects – licensed car manufacture and exports, optical equipment exports, radio and television, etc. – is a screen for something far more far-reaching. The top Japanese negotiators will discuss, and possibly sign a contract to buy a big chunk of, Britain's North Sea Oil for the next quarter of a century.

'As you know, the discoveries in our designated waters have exceeded all previous estimates. We have a comfortable surplus. The Japanese have no oil. This agreement can control the balance of trade between the two nations more than all the other commodities put together. It is of vital importance, especially right now, because the current unrest in the Middle East has blocked off the Straits of Hormuz, and cut off about two-thirds of Japan's oil imports. So you can imagine why the Japanese are here, judge the delicacy of the situation, and realise why the stakes are fantastically high.

'Now listen carefully to the following facts: One: the Japanese are staying at the new Palace Hotel, in Curzon Street, a short stone's throw from Berkeley Square. Two: the main rival to Britain in securing the long-term Japanese contract is the German-Danish North Sea Oil Exploration Corporation, based in Copenhagen, and representing certain Norwegian and German interests. Three: all three countries have made good discoveries in their sectors of the North Sea and this puts them seriously in competition with British interests.

'I do not need to tell you that there is a great deal of significance in putting all the known facts of your four-man arson team together. If they could succeed in sabotaging the success of the Japanese Trade Delegation to London, even to the extent of blowing them all up, the chances of a long-term oil agreement with Japan could be nil.'

Jim Marshall was not usually given to drama, but intentionally or not, he had succeeded in completely silencing all three of his listeners. No further discussion was necessary. 'You know what you have to do,' Jim concluded. They did.

Chapter 14
Echo Answers 'Where?'

Arrangements had been made to extend the scope of the protection squads, and to concentrate on the Palace Hotel. The search was intensified for a pub with a barman named Eric, so the four members of the arson investigation team decided to call it a day. They broke up at five o'clock on what had been an unprecedented Sunday afternoon. There was not much left of the weekend, but after David had showered, made a cup of tea, and pondered over the case, his thoughts turned to Elizabeth. He speculated on what she would think, and what conclusions she would draw from the fresh information. His mind wandered to visualizing what she would look like while thinking, and how he would feel while watching her think. At eight o'clock, on impulse, and risking admonishment, he telephoned her.

'I wonder if you would be interested in hearing about the latest developments? I think we have a break.'

There was a pause on the line which David interpreted as a hint that he was pushing his luck at this time of a Sunday evening, but which was Elizabeth taking a grip on herself to avoid the impression that she had been hoping that he would call.

'Of course I'm interested, considering it's my case. You owe it to me to keep me fully informed. What startling discovery has

H Division now made?' There was a hint of sarcasm in her voice.

'It's a long story. I was rather hoping... that is, if you aren't too busy... that we could kind of... well, I'd like to tell you personally, because there's a lot to tell, and it's top secret, and... is it too late for a dinner tonight?'

'So even on Sunday evening, you want to talk shop?'

'I didn't mean it that way. But I know something that you don't; and hell, I'd like to see you anyway.'

Another tantalizing pause. 'I can't come out tonight. I've just washed my hair and I don't feel like dressing up.'

David refrained from making an obvious suggestion, but merely commented, 'I'm disappointed.'

'Is that all?'

'Well, devastated.'

'Really?'

'Damn it, I need you as a consultant, and furthermore, I desperately need to see you anyway. Of course, if you feel tired, and would rather have a quiet night indoors, I won't pester you.'

Elizabeth put David out of his misery. 'For a detective, you are not as logical as you ought to be. Consider the facts, as you are never tired of telling me. First, I don't want to come out. Second, you have something important to tell me. Conclusion: you must come over to my place.'

One or two passers-by along David's road in Shepherd's Bush were surprised to see a man charge out of a house and leap into an open sports car without going through the motions of opening the door, and then doing a passable impression of Jackie Stewart getting away from the starting line at Silverstone racetrack.

* * *

115

David was in an easy chair, enjoying a Harvey's Amontillado, but feeling as though he had had several, as Elizabeth had welcomed him warmly, and was prattling away about the weather, the wine, the cricket, and hair dryers, everything except arson. He had dogged her footsteps into the kitchen, where he discovered that a meal was in preparation – grilled chicken, in an exotic sauce, for two people, no less. Light had dawned. He suggested mildly that she had gone to some trouble, and dare he presume that she was expecting him?

Elizabeth's simper was irritatingly smug. 'I thought you would never call. What kept you?' Her smile was captivating.

This was obviously the moment, if never again. David did what was expected of him in the circumstances. Elizabeth had refrained from putting on make-up, which allowed for a certain flexibility. Protests about difficulty in breathing eased his hold as he held her at half arm's distance, completely enraptured.

'I never expected this,' he said, 'not for many moons, anyway. I thought you might regard me as just another plainclothes policeman.'

'I treat all policemen like this,' she burbled.

'Including Guy Sanders?'

'Well, I don't really know him yet.'

'To use his language, you're not bloody well going to.'

'Don't worry, David dear, I can only manage one at a time, especially if he's Welsh.'

The exchange of endearments had to end, as Elizabeth had to attend to some of the practical aspects of the evening. The chicken was a complete success, and her coffee excelled the Colombian Coffee Shop's finest brew. As David waited for her to close the kitchen up for the night, he pondered on his astonishing good fortune. She pulled a pouffe over to the side of the chair, and nestled beside him, with his arm around her.

'I don't wish to dampen a lovely evening by talking shop, but could you bring me up-to-date, as you promised? Perhaps a little dampening of your ardour might be safer for both of us; otherwise the investigation of our four arsonists will be severely jeopardized.'

'Our "Four Just Men", you mean?'

'Our what?'

'"Four"... oh, of course, you haven't read the poem.' As best he could, David recounted the results of the searches of Bill Castleman's and Frank Eastwick's flats. Fortunately, he was able to recite almost word for word the amended lyrics of *There'll be a Hot Time in the Old Town Tonight*.

Elizabeth was fascinated. 'This sounds like one of the classic examples of the voluntary admission-of-guilt complex. There are certain criminal types who actually tempt fate, because subconsciously their inner selves know that they are doing wrong, know that they ought to be apprehended, and sometimes without knowing it, become careless. Occasionally this assumes the form of taking unnecessary risks by excessive displays of over-confidence, ostentation if you like; and Bill Castleman's poetic interest got the better of him. And please watch your current display of over-confidence, if you don't mind.'

David released his grip which was close to being an embrace. He was doubtful. 'Psychology isn't my field, but I think I know what you are talking about. But the explanation of their motivation is probably far simpler. They all seem to need money; and they have all turned to crime when an opportunity has arisen; especially if it appears to be particularly lucrative. And this has something to do with a man called Heinemann who has something to do with a Danish oil company which is seeking a huge Japanese contract. Oil is big money. Remember that their plan has been smoothly methodical, and as far as they know, nobody suspects them. Hence Bill Castleman simply indulged in a little light-hearted fantasy.'

Elizabeth gently took hold of David's hand, which was straying dangerously. 'Well, whatever the reason, the clues he put in the last verse, with "Eric's Bar" and everything, make me feel that someone is planning another Fire of London. When do you think they will be back from the Continent?'

'As a matter of fact, we don't know for certain that they are all in Europe. Remember that Castleman's ticket was still in his desk.'

'But Castleman wasn't at home. So where was he? If he was in London, he would almost certainly be at home. Was there any sign of his presence at the flat?'

'No. The kitchen was quite tidy, everything put away. Bed made. I'll swear that nobody had been in the house for a couple of days or more. But then, I'm in London, but right now I'm not in my flat either, I'm delighted to observe.'

Elizabeth disengaged her head from David's shoulder, and looked up. 'Do you realize that all the assumptions that led us to believe that our men are across the Channel could be false? We all jumped to the conclusion that because Big Jim asked his way to the Dover cross-Channel Ferry terminus, therefore he and Frank Eastwick caught the boat. They could just as well have caught the train back to London, via Dover Harbour railway station.'

David did his best to digest this revolutionary idea.

'My God, you're right. The drive to Dover could have been a precautionary move to put any possible investigation, however flimsy, off the scent. But why such an elaborate ruse? We believe that they have not suspected us yet. And why sell the car?'

'Because in this case they were not careless, and left absolutely nothing to chance. Suppose I'm right, and they did come back to London. Can we be a hundred percent sure that they don't suspect a possible detection? What about Walter Dudman? What firm evidence do we have that they caught a plane to Copenhagen?'

'To be honest, I can't tell you. All I know is that Guy Sanders was cursing the fact that he practically saw him on to the aircraft. If you promise to keep quiet, I'll telephone him now.'

Sanders confirmed that, although he had not personally escorted Walter Dudman up the aircraft steps, he had checked with Scandinavian Airlines and a Dudman, Walter, was definitely on the passenger list, and they were sure that he had not got off again, because he had checked in some excess baggage. That would have been his archery equipment. 'Call up S.A.S. yourself, if you want to double check – that is, if you've got nothing better to do on a Sunday evening.'

David did not enlighten him, but telephoned S.A.S. just the same. The records showed that a Walter Dudman had boarded the aircraft, and that the only possible way that he could not have travelled was if he had dashed off at the last minute before they closed the door, and the entry on the passenger list had not been cancelled. That was possible, if a clerk was negligent. But the excess baggage must have gone through.

David resumed his position in the chair, within neck-stroking reach. 'You know, you may be right; but I do think it's unlikely. The baggage could have been a clever ruse. They could be holing up somewhere here.'

'Not in the Palace Hotel, I hope. And Eric's Bar is unlikely to have overnight accommodation. Hold on though, what is this Cabin word? Doesn't that suggest some kind of camp-ground or country resort – you know… the rural touch?'

David was alarmed at this omission in their previous thoughts. 'That's an interesting possibility. I'm afraid we didn't focus on that Cabin word too much. We had better include all the holiday camps within an hour or two's reach of London. But how do you reconcile a cabin with a palace? I suppose, however, that the nightingale and the timber would be closer to a cabin than a palace? We need a cryptologist. Hell, they could be all booked into the Palace Hotel, under false names. But then, they wouldn't need Walter, with his bow and arrows, to shoot the pipe-bombs.'

'But suppose they are in striking distance of the hotel! They could be staked out in a building, and just like Ashmore, Walter could aim his missiles into a vulnerable spot or simply wait to make a direct hit on the delegation as they leave the hotel.'

David detached himself, somewhat reluctantly, to make another telephone call, this time to Scotland Yard, to initiate an immediate check on the identity of all the guests at the Palace Hotel, and a similar check on the nature and activity of all the inhabitants of the buildings in the vicinity, especially those with windows on the same level as the most expensive suites. A watch was also to be made on the gardens of Berkeley Square, whence part of the Palace Hotel could be sighted between the roof-tops.

The realisation that, however improbable, Messrs Dudman, Castleman, Smith, and Eastwick could all be in London, brought the improving relationship between Inspector Thomas and Miss Lloyd to an end, at least for the time being.

'I must ask you before I go,' David said, '…and I do have to go. What has transformed your attitude? You were mightily suspicious at the King John Inn. What has melted the ice? I'm still bewildered. Happy, but bewildered. And no complaints.'

Elizabeth's smile was radiant, and positively encouraging. 'It was your dealing with Mrs Dudman. I expected a cold and heartless approach, but you were decent and kind. I like kind men, especially when they are passably handsome, and reasonably honest (which you, of course, have to be) and particularly if they are Welsh, and have a sense of humour, distorted though that may be.'

Chapter 15

Meeting of the Minds

By the time David reached Curzon Street the Yard was out in full force already, combing every building that could conceivably be used as a potential sighting point for shooting fiery arrows at the Palace Hotel. The searchers were reinforced by the Special Branch men already assigned to chaperone the Japanese Trade Delegation, whose members were now safely in their beds, trying to readjust to ten hours of jet lag, and oblivious to any possibility of threatened danger.

Only two buildings could, by any stretch of the imagination, be used by an archer aiming to penetrate the windows of the Palace Hotel. One was an empty office building which gave forth an ear-shattering din when the burglar alarm sounded as the police attempted to enter. The other was a block of expensive flats. Some were occupied partly by several well-to-do families who were indignant at being interrupted late on a Sunday evening. In the others a number of ladies who described themselves as models were also about to turn in for the night, if their apparel was any guide, and who also seemed annoyed at the appearance of the police. Their answer to the question 'Are there four men in your flat?' drew a number of interesting replies.

The whole of Berkeley Square was diligently and meticulously searched, and nothing suspicious was found, not even the odd nightingale.

David returned to Shepherd's Bush, somewhat deflated, and feeling rather embarrassed at having stirred up a complete mare's nest. His thoughts alternated between wondering what Sanders would have to say; and the memory of Elizabeth's head nestling by his side; but above all, keeping him awake, his exasperation at the determination of the four fire-raisers to stay completely out of sight.

They were clearly trying to avoid detection. One, or even two, men taking a weekend off might disappear from all human ken for a couple of days, for no sinister reason, except that they had just forgotten to tell anybody. But for four specific people, with some association with each other, to do so seemed distinctly unlikely. He could pick ten names, or even twenty, at random from the telephone directory, and guarantee to locate their whereabouts within 24 hours, or near enough. Yet Messrs. Dudman, Eastwick, Castleman, and Smith were defying the combined efforts of half the police forces of southern England, to say nothing of Interpol and the Copenhagen police, to find them.

Damn it, he must have looked a bit of a fool to cause his colleagues to chase around Curzon Street looking for a man with a bow and arrow! There's a point, though... a man... could it not be more than one? Could Walter Dudman have trained the other three? No, impossible. Archery could not be learned so easily. Such a refined, technical pastime took years of patience, stamina, and discipline. It had to be only Walter Dudman.

What about the targets? One aspect that had struck him while inspecting the scene in Curzon Street was that flaming arrows, in the old Wild West tradition of Red Indians setting fire to a fort or an encampment, were all very well as long as the target was made of inflammable material – like a collection of old wooden huts, for example. The sites at Adelaide Street and Ashmore were perfect examples of such buildings that were vulnerable in the extreme. But the solidly-built, steel-superstructure, pre-stressed concrete of the Palace Hotel was a different proposition. No flaming arrow was going to beat the fail-safe anti-fire sprinkler systems and fire-proof automatic door devices with which the hotel was sure to be equipped under the strict London Council fire regulations.

Firing into individual rooms, rather than at stone or concrete walls at random, was at least more plausible. If the arrows could penetrate the windows, and then act as incendiary bombs on impact, they would make quite a mess of anything and anybody inside the rooms. If a Japanese trade commissioner was asleep in his bed, such a missile would give him a nightmare, or at least a headache.

With the ebb and flow of such speculation, David eventually fell asleep with his own private nightmare, dreaming of men shooting flaming arrows at an enormous nightingales' nest in Berkeley Square, with Elizabeth screaming for help, with Mrs Dudman putting out the flames with buckets of Young's Bitter supplied by a chain of men, all named Eric.

* * *

The next day, Guy Sanders – surprisingly tolerant of the Berkeley Square incident of the night before – joined David Thomas and the combined police forces of the London area in interviewing all the barmen named Eric, who could be candidates for an honourable mention in William Castleman's latest literary effort. One by one, each was eliminated, and while some pubs had a Four-Ale Bar, none was called a Cabin. The list of remotely-possibles was whittled down to two, a barman just hired at The Railway Arms in Kentish Town, and the proprietor of the Red Lion in Soho's Wardour Street. One singing quartet had attended the former every other night within living memory, but their sentimental repertoire bore not the slightest suggestion of a Hot Time of any description; the latter Eric had remembered a tall man with glasses and a short man who kept talking affectionately about his "'arrers" but further enquiries of the Red Lion's clientele revealed that this referred to his cherished set of darts.

'We had better get back to Marshall's office,' Sanders grumbled. 'I'm told that he won't have much time for us, much as he's interested, because he's tied up with this Japanese Trade bunch in protocol matters. Let's pick up Mike Bridgeman and present ourselves.'

The three found Chief Superintendent James Marshall in an uncertain frame of mind. 'Look here...' he began somewhat ungraciously, '...I'm not at all satisfied with the way things have been going. After my confidential briefing on Sunday afternoon at H Division – at H Division...' he repeated the words to imply that he did not habitually consume his valuable time visiting the Divisions during the weekends... 'I was expecting at least the glimmer of something, anything, by now. But what do we have? Sweet Fanny Adams.'

As the Yard representative, Mike Bridegeman took up the challenge. 'With respect, Sir, we have reinforced our conviction that the four men are concentrating on London. We are still mystified as to the precise message implied by Castleman's doggerel, but the theory put forward by H Division that the men have never left the country seems to hold.'

'You mean that Castleman never used his airline ticket, Smith and Eastwick never caught the ferry at Dover, and Dudman never boarded the aeroplane? Have you checked beyond all reasonable doubt? What happened to the excess baggage that went to Copenhagen? The aeroplane flight should be the key. So, Sanders, check with Scandinavian Airlines again. Now.' Marshall's order was both patronizing and authoritative.

Sanders called S.A.S., and after a brief conversation, put the receiver down, deflated. His moustache almost drooped. 'S.A.S. is prepared to lay its reputation on the line that Walter Dudman was on the flight to Copenhagen . The passenger manifest has been checked both in London and in Copenhagen. Dudman's name was on it from start to finish. What's more, the excess baggage that he checked through was extra proof.'

Marshall mellowed slightly. 'That disposes of that little London theory,' he declared complacently, pleased that something definite had quickly been achieved at his instigation, and moreover with a simple telephone call, without the help of half the Metropolitan Police Force. 'Now, what about Copenhagen? Any sign of anything at the German-Danish North Sea Oil Exploration Corporation?'

Mike Bridgeman admitted that finding only locked doors at the premises had led him to the wrong conclusion. Marshall leaned back in his armchair and sucked his pipe for several minutes, his eyes fixed on an indefinite point on the ceiling. He finally gave his verdict.

'In short, we're still where we started. I was going to say "back where we started" but we would then be flattering ourselves that we actually got across the starting line. All we have done is to flail around, hoping to pick up some crumbs that these masters of the disappearing act might have dropped. The idea of an attack on the Palace Hotel – or any other palace, for that matter – just won't wash. Think of the implied motive. This is not a murder case. Even if it was, what good would it do to kill the Japanese delegation? Others would take their place and the trade discussions would go on.

'This is arson, and the objective must therefore be something arsonable, if I may use the term. We have been treated to several experimental fires, all involving wooden huts, with the apparent purpose of devising a method of rapid, almost instant, combustion. By piecing together the evidence of the manufacture of the arrow-like pipe bombs, we can assume that the incendiary devices are to be fired from a bow, by an expert archer. The first experiments around London were to test the effectiveness of the basic pipe-bomb design, and possibly the efficiency of the incendiary material in the bomb; the last experiment, in the West Country, was to prove that these ingredients could be adapted to an arrow-like design. Do you remember that the first device found by the Dorset police was of the earlier type? It was close to the camp gate, and probably used first, to provide enough light – remember it was pitch dark – so that the archer, Walter Dudman presumably, could see where to shoot.

'The main point that I am trying to make is that buildings made of bricks or stone or concrete are unlikely targets. Equally, metal structures such as oil rigs, even pipe-lines – in case this has crossed your mind – would be difficult. And in any case, if it was a solid building, or a rig, or a pipe-line, simple explosive would be far more effective.'

This was the extent of Jim Marshall's ceiling-inspired summing up, but David ventured to state the thought that was on everyone's mind: 'Where do we go from here?'

Marshall put down his exhausted pipe, rose from his chair, and paced the room slowly. 'This is one of those exasperating cases where we just have to sit and wait for the breaks,' he said. 'Perhaps something will turn up from Copenhagen, or the docks, or London Airport. I'll swear that Dudman can't slip back through there.'

He paused, looked at his watch, and moved to the door. 'Look here, I have to attend to this delegation from the Tokyo Police, and talk about our police methods. I shall not mention Berkeley Square as a sample. Have you done your homework on their standards of law enforcement, Mike?'

Mike Bridgeman ignored the sarcasm, and assured his chief that, if necessary, he could quote the maximum penalty in Japan for knocking off a policeman's helmet, and could provide from memory the average annual number of suicides from drowning in lakes, rivers, or waterfalls, or by jumping off high buildings, analysed by occupation, including taxi drivers.

'Good, you'll probably need something like that. I'd like to cut a shine with the Japanese. These chaps are supposed to be completely inscrutable, hardly say a word, except to grunt – politely – to assure you that they are listening, probably record everything we say in a microphone disguised as a tie-tack, and show no enthusiasm, simply polite agreement. I find that routine discouraging, so I want to make an impression. I want you to back me up, Mike, and emphasize the way we go about our routine business, for example in this arson investigation. Who knows, they might have an arson man with them. I want to emphasize that most crimes are solved by painstaking, soul-destroying, monotonous, patterns of investigation. Only rarely is a crime solved or a murderer apprehended by a flash of inspirational genius of the Sherlock Holmes' variety. Take our fingerprinting, for example, now being augmented by voice-printing. We can make a good case.

'I'll quote the case of the Blackburn murderer some years back. We knew from other evidence that the suspect had to be a resident of the city, and we took the fingerprints of everyone living in Blackburn, and finally nailed him. Now, to add a little spice to the review, I can quote our current case, in which we are interviewing every barman named Eric within 50 miles of London, and that we are checking all the ports. That should appeal to them, as a seafaring nation.'

Bridgeman, Sanders and Thomas wandered off for a quick bite at the Yard cafeteria.

David suggested that the Super's pipe could be the secret weapon that might penetrate the air of oriental inscrutability, and all agreed that the occasion would be diverting, if not entertaining. They prepared themselves for minor walk-on roles in the forthcoming afternoon matinee.

Chapter 16
The Twain Shall Meet

The Japanese won the first round in the sparring for points in lifeman-ship. Chief Superintendent Eiichiro Yamazawa and Chief Inspector Akio Takata had been escorted into Jim Marshall's office at 2.30 with the proper propriety and dignity by two Inspectors of the C.I.D.'s Special Branch. They had both bowed deeply, to the level accorded to Marshall's rank of Chief Superintendent, and had also shaken hands. Jim had been taken slightly off guard, and had probably bowed either too deeply or not enough, depending on where he ranked in the pecking order. The visitors exchanged verbal greetings in excellent English, and had then, following age-old Japanese custom, produced a small gift, as a token of friendship and to commemorate the occasion. The gift was not intrinsically valuable – that would have been ostentatious – but it was appropriate: a small facsimile of the badge of the Tokyo Police Force, neatly mounted in a little Damascene frame, contained in a perfectly-fitting transparent plastic box, and the whole artistically wrapped in gold paper and tied neatly with red ribbon. Not only did Jim have nothing to match such an elegant gesture; he had nothing at all. He mentally kicked himself for having stressed the need for Mike Bridgeman to do his homework, but having omitted to do his own.

The delicacies of the first introductions passed, they then settled down to another age-old Japanese custom: that of spending at least twenty minutes at the start of a business meeting without ever mentioning the subject or its purpose, in this case the details of British police procedure. They covered the weather; the standard of service in London hotels – which, to Jim's surprise, received full marks – the oil crisis and the width of the Straits of Hormuz; a comparison of the smog between London and Tokyo – more full marks to London – the Olympic Games; and a debate on the relative merits of Wedgwood and Royal Doulton china. Eventually, by a twisted form of logic known only to the Japanese, the conversation steered towards the detection methods of the London and Tokyo police.

During the exchanges, Jim Marshall regained some equanimity by going through his pipe-lighting ritual, as a diversionary tactic. The Japanese eyed the shredded tobacco suspiciously, watched warily as Jim lit up, and flinched slightly as, after the first satisfying draws, the resultant clouds of smoke wafted across the room like a personal smoke-screen. Yamazawa then elaborated on their admiration of police routine in Britain, and explained that Takata was especially interested in arson cases, because they were afraid that radical groups in Japan would turn to fire-raising as a political pressure tactic. Except for construction in the big cities, Japanese building methods and materials were especially vulnerable.

Marshall gave them his well-rehearsed account of the Blackburn murder case, and emphasized the need for constant vigilance by the lowest members of the force, and the value of exhaustive and comprehensive routine analysis. 'Our much-maligned and often-ridiculed London Bobby,' he said proudly, 'has probably been responsible for more successful crime detection than any other police force in the world, because he is trained to watch for details, is expected to use his initiative, and above all, is a member of a criminal detection system that works smoothly from top to bottom, and is fully integrated, vertically and horizontally.' Jim was not sure what this last claim meant, but it always went down well, and sure enough, again following Japanese protocol, the visitors had grunted in between Jim's pauses to reassure him that they were listening intently, and at the end nodded sympathetically.

Chief Superintendent Yamazawa returned the compliment by agreeing on the importance of routine work (he would not have openly disagreed, even if he had privately thought that Jim was talking a load of honourable codswallop) and, in turn, recounted a case of running down a Yokohama jewel thief who always used hired cars under a variety of false names. The police had conducted an analysis of every journey made by every hire car company over a period of six months, and tracked down the quarry by matching up hirings with incidents. This, he said, had been possible only because Tokyo hire car companies had to keep meticulous records.

This gave Jim the opportunity to introduce the subject of the current case study and he asked if they would be interested to be brought into the picture by an up-to-the-minute report from the men working on the case, and following the principles of strict, though boring, routine. The tall, bespectacled, distinguished-looking Yamazawa bowed slightly in a polite gesture to signify agreement. Jim rang the bell on his desk, and Mike Bridgeman came in to be ceremoniously introduced.

He was followed in, less ceremoniously, by the tea lady, who had decided to arrive at the same time. She plonked the tea tray on the Superintendent's desk in a cavalier gesture. 'Made an extra big pot today...' she announced loudly '...seein' as 'ow you 'ave visitors, and I brought some cakes to go wiv it.' Jim Marshall was not sure whose round that was. He glanced surreptitiously at the two Japanese who demonstrated the notorious inscrutability of the Orient in their reactions to the English afternoon tea ceremony, so different from their own.

Mike did the honours of pouring the tea, and taking over from Jim's narrative, explained that the chance discovery of a frivolously-written poem had led them to put in an intense search for a bartender named Eric, almost certainly from the London area. Yamazawa commented that, in a city of ten million people, there would be hundreds of Erics, but Jim pressed on. 'Ah, but you see, this is where our amateur poet helped us; he actually mentioned, or suggested, the name of the bar or pub, and this narrows down the field. We ought to run this down to earth very soon, especially as there can't be many bars or pubs named Eric's Cabin. Maybe it is a special lounge in a hotel. But we're checking them all.'

Chief Inspector Akio Takata, a short, stocky, round-faced man, hesitated for a moment, then summoned up the confidence to make a statement, having carefully weighed up the pros and cons of whether or not he would lose face by speaking irrelevantly, or even worse, appearing to be facetious. 'With greatest respect,' he said, 'if name Eri, not Eric, can locate bar precisely.'

To state that the two Englishmen were caught off guard would have been the understatement of the year. Both minds mentally pictured William Castleman's typewritten poem, and both simultaneously remembered the hitherto assumed mis-typing of the word Eric. Jim Marshall lost his grip on his pipe, and Mike Bridgeman almost dropped his teacup. Both stared incredulously at Takata, who misinterpreted their expressions of concern, and held up his hand in a defensive gesture.

'Very sorry,' he said apologetically. 'Not mean offence, or joke; Eri's Cabin is name of bar in Roppongi District of Tokyo. Good English beer and board for arrows. Very popular with English businessmen who visit Tokyo.'

Jim Marshall finally found the breath and voice to speak intelligibly. 'Please do not apologise. You took us by surprise, because in the poem, the name is spelled Eri and we thought it was just bad type-writing, especially as the writer did make other spelling mistakes.'

Takata was relieved. 'Assure you Eri's Cabin is pub in Tokyo. Many English and Australian peoples go there. Play games and drink much beer. Sometimes get drunk and Eri calls police. But Eri OK. She respectable.'

'You mean this is a pub like in England?'

'Oh yes. Very good pub. Serve Bass and Newcastle Brown and Foster's.'

The full impact of this astonishing revelation was infiltrating Jim's and Mike's minds. They sank their respective teas to regain stamina, poured second cups, and Jim rang his buzzer again. 'I think you had better see a copy of this poem,' he said.

David Thomas came in, armed with a facsimile of the Castleman epic.

'This Eri,' Mike enquired, 'you said she was a lady?'

'Yes. She very nice. Make good fish and chips. But customers sometimes make trouble over game. We put two in prison one night for bad language.'

'Not too offensive, I hope,' murmured Mike.

'Oh no. They explain that "Up Emperor" is English way of saying "Raise glorious flag high".'

Jim suddenly found difficulty with his pipe, Mike bent down to fasten his shoelace, and David stifled a sudden fit of coughing. None of them dared to look at Superintendent Yamazawa, who had so far maintained a hundred per cent record of inscrutability. The British contingent made a disciplined effort not to display the realisation that in the last five minutes, Inspector Takata had possibly unravelled more of the arson mystery than the entire British police force had done in the last five days.

Mike handed the poem to Superintendent Yamazawa to relieve the tension. The Japanese policeman read it carefully until, at the end, his eyes ran quickly over the last verse again. At that moment, the British trio were treated to a performance of oriental emotion that they were unlikely ever to witness again. The Superintendent dropped his mask of inscrutability. It may be recorded that he completely lost his scrute. His hand shook, his mouth opened, then shut again, and he looked around, wide-eyed, at the assembled company. Without a word, he handed the poem to Inspector Takata, who echoed the almost theatrical performance of his chief. They both forgot the rules of courtesy that demanded that they should always speak English, because the English never spoke anything else. They babbled away in Japanese at a high rate for several minutes, until Superintendent Yamazawa pulled himself together.

'Apologise for lapse into native tongue,' he said, with a slight bow, 'but interpretation of poem very serious for us. Please to telephone Tokyo. Must speak immediately to Chief of Police. While you get number...' he handed a card to Jim Marshall '...I will explain.' Jim resigned the chairmanship of the meeting. Yamazawa was now in charge.

David Thomas read the poem out loud again:

The nightingales no more will sweetly sing
The Palace's old timbers will all be smoldering
In Eri's Cabin-Bar we'll have our final fling
There'll be a Hot Time in the Old Town Tonight.

'Is it something to do with nightingales and palaces?' he asked.

Yamazawa chose his words carefully. 'Coincidence of references too strong for doubt. Palaces refer to buildings of old Ninomaru Palace at Nijo Castle in Kyoto, because built of timber. Old buildings in Kyoto, and like many in Japan, built of wood, with paper or wood walls, and thatched roofs. Ideal target for arson. Kyoto very old city, founded more than 1,000 years ago, and capital of Japan for most of that time – thus "Old Town" in poem.'

'But what about the nightingales?'

'Most important clue. Establishes Palace at Nijo Castle as target. In former days, shoguns ruled Japan. In Kyoto, Nijo Castle like palace to famous shogun and...' he paused, seeking the correct words... 'he protected innermost sanctuary by curious warning device. All corridors leading to shogun's personal rooms made of wood planks supported by beams which make squeak when pressure put on, such as when person walking in corridor. Sound like birds, and usually called nightingales, because danger most likely in night. Can still be heard today, for tourists.'

'But Eri's Cabin is in Tokyo, not Kyoto.'

'Kyoto only two and a half hours by train or air from Tokyo. Foreigners in hotel in Tokyo would not be connected with danger in Kyoto.'

Tokyo came on the line. Yamazawa spoke rapidly and intensely for a few minutes, and turned to Jim Marshall. 'Thank you. Have alerted Tokyo and Kyoto police to grave danger. They will search every hotel in both cities for four men whose descriptions will be supplied over telex wire immediately.' He raised his eyebrows and Jim nodded assent. 'Special guard on Nijo Castle, Imperial Palace, and other shrines in Kyoto. No English person or persons can enter grounds of palaces or famous buildings without search. Plainclothes men also in Eri's Cabin.'

Jim Marshall sensed that perhaps a little of the initiative should flow back to the English side of the exchange of revelations. 'I hate to disillusion you,' he said politely, 'but it is not enough to protect grounds of palaces. We are almost certain that the method of fire-raising has been perfected that will permit the arsonists to make their strike without being inside the grounds, or possibly not even immediately outside them.' He went on to outline the technique of pipe-bombs disguised as arrows which had apparently been devised by the Four Just Men, and the expertise of Walter Dudman, the experienced archer.

More mopping of brows. 'Ah so. Like cowboys and Indians with better technology. Do not like this at all. With such method, entire city of Kyoto could be vulnerable.' He reiterated that, unlike all other large Japanese metropolitan areas, the old city of Kyoto, resplendent in crafted wood and thatch, had been faithfully preserved as much as reasonably possible against the ravages of modern concrete and steel development. Kyoto was still the Old City, with a thousand temples, palaces, and shrines, revered by the whole nation. Its value was such that, even in the darkest days of the Second World War, when severe sacrifices were being made for the war effort, time, labour, and money were still found to build wide boulevards strategically placed to act as fire-breaks in the unhappy eventuality of an incendiary bombing raid, which fortunately never came to pass. But, he explained, their fears were not without foundation. More citizens were killed in the incendiary raids on Tokyo than in the atomic holocausts at Hiroshima and Nagasaki combined.

Mike Bridgeman volunteered an analysis. 'It seems to me that, just as we had concluded that we must apprehend our criminals in London before they got down to their dirty work, nothing has changed except that the area of search has been dramatically transferred to Japan. And we shall have to look into the Copenhagen connection.'

The Japanese Superintendent nodded, with another quick bow. 'Completely agree. Problem now part English, part Japanese.' He turned to Jim Marshall. 'Because of emergency, I ask big favour. No time to lose. Four Englishmen conspiring in arson in my country will raise enormous problems, including difficulties in international relations. But biggest problem is to identify criminals. Very difficult for Japanese as – please forgive – all Caucasians look alike. Can you assign one or two of your men to go to Tokyo immediately to assist in pursuit of arsonists? Because of shortage of time, almost impossible to circulate descriptions with enough detail to permit reasonable chance of apprehending crisis. But one of your men, already familiar with the case, and who has actually seen some of them, could recognize them and increase chances of arrest.'

Superintendent Yamazawa could not have done better if he had been the Japanese Ambassador.

Marshall fussed with his pipe, now requiring the services of a vicious-looking instrument of torture guaranteed to rid the bowl of unwanted dregs. If he recognized the irony of the reference to Caucasians, he did not reveal it. 'I suppose I have to agree with you on the urgency of the situation,' he said amiably. 'Even though we have no idea of the timetable of our arsonists, we cannot take chances. It would help if we could arrive before they do. This emergency will need our joint resources. These amateur criminals have so far done a masterly job in eluding us, and our meeting today has been an act of Providence. It was sheer luck that the subject should even have arisen. We must follow our luck and put into practice some of the methods that we have been discussing. I can certainly promise you one of our people straight away, as he has been the main investigator in the case. I assume that you can take care of him in Japan. I don't think he has been further away from London than his ancestral home in Wales.'

He turned to Mike. 'See what Guy Sanders has to say about the idea of sending Thomas to Tokyo. I don't suppose he will be very enthusiastic. He'll probably want to go himself.' Surprisingly, he was wrong. Sanders was due to give evidence in court concerning two robberies and a multiple rape. In the latter case, the Crown regarded him as a key witness, and he ruled himself out. Sensing the situation accurately – Sanders was no fool, and in spite of his outward bravado, he knew what to do – he recommended that Inspector Thomas would be the best man for the job. 'I am sure he is fired with enthusiasm to see it through to the end; and most important, he has been watching the men closely, and has their descriptions indelibly printed in his memory. He would recognize Eastman and Dudman without hesitation. What do you think, Mike?'

Mike nodded. 'I agree. It is most irregular for a Divisional Inspector to go charging off outside his own jurisdiction, even in Great Britain, much less a foreign country. But special circumstances demand special solutions. InspectorThomas has seen the men. He's the obvious choice.'

Yamazawa bowed again. 'Tokyo Police honoured to have Inspector Thomas as guest in our country. His presence will be very important just for recognition. Japan Air Lines will arrange flight; he will stay in first-class hotel. We appreciate your support in our sense of urgency, and I offer grateful thanks to Scotland Yard for cooperation.'

Chapter17
Motive Power

'I'm coming over? The sky's just fallen in.' David's excited telephone call to Elizabeth was received with less than his expected enthusiasm. She had just arrived home from the office and raced up the stairs, having welcomed Mr Braithwaite back from his conference. She had taken up a good two hours of his time in narrating, with considerable self-satisfaction, the developments in the west London arson case. Although he had been disparaging about her ideas when he left, he was now gallant enough to congratulate her, and expressed the hope that Messrs. Martin, Smith, and Jenkins would recognize her efforts appropriately.

'Do you mean now?' she said petulantly. 'I've only just arrived home and I'm in a mess.'

'Never mind the mess. You'll never guess where I'm going.'

'Back to your beloved Dorset, I suppose. Piddletrenthide, probably.'

'Cut the sarcasm. Considerably farther than that.'

'Don't tell me. Your Welsh Wales, I suppose.'

'Would you believe Tokyo?'

'Tokyo, Japan?'

'What other Tokyos do you know?'

'You'd better come over. Right now.'

* * *

After a generous welcome into the mews flat, as compensation for the abrupt reaction to his call, David brought her up-to-date with the dramatic outcome of the Anglo-Japanese meeting that afternoon, leading up to the point when he had been selected to represent Her Majesty's Metropolitan Police Force in Japan. Fortunately, having taken a quick trip to Paris and a package holiday week in Majorca, his passport was in order, and his inoculations were, following regulations, up-to-date. All he had to do was to draw some travellers' cheques from the bank, and Japan Air Lines had a ticket ready for him at the airport. He was surprised how easy it was. He did not attempt to conceal his excitement, either in the position of authority that had been thrust upon him, nor in the prospect of visiting a country that he had read much about, but which he had never dreamed that he would ever visit.

Elizabeth shared in his exuberance from the kitchen where she had started to brew a pot of tea, but changed course in favour of two gin and tonics. Then she sat down and considered the implications. 'You could be gone a long time, just when I am getting used to having you around.'

David took the hint, and put an arm around her shoulders, remarking flippantly, 'I'll ask Mr Braithwaite to be specially kind, and to look after you on my behalf while I'm away.'

Elizabeth was not amused. 'Forget Mr Braithwaite. And what will you be doing? In a couple of days, you'll have all the Japanese girls saying "Hai".

'Just like a woman. Here am I, stepping forth into the unknown, risking a fiery death from a gang of ruthless arsonists, and all you think about is the girls.'

'I don't question your role as a policeman, but your defences against the fascination of oriental maidens might not be so resolute. You haven't been too defensive lately. How soon are you going, by the way?'

'Tomorrow afternoon. The 3:25 'plane arrives next day, Wednesday that is, at 5.10 p.m. Tokyo time. Superintendent Yamazawa arranged for instant free flight, and would have got me on board today if he could, but there was no time. Marshall did not wish to give offence by suggesting tonight's British Airways flight. Tomorrow morning, I have to go to the Yard, for a full report from Copenhagen. The lines have been red hot these last few hours, and Herr Heinemann has been treated to a severe cross-examination by the police there.'

'Obviously the Japanese are taking this next fire extremely seriously.'

David almost took his arm away from its strategic position. 'Next fire! This isn't just a next fire; it could be the conflagration of the century. In their efforts to preserve all that is gracious about an old historical city, the Japanese have maintained Kyoto with a disproportionate amount of wooden construction. Even in normal times, and even with a climate similar to England's, the fire brigades have to cope with more than the normal frequency of alerts. Inspector Takata explained that they already have to guard against political protesters who resort to petty acts of arson. But if Walter Dudman can shoot his flaming arrows all over the place, including the palaces, the whole city could be ablaze in no time.'

Elizabeth digested this succinct speculation of an impending inferno. 'Of course. I should have realized. I can understand the concern. When I was at Cambridge, my friend Chieko told me about Kyoto and the way that the nation reveres it as the traditional capital. Tokyo may be the New York of Japan, but it is a big, busy, crowded, smoggy, overgrown city.'

'Yes. To destroy a cherished ancient city like Kyoto would be a massive national disaster. To destroy it would be like blowing up the Houses of Parliament, Westminster Abbey, and Buckingham Palace all at once. Even worse than kicking a football in the Long Room at Lord's.'

'Especially if it was by a gang of anti-Japanese agitators.'

'You've touched a raw spot there. Imagine if this blaze did occur, traced to British hands, and possibly given the appearance of quasi-official cognisance, the diplomatic fat would be in the fire, with a vengeance, if you'll excuse the metaphor.' Following Jim Marshall's instructions, David refrained from telling Elizabeth about the link between the closing of the Straits of Hormuz and the Japanese oil talks.

'Certainly I'll excuse it. If you'll excuse me reminding you of the "Made in England" stamp that we found on the later models of the Dudman Device, and which we thought to be an unnecessary embellishment.'

'My God, I'd forgotten that.'

'You see? You just can't do without my assistance. No wonder there are so many unsolved crimes, with the police only half-awake most of the time. If I were...' Elizabeth's intended dissertation on the inefficiency of the police force was interrupted by a demonstration that was second to none in one department, namely bringing a struggling female to submission in unarmed combat with no trouble at all.

After rearranging hair, earrings, make-up, and buttons, Elizabeth resumed the verbal attack. 'Obviously you need help. I shall have to come with you.'

This bombshell in the discussion saved Elizabeth from further depredations.

'You can't mean that.'

'Why not? You have just told me how easy it is.'

'But I had top-level official sponsorship. How could you get away from your work? Think of the expense. What will Jim Marshall think? What will Guy Sanders say? Hell, Elizabeth, I know this is the age of women's emancipation, but you just can't go chasing off half-way round the world on a sudden impulse. And you haven't got a passport.'

Elizabeth's eyes flashed, as did her choice of words. 'Codswallop! and furthermore, Balls! I am not in the habit of leaving things unfinished, and I have more than a passing interest. I do have a passport. And if this was a commercial exercise, I would be a major shareholder. To start with, I can talk old Braithwaite round, especially as he was most amiable this afternoon, and said that he hoped that I would follow the case through to its conclusion, for the reputation of the firm's insurance record. He even…'

'Go on.'

'No. You'll laugh, and I'll never hear the last of it.'

'I solemnly swear, by the bones of Owen Glendower, that I will not laugh. Trust me.'

'He said that if I pulled this off on behalf of Martin, Smith, and Jenkins, I could call myself Miss Lloyd of London. You promised you wouldn't laugh , you bastard.'

After another round of all-in wrestling, she continued. 'Anyway, I'm coming. Jim Marshall will just have to agree, and anyway, he can't stop me, as a private citizen. I can pay my own way. I always did promise Chieko that one day I would come to see her in Japan, but never thought seriously about it – just like you did. I may not be able to get there as soon as you, but I shall have a damned good try.'

'When did you get a passport?'

'I went to Paris with a friend. And that's none of your business.'

The full implication of what might be in store sank into David's head. He looked into her green eyes with more than mere acknowledgement of promised assistance. 'My dearest dear,' he said, 'to have you with me will be idyllic. But we shall have to keep our minds on the job – the arson job, that is.'

'I protest that I do not know what other job you may have in mind; but I too shall, as you so crudely put it, be on the job, mainly because I do not think you will get very far without me.'

With which parting shot, David had, reluctantly, to leave, but was persuaded to stop off on the way to prepare for the next day's critical briefing.

* * *

David made sure that he was early for Jim Marshall's meeting on Tuesday morning, even though he had stayed late with Elizabeth. They had attended to the material things of life at a French restaurant in the King's Road, and by mutual agreement went their own ways home. That David had not gone back to Elizabeth's was the joyous realisation that, with any luck, a lifetime together might lie ahead. He needed some sleep before the coming assignment, and had he returned to Chelsea, the chances of a night's sleep might have been highly doubtful.

'Looks like it's a case of the Four Just Men against the Four Just-Been-Had Men,' Mike Bridgeman commented, as he assembled four steaming cups of coffee from a flask. The meeting with Guy Sanders and David Thomas was once again presided over by Detective Superintendent Jim Marshall, and was sanctified by his pipe, which was going full blast on a crisp March morning.

'You're dead right,' Sanders observed ruefully, 'almost every theory we've had about these bastards has gone completely down the drain, while two smoothies from the Land of the Rising Sun walk in here and practically solve the case for us.'

'Steady on, now,' Jim relinquished his affectionate grip on his pipe for a moment, and reached for a sheaf of papers, 'we've a long way to go just yet, and so have they. We had better look sharp. The plot has thickened considerably, and we have to keep pace with its momentum. I'm very pleased, incidentally, that you, Thomas, will be on the case. You have pursued the foundations of where we got started with some diligence, in spite of a shaky beginning. You did the groundwork, and taken to the extreme, you may have been instrumental in saving damage to one of Japan's national shrines, and God knows what the implications will be if that happens. It is absolutely imperative that we stop them in their tracks.' He smiled at David. 'I understand that you had some help from Haydn Lloyd's daughter too.'

David thought it advisable not to go into detail, nor to mention Elizabeth's plans. He simply enquired if there was any news from Copenhagen.

Marshall referred to his file, stuffed with telex messages. 'Plenty. One mystery is solved. While we have been searching pubs and watching ports, these four have been in conference in Copenhagen , and as far as we can tell, have no intention of returning, at least not yet.'

'All four, Sir?' Guy Sanders remembered that Jim Marshall did not approve of strong language, although he was tempted to use it.

'Yes, all four. We ought to be kicking ourselves for not following the one sound lead that we had, Walter Dudman. We were told that he went to Copenhagen, we checked that he went to Copenhagen, we even double-checked; but simply because we had a forwarding address, we did not bother to make a hotel search until it was too late. He was in the Hotel Scandinavia, under his own name, all the time. And so were the others.'

This time, Sanders reacted. 'Christ. Big Jim and Frank Eastwick did catch the cross-Channel boat?'

'Yes, just as we originally thought. The difference was that, when they left Dover, they took the ferry to Dunkirk, not Calais; and took the train to Copenhagen, not Paris.'

'And Castleman?'

'Same route, we believe. Anyway, that is now irrelevant. But that is one straw that we have to clutch. They may have been covering their tracks, and they may have just decided to go to Copenhagen by their own preferences, but the fact that they registered under their own names means that they do not suspect that we are aware of them, or their associations, or their plans.'

'How did the Danish police find them?'

'Good old routine. They simply started with the big hotels, and soon found all four names together in the Scandinavia. Plenty of Smiths, but only one each of the others.'

'Are they still there?'

'Unfortunately no. The birds have flown, quite literally. They checked out normally, and caught the noonday S.A.S. plane to Tokyo on Sunday. They just ordered a taxi. The hotel porter remembers them well. One of them had a long black case, and the others had some odd-shaped cases too. Just think: while we were still interviewing barmen named Eric, they had actually arrived in Tokyo. And before you ask, the Tokyo police have checked every hotel in the city. And there was a report from Eri's Cabin that four men were singing lustily there last night.'

'But what about all that paraphernalia, the bow, the crazy arrows, and everything?'

'Simple. They had done their homework and planned their timing well. There is an international archery meeting in Tokyo next week, a sort of Archery World Cup. Dudman could easily show that he was a member of the British archery team, and had fooled the customs people quite easily. They inspected the contents of the boxes only cursorily, as the Japanese Archery Club was on hand to greet Walter. But they were so interested in his demonstration of the bows that they did not notice anything strange about the arrows. Only an expert archer would know the difference, and you can bet that they had been pretty well disguised, probably with a stack of real arrows on the top.'

Mike Bridgeman poured out some more coffee. 'What beats me about this whole set-up is that these chaps are all amateurs. It's almost bizarre. Clean sheets, every one, yet they are on their way to commit what might be the crime of the century and even start an international diplomatic incident of the highest order. Just think: the discovery of the pipe-bombs "Made in England" and who knows, other incriminating evidence of a possible British plot. Makes the Great Train Robbery seem tame.'

Jim Marshall repacked his pipe, ignoring the grimaces of his colleagues. 'It's damned clever, when you think about it. Just put yourself in the position of the outfit that has sponsored them. They could have hired professionals, but that would have been risky, because professional arsonist "torches" might well have had police records, and there would have been a chance that one would have been picked up and it would only need one to blow open the plot. On the other hand, if you examine the qualifications of these four, they combine to form a very efficient team.

'Eastwick, you see, is the team leader who had met Heinemann, who had dreamed up the whole scheme, and presented it to his principals, whom I shall come to later. He was the coordinator, negotiator, and, through his sponsors, the financier. Castleman made the travel arrangements, and he knows the country well. Smith is the wheel man, so that they are completely mobile, and Dudman is the key to the whole enterprise. He can set fire to a building without even going close to it, by a sophisticated, yet basically simple, modification of the ancient fire-arrow application of siege warfare. It all fell into place nicely: elementary organization, careful instrument-type metal-working, and the simple mixing of the incendiary ingredients.'

'You mean that they made their own fiery mixture?'

'Almost anyone can make an incendiary bomb. Our experience in Northern Ireland has taught us that. Many a common fertilizer contains most of the necessary elements, with a little sugar added, I believe. Alternatively, powdered aluminium or magnesium mixed with iron oxide – common-or-garden rust to you – make a very effective blaze, if detonated. The secret is the detonation . None of these mixtures is harmful, unless sparked off by a small explosion, the detonation. Most of the skill lies in the design and application of the detonator. That's tricky, but not difficult to a skilled craftsman like Walter Dudman. Remember his radio repairmanship, a bit of a lost art nowadays when nobody mends anything anymore. Detonators would come easy for him. Jim Smith made the tubular part of the device, probably did the filling too; Dudman finished them off in his Putney workshop. We're having that checked, by the way, although that is now a redundant exercise – shutting the barn door after the horse has bolted.'

Jim consulted another folder in his files. 'We have strong grounds to establish that the people behind this systematic programme of international arson are the Danish-German North Sea Oil Corporation, with headquarters in Copenhagen. Gerhard Heinemann, who Mrs Dudman nominated as a contact man for her husband, is a Dane from Schleswig-Holstein, hence the Germanic name. He is in charge of international affairs for the company. His business card obscures the fact that part of his job is to supervise, even organize industrial espionage, and that includes the Department of Dirty Tricks.

'Heinemann has a record. Not much of one, but enough to keep him in the files of the Copenhagen police. He was mixed up in a financial swindle a few years back, and his job was partly as a bag-man, carrying money across borders, and involved in it enough to get him a light jail sentence. It was a narrow squeak for him, and the short sentence was thanks to a technicality which seemed to prove that he was just a courier. But the oil company's lawyers did work extremely hard to ensure some leniency, more than you would expect for a mere courier.'

David posed a question: 'Would a large oil company of international status and repute get involved in a criminal exercise of this kind? It seems unbelievable. I would have thought there was too much at stake for them to risk discovery, quite apart from the lack of ethics.'

'Thomas, you have no idea of the extent of illegal activity that goes on in the highest levels of big business. The Swiss banks could tell you a few tales that you would not believe. There are cases on record that no publisher would care to accept as fiction, much less fact. When oil is involved, the stakes are the highest in the world. Most of the biggest corporations are the oil companies, or companies dependent on oil: Exxon, BP, Shell, etc. The world moves on oil. Take it away, or create a shortage, and you can change the fortunes not only of a nation, but of an entire geographical region. Look at the fuel crisis of 1973. Cut off the oil, or even just reduce it, and the wheels of industry stop turning, the price of petrol soars, transport slows down, and in the extreme, in the industrial countries, their whole economy and standard of living are affected, and even the balance of power can be jeopardized.

'Now, consider the specific situation that faces us right now. The Middle East War has closed down the Straits of Hormuz. Japan's industry is about to come to a grinding halt if it cannot reinforce its oil supplies, or even establish an alternate source. And so it has realized that its 80 percent dependence on oil from the Gulf and the Arab world is a formula for possible disaster. With the Middle East problems, it has turned its attention to the North Sea, and apparently there is a straight fight, probably with no holds barred, between Britain and a German-Danish-Norwegian consortium for a long-term contract to supply oil to the world's second largest industrial power. The internationally-agreed North Sea oil concession areas are split between the U.K., Norway, West Germany, Denmark, and the Netherlands. Britain has come off lucky, because we have the lion's share of the known reserves, and also we share with Ireland the seas off our western coasts.

'So the Japanese are out shopping. Recognizing our strength, all the other North Sea oil nations except the Netherlands have got together to produce a package deal. The Netherlands probably had to abstain because of its majority ownership of Shell, although that does not seem to have been a factor on our side. But the pieces fit together; that is why there was so much importance and security attached to the Japanese trade visit to London.

'Frankly, we cannot see how the rival group can beat us, but complacency can be as bad as sabotage. The deal is for 25 years, and it could involve more than just oil. It could help to revitalize our ailing ship-building industry. But even more – and you cannot put figures to this – the deal could symbolize a long-term trading understanding between Britain and Japan, contribute to erasing the worst memories of the War, and indirectly affect the course of international commerce of the civilized world for the next half-century.'

Jim Marshall felt that this peroration deserved another elaborate pipe-filling ritual, and the meeting paused for some more coffee. When they resumed, Mike Bridgeman took up the briefing.

'This act of arson, with the British deliberately implicated, could put back post-war Anglo-Japanese commercial and diplomatic relations by at least a decade. In spite of the Second World War, many in Japan prefer to look upon that as an inexplicable, even inexcusable, military aberration. They remember that in the First World War, they were on our side, and as an island nation, they see many similarities between our two maritime nations. The whole theme of this massive arson plot is, I am sure, to discredit the British to such an extent that the potential success of the current trade negotiations will be irrevocably undermined. Much will be made of the revenge motive of four Japanese-hating Englishmen, and false stories will no doubt be spread to implicate the British Government.

'Do you remember the Zinoviev letter? In 1924, a forged letter was allegedly sent from the Soviet Union, signed by Zinoviev, President of the Communist International, purportedly to spread communist propaganda throughout Britain. It was later proved to be a forgery, but its publication did much to bring about the downfall of the Labour Government and possibly changed the course of European politics for several years. So don't underestimate the potential of falsification on a grand scale. If a piece of paper can bring down a government, what might the burning down of a cherished city do?'

'And this outfit in Copenhagen is behind it all?' demanded Sanders.

'No definite proof, but this is one hell of a motive. If the British can be completely discredited, then I don't give much for our chances of a long-term oil contract. The dirt sticks. and "no smoke without fire" is an apt metaphor in this case.'

'And Eastwick's Gang of Four is this oil company's dirty tricks department?'

'Absolutely. The Copenhagen police worked on Heinemann, promised him at least some freedom for the rest of his life, as a choice against spending his remaining years behind bars. But he's tough. They had nothing but circumstantial evidence, and pretty slender at that. He called their bluff, admitting a loose connection with Eastwick and was trading in pornographic literature, which in Copenhagen is about the equivalent to snatching a bag of bull's-eyes from a sweet-shop.

'Carrying a British passport, he used to travel by rail and join the regular cross-Channel Ferry at Calais, looking like a typical holidaymaker returning not from Denmark, but from France, with the usual bags full of souvenirs. Frank was his distributor in London, working through contacts at the White City Dog Track. We believe that he became aware of Frank's hatred of all things Japanese, and the idea gradually evolved of using this for the advantage of his official employers. They talked about how they could sabotage the Anglo-Japanese negotiations, and next thing you know, a plan emerges, and they're in business. But damn it, that's all surmise. We haven't a shred of evidence.'

'And what's the payoff? People don't just develop a conspiracy on this scale for pennies.'

'Quite. The Copenhagen police leaned on Heinemann's secretary, who revealed that he drew out a considerable sum of money from the bank last week, all in sterling. He said he needed it for a business deal in England, but we believe he paid it to Eastwick – a cool £350,000, by the way – as a down-payment to seal the contract. We can't prove that Eastwick got the money, but the coincidence of timing is there.'

'£70,000 each, with two shares for Frank, I suppose.'

'That's about it. Just think: the four were either stony-broke or deeply in debt. The temptation to retire for life on a comfortable nest-egg – and repay some old scores into the bargain – was too good to miss, even for Walter Dudman.'

'Why even Walter?'

'He is far from being a criminal type, whereas the others are all at least street-wise. But his worries ran deeper. He couldn't face the shame and misery of having to tell his Gladys that they would have to go bankrupt and jeopardize their dream of retiring in a cottage in the country. He probably doesn't regard the burning down of a palace in a country that had, in his mind, caused his business to fail, to be absolutely immoral.'

'Same with Castleman, I suppose?'

'Yes. He seems to have regarded the whole affair as a bit of a lark. But I don't think that either of the other two had too many pangs of conscience. Frank Eastwick still has the marks of barbed wire all over his body.'

'You said "down-payments". Will there be more?'

'For such work, almost certainly. The final payout, assuming that the four succeed, could be three or four times that amount. For the stakes involved – trillions of pounds of oil contracts – that would be small change for Heinemann's people.'

'Not bad for a bunch of amateurs, all with a clean record.'

'Get your definitions right. This point has been made before. In their own fields, each one is a professional. Castleman organizes the logistics; Smith is the perfect "wheel" man; and Dudman was close to being an Olympic-standard archer. Eastwick has a perfect team. Yet even he is an amateur in one respect, as he is just a tool of Heinemann, and he may not know what the whole idea is about.'

'But they did throw us off the scent, with car auctions, and the like.'

'I don't think that "throwing off the scent" is the right metaphor. They simply took reasonable precautions, mainly to cover up their movements from their close acquaintances, including Gladys Dudman. The balladeering at the Old Comrades Club was just a bit of harmless bravado which they never dreamed would mean a damned thing to anyone else. But, as we have always felt, they do not know that we are on to them, so we have an advantage, especially as the Japanese police forces are alerted too. This could be a close thing. By the time you get to Tokyo, Thomas, you may be too late, as they may already be behind bars.'

David had listened thoughtfully during this comprehensive review, and the full responsibility that was on his shoulders started to hang more heavily. He ventured to add his own summing up of the situation. 'With respect, Sir, you seem to be over-confident that we shall apprehend the four men.'

'What do you mean?' Superintendent Jim Marshall's voice had an edge to it.

'I mean that the method they have selected to set fire to their target or targets gives them a special flexibility. The arrows can be shot from almost anywhere, and they don't make any noise to direct attention. Further, if at night, they cannot be seen. Walter Dudman doesn't even need to see his target. He could do an indirect shoot, just like machine gun firing patterns were developed to saturate a target on the other side of a hill or obstacle. He would just need to identify a couple of reference points during daylight hours.'

'Well, it's up to you, Thomas. You'll be on your way this afternoon. The entire police forces of Japan have been mobilized, so you have plenty of support. Takata will be coming with you, and you're acting as a special consultant. But you may find yourself playing a key role as your two eyes are vital. You're the only one who can spot the men in a crowd. Don't be afraid to ask for extra assistance, including the Self-Defence Force, if necessary.'

'The what, Sir?'

'Self-Defence Force. That's equivalent to our armed forces. Under the Japanese Peace Treaty, they are not allowed to organize militarily in a way that could appear to be aggressively inclined. Thus their quasi-military force has this polite and very correct name.'

'Er… I think I should mention that I may also be having some assistance from another quarter.'

The silence was deafening, until Marshall said, 'Oh?'

'Miss Lloyd has decided to accompany me. I did not encourage her, but her boss at the insurance company did. He looked upon her as the insurance world's equivalent of a Sheriff's Deputy, charged with running down the arsonists, and winning a great deal of kudos in the competitive world of high-rate insurance, not to mention the money itself. As you must know, she can be very determined, and this is on her own private initiative. Is there any official objection?'

'God bless my soul, what will that girl get up to next?' Marshall paused, and then added, pointedly, 'Is there anything going on between the two of you?'

'Well, in a way.' David explained that Elizabeth's visit to H Division had, after a false start or two, developed into a closer relationship – without elaborating on <u>how</u> close.

Mike Bridgeman looked quite pleased. Guy Sanders was unusually quiet, possibly because he couldn't believe it. The Superintendent questioned him, almost like a prosecuting counsel.

'Does her father know?'

'Do you mean about us, or about going to Tokyo?'

'Both.'

'She has spoken to her father about meeting me, and we were going down to Wales soon to meet him. But Japan has come up and she was going to telephone him today as soon as her ticket was confirmed by the airline.'

'Look here, young man, I'm speaking to you not as a Scotland Yard Super to an H Division Inspector, but as one man to another, with an admitted difference in ages. I have no authority whatsoever over Elizabeth, and she can, and I am sure, will, do as she pleases. But her father was my best friend in the force, and I regard her almost as one of my own. So forgive me if I appear to show an exaggerated concern. You are charged with an extremely important official duty. It now looks as though you have another duty. Do, I urge you, take special care of this young lady, whose intellect occasionally finds an outlet in headstrong escapades. I don't mean to suggest that this is an escapade, but do keep an eye on her, won't you? These Four Just Men may be amateurs and they may be harmless, except for their arsonist inclinations. But we cannot be complacent. There may be dangers that we don't know about. You had better bring her back without a hair of her head out of place.'

The Superintendent's obvious sincerity was such that David did not feel in the least embarrassed in assuring the assembled company that not a single one of Elizabeth's auburn tresses would be endangered. He even hinted that he hoped that this special care might continue for the rest of their lives.

The meeting broke up, with warm good wishes for the traveller from all his superiors, and David rushed off to Shepherd's Bush to pack.

Chapter 18
Fish and Chips
for Four

The teeming cosmopolitan centre of the Tokyo metropolis boasts many hundreds of night-clubs of all sizes and quality. A better – and almost certainly cheaper – way to spend an evening is to enjoy the cuisine at one of the many restaurants, offering not only the various Japanese menus, but also superb selections from almost every country of the world's national dishes. The night-clubs are of a general pattern, equipped universally with the same gin-and-tonic type of bar, the same type of barman, the same type of bar-girl (euphemistically described as a hostess), and the same outrageous prices; but the restaurants are another matter entirely.

The discriminating diner can choose tempura, sukiyaki, sushi, yakitori, shabu-shabu, and other dishes from the Japanese; but also steaks from Argentina, Brazil, or Texas; the ambience of Paris, the ebullience of Naples, the dignity of Geneva; or the joviality of Munich. The evening air sometimes catches the pungency of Moscow or the spiced warmth of Athens. Flamenco dancers entertain at the Andalusia, there is can-can (and other variations) at Maxim's, belly-dancing at the Casbah. Chinese and Korean eight-page menus, Indian or Pakistani curry, Indonesian or Thai rice dishes, Mexican enchiladas: you name it, Tokyo has it.

Not surprisingly, therefore, the city has its quota of English pubs, and the best of these is Eri's Cabin. Eri was a former hostess who, like so many others of her clan, had assiduously saved enough money to become independent. Intending to open yet another night-club bar in the Ginza or Akasaka districts, she had been persuaded instead by some of her former English and Australian clientele to risk her investment in an English-type pub.

From the central part of Tokyo, skirt the southern edge of the Imperial Palace moat, and follow the road underneath the elevated Shuto Expressway. Do not expect to find many directions as the Japanese are not at their best with road signs. General MacArthur tried to introduce some alien ideas like street names, but the locals had always got along very well, thanks to postmen who were born navigational geniuses with photographic memories. Only the big boulevards are readily identifiable by name. Still, the road beneath the Shuto Expressway is quite straightforward, and any taxi-driver will know how to get to Roppongi Corner, blindfolded.

Turn right at the corner, pass by a few shops and cafes, turn right again into a narrow street, down a slight hill. Opposite the headquarters of the Self-Defence Force, a flight of stairs ascends at the side of a ramshackle looking, shapeless wooden building. Through a door at the top of the stairs, Eri had converted a floor into a passable replica of an English pub, which she called Eri's Cabin.

On any night, this is a favourite rendezvous for itinerant Englishmen, Scotsmen and Irishmen, and Australian or Hong Kong aircrew. Together with some of the local English-speaking foreign residents, they can seek solace from their busy oriental world by enjoying a pint of British beer. Posters of familiar English scenes, quaint notices in Gothic script, a motley assortment of yard-of-ales and pewter tankards, all donated by appreciative customers, embellish Eri's Cabin with the atmosphere of genial friendliness which is the

157

special flavour of the typical English pub. Eri dispenses beer, cigarettes, and – her speciality – English fish and chips – with a special blend of Japanese hostess charm and English barmaid perkiness. The conversation is of tramp shipping, airline schedules, football scores, and cricket results. The regular drinkers lean on the bar; the hungry ones eat their fish and chips at the tables; and some of the regulars play darts, with their own sets of "arrows" which Eri keeps in a safe place.

Into this home-from-home one Monday evening in March, at about ten o'clock, came Bill Castleman to introduce three friends who were on their first visit to Japan. (Simultaneously, some 8,000 miles away in London, where it was only two in the afternoon, Jim Marshall was trying to persuade the delegation from Japan to get to the point.)

Eri greeted her old friend, Birro Casterman. During his travels to the Orient, Eri's Cabin had been a refuge where he could avoid indiscretion, yet have an enjoyable time in good company. He knew Eri well enough to bring her the odd gift from England, such as a long-playing record of barrack-room songs, with which she entertained her customers from time to time. On this occasion he presented her with a small package which she happily opened to find a small bottle of duty-free Arpège; and courtesy demanded that although she already had a stack of such gifts, she should make as much fuss as though it was the first she had seen.

After Bill had introduced Frank, Jim, and Walter, the four retired to an alcove table, and did justice to four pints of Double Diamond.

'I've asked Eri to save us some fish and chips,' began Bill, 'so we have time for a couple of rounds. Nortmally it's first come, first served, before she runs out of fish, but we shall be looked after. Makes a nice change from the Old Hammersmithians.'

Frank Eastwick seemed happy. 'I must hand it to you, Bill, you know your way around here. I wasn't exactly looking forward to a meal of raw fish.'

'I thought you would all like it,' Bill beamed, 'remember, we have to sing our anthem, and I can't think of a more appropriate place. Now you can see the reference to Eri's Bar for yourself, but we can't do it on a Thursday evening this time.'

'Can't argue with that. You're the tour guide, and you've done us proud. Not a hitch.'

Walter Dudman spoke up: 'Let's drink a toast to the Japanese customs. If they had been tougher, we'd have been in real trouble.'

'You under-estimate your own talents, Walter. You did a beautiful job. Only an expert would have noticed that the arrows at the bottom of the box were a bit larger than the ones on top. And they didn't look anyway. They were too interested in the bow that you showed them, and your chat about the samurai and their archery skills. Your diversionary tactics worked perfectly. You should have been on the stage.'

Jim Smith sank the remains of his first pint. 'You really had them interested, Walt, what with all that stuff about Genghis Khan and the lamination techniques. You gave quite a lecture. I was afraid that they might have got too interested and asked us to demonstrate. In fact, you got me interested too. Deadly as a sniper's rifle, you said?'

'Abso-bloody-lutely!' Walter was slightly on the defensive. 'And let me remind you that, unlike the rifle, at night-time, there is no flash to locate any visible source of the missile Not only that, the bow is completely silent, except for the "twang" when I release the bowstring. But two or three hundred yards away, nobody's going to hear that.' He paused and grinned. 'And Nobody heard the Twang. Good title for one of your songs, Bill—'

Frank Eastwick interjected. 'Before any more songs, we have a job to do. We can't count our chickens until they are hatched. Drink up, it's my round, and we'll go over the plan again.'

Eri caught Bill Castleman's eye and four more pints were forthcoming. 'You want fish and chips now?' she asked.

'Might as well, Eri, we're going to talk for a while. Any chance of getting on the board?' He glanced at the dart-board, where a needle match was in progress between Cathay Pacific Airways and Qantas.

'Never mind darts,' Frank Eastwick warmed to his task. 'Remember that our watchword is minimum exposure. We move in at dusk on Thursday, weather permitting, and only a tornado is going to prevent our pipe-bombs from being effective. At that time, the streets will be full of rush-hour traffic, and the tram-cars and tram-stations will be crowded with office workers returning home. The fire-engines will thus be held up by the snarled traffic, whereas, during the daytime, the traffic is lighter, and during the night-time as well, they would have a clear run. But just at dusk, those Kyoto tram-cars are on our side.

'The twilight hour makes it easier for us. As Walter points out, his bow is near enough silent, and we can make it invisible. Our secret weapon. Nobody is going to see or hear the arrows in flight. Even if, before or after, anyone saw us with a bow, they wouldn't connect us with the fires.'

Eri brought their fish and chips to the table, and Bill thanked her with 'domo arigato'. A man in a business suit passed by their table, and Bill motioned for them to keep their voices down. Frank dropped his lecturing to a whisper.

'Timing is absolutely important. We have to be in position at the precise points just as twilight sets in. If we act too soon, when it's still light, someone might just see the arrows. If we wait until complete darkness, Walter's aim might be off. Have you double-checked the time of sunset, Bill?'

'Yes, and double-checked the itinerary from Nagoya, too.'

'All right. We have to overnight there, not in Kyoto itself. We shall keep off the scene until the vital hour. Once aboard the strike vehicle, there's no substantial difference between driving 75 miles from Nagoya as from a base in Kyoto. Then it's a commando raid: in quick, strike, and out again quick. But we all have to play our parts precisely. One slip and the whole plan's up the creek. But we have one advantage: nobody knows what we're up to, but it would be foolish not to take maximum precautions.'

'As the actress said to the bishop,' remarked Walter, now back to his old cheerful self.

'Quite. The English newspapers did have a paragraph or two on our experiments. But only a couple of lines or so. Even if they do find anything suspicious in Dorset, they will put it down to some political crazies.'

'Wessex Nationalists would be a natural for Ashmore,' observed Bill Castleman. 'Local environmental protest group setting fire to an army camp.'

'Yes. It's all very comforting. And nobody has, to my knowledge, made any enquiries as to our whereabouts. I didn't speak to my land-lady, bless her soul, after getting back from Ashmore on Thursday night. In fact, I never spoke to anyone until Jim picked me up next morning. Unless you count the wrong number on the telephone.'

'Wrong number?' Walter Dudman looked up quickly.

'Yes, somebody got the wrong name in the book.'

'That's damned funny. Someone did the same to me, just as I was leaving for the airport on Friday. Did your call come in about 9.30, just after breakfast?'

'Can't say exactly, but it was about then. Probably just a coinci-dence. But it does emphasize the need for vigilance.'

Walter looked worried, and Jim patted him on the back, encouragingly.

'Don't worry Walt. Like Frank said, just a coincidence. If they were on to us, we wouldn't have got out of the country.'

'It doesn't actually follow, to be exact.' Frank shook his head. 'We

161

covered our tracks pretty well by taking indirect routes, even though it didn't appear necessary. Sort of instinct. Except you, Walter. And you had a cast-iron reason for going to Copenhagen, so it's unlikely that they will trace us to there.'

Walter seemed relieved. He decided not to mention Brussels. 'Not cast-iron. Good mountain yew, perhaps.' He gestured as if to draw a bowstring.

'That's all right then. As I was saying, following Heinemann's advice, we cover our tracks, without actually going into hiding. Like not staying in the larger cities.'

'Yokohama and Nagoya are not exactly villages,' commented Walter.

'Well no.' Castleman provided the local intelligence. 'Yokohama is one of the largest cities in Japan, but its proximity to Tokyo, yet not part of the Tokyo city itself, is a neat distinction. And it's convenient for getting to Nagoya, our main operations base, tomorrow. Only 80 miles from Kyoto. In both cases, we're booked into smaller hotels, less likely to be identified.

'But just remember, four Anglo-Saxons are more likely to be conspicuous here than in Copenhagen. I am just being more careful as we approach the final countdown. Now listen. We're getting side-tracked. Let's get back to our timetable. We leave Nagoya at 2 p.m. on Thursday. We pace ourselves to arrive in Kyoto just as the light begins to fail. Fortunately, Bill knows Kyoto as well as he knows Earl's Court.

'The negotiations for borrowing the vehicle and familiarization with its driving characteristics must be completed in Nagoya no later than 11 a.m. on Thursday. We shall have a letter of introduction from the British Commercial Attaché at the Embassy. That's been arranged, so there is no problem there. You're all set to take care of that, Jim?'

Big Jim Smith had been patiently waiting for his cue. 'I have an appointment with Toyota tomorrow morning, Tuesday at 10 a.m.

I spoke to one of the assistants this afternoon, and he assures me that the company will allow us to conduct our own tests, with his letter as a guarantee of good faith. He expressed the hope that our purchasing plans for Japanese vehicles would involve some reciprocal trade that would help Britain's export drive to Japan. I can't see any potential hitch in getting what we need.'

Eastwick took over the discussion. 'Right then. Tomorrow morning, we'll go over Bill's large-scale maps of Kyoto just one more time, to be certain. We'll prepare the letters for posting to all the big newspapers on Wednesday night. Jim will get in some driving practice around Yokohama and the centre of Tokyo – if he can drive there, he can drive anywhere. Walter, you won't be able to get in any practice, but I think you don't need any.'

'In this case, the targets are much bigger than the ones I am normally challenged with. I can hit a roof, even in the dark. I shall score, don't worry.'

'That's about it then. After lunch tomorrow, we'll all take it easy and catch up with the jet lag. We shall have to be up early for the train on Wednesday morning. Have you booked the tickets yet, Bill?'

'Four seats on the 7:13 Kodama bullet train out of Shin-Yokohama station. Seats on the right side, so that we can enjoy the view of Mount Fuji. Leave the hotel absolutely no later than at 6.30.'

'Any chance of the train being late?'

'You can set your watch by them. I hear that the drivers are fined if they're a minute late or a minute early.'

'Good. Any questions?'

'What about that idea of leaving a couple of unprimed incendiaries at the Embassy?'

'Thanks, Jim, I nearly forgot. Bill has made preparations, and Walter has already given him the pipes. Right, Bill?'

'Right. They're in a cardboard tube, like rolled-up documents.

163

I'll see that it is hidden somewhere in one of the outer offices of the commercial attaché's department. Unless someone gets really curious, the tube looks just like rolled-up maps or charts.'

'Take care you don't drop them on the end, just in case.'

'You bet.'

Bill Castleman stood up. 'We've done enough talking for tonight. Hope you enjoyed Eri's fish and chips. Let's relax. We can sing our song in a minute. It seems to have brought us luck so far. Let's see if these locals are ready for a real darts team.'

Frank Eastwick felt that he should close the meeting. 'Why not? Relax it is. Thank our lucky stars that the police haven't the foggiest notion as to what we're up to and that they haven't a clue as to where we are.'

Chapter 19

Up and Away

By mutual consent, David and Elizabeth arranged to meet at the Japan Air Lines ticket counter, London Airport, at 2.30 p.m. on Tuesday. Superintendent Yamazawa had organized David's ticket, first-class, which was waiting for him at the check-in counter. On arrival, his suitcase was whisked from his hand, labelled, and deposited on the baggage conveyor belt almost before he reached the counter. The station manager escorted him to the V.I.P. lounge, where the lady at the bar mixed him a large Suntory and soda to ensure his comfort before being called aboard.

Elizabeth arrived shortly afterwards, checked into economy class, and stood waiting. David emerged, rather shamefacedly, from the lounge, where he was struck by the contrast between such courtesy and the melee when he had taken an inclusive tour from Luton the previous September. He had enjoyed a second Suntory before remembering the time of his date at the ticket counter, and was prepared for a verbal onslaught. He was not far wrong.

'Where the hell have you been?' demanded Elizabeth.

'Er... I've been organizing a comfortable place for us to wait in until the 'plane leaves. The airline took me to the lounge and I've asked them if I could bring a friend in from economy class.'

'You travel in style while I go steerage. Excuse me while I get myself a Coke.'

Fortuitously, Inspector Takata turned up at that moment. He bowed graciously to David, and a little hesitantly to Elizabeth. David bowed back, carefully, knowing that about ten pairs of Japanese eyes were checking out his etiquette. He hastened to explain her presence.

'This is Miss Elizabeth Lloyd, of Martin, Smith, and Jenkins, the famous insurance company, of Lloyd's.' With a sly glance at Elizabeth he added, 'Of London.' He went on to explain her association with the case, giving her full credit for her contribution, and implying that she was a direct descendant of Edward Lloyd himself. Takata was impressed, and spoke quietly to the J.A.L. ticket agent at the counter, who then addressed Elizabeth.

'Excuse, please, but economy class fully booked, no seat available; we must upgrade you to first class.'

Five minutes later, a slightly bewildered, but far more contented Elizabeth, was confronting a giant gin and tonic in the V.I.P. lounge. The subject of class distinction and Coke was forgotten, and David was obviously forgiven. To their surprise, the door opened, and Inspector Takata came in with Mike Bridgeman.

'Had special instructions from the C.I.D. Commander to see you off,' he beamed. 'It's not every day that Scotland Yard gets a chance to help our friends in the Orient. I have a useful dossier for you, Thomas, which Jim Marshall has put together. Also, Inspector,' he turned to Takata, 'perhaps you would convey this letter from our Commissioner to your chief? As you know, we are charged with taking care of a very important delegation from your country, and we must see it through until the politicians are finished. If things go well, we should accomplish that by the end of the week.'

Takata bowed again slightly. 'Tokyo Police grateful for offer of assistance. Will convey letter to headquarters immediately when we arrive in Tokyo.'

Mike elaborated. 'There is not much we can do right now. I have sent a full report to the British Ambassador in Tokyo. We have a grave responsibility, with four Englishmen on the loose in your country and planning God knows what. His Excellency can't do much either, but we'll make sure that he is completely informed immediately of anything we can pick up at this end. But Inspector Thomas, with his better knowledge of the whole case, and of the four men, is the best contribution we can make. And...' he smiled, 'he will have specialist assistance from Miss Lloyd. I hope you will take care of them.'

David and Elizabeth hastened to assure Mike that they were already being well looked after. Takata added, 'I think treatment OK so far. And will get better.'

'How much time difference is there?' David asked the J.A.L. Station Manager, who had also joined the party.

'Eight hours. It is now already 11 p.m. in Tokyo. You will land at Anchorage, Alaska, en route. He explained the geographical peculiarities of the Polar Route, and mentioned, in a slight lapse of his English, that they would be well fed up during the flight.

Takata joined in the conversation. 'Also,' he said, 'I will take care of honoured guests.' He gave a semi-humorous bow to the Station Manager. 'I also up-graded.'

Mike Bridgeman put a friendly hand on Takata's shoulder, and took the opportunity of assuming a take-charge position, without giving offence. 'Marvellous. You will be a great team, with your local knowledge and expertise, Inspector Thomas's familiarity with the characters we are looking for, and Miss Lloyd's unique contribution. As you know, we owe it to her for discovering the plot in the first place.'

Takata nodded. 'In England, women completely em...?' He sought the word.

'Emancipated,' said Elizabeth firmly.

167

'Thank you. Not so much in my country. But changing, especially in big cities. Girls work in offices and factories, and wear kimono only on special occasions.'

It was time to go. The V.I.P. treatment continued as the three now-distinguished passengers were escorted on to the plane, and directed to the front section, where three smiling stewardesses awaited, to offer all the accoutrements of first-class travel, including the oshibori – warm towels – and happi-coats, those loosely-fitting casual garments which help to prevent normal attire looking like dishrags by the end of the journey.

They climbed over Windsor Castle and headed north along airway Amber One. It seemed odd that Manchester, northwest of London, should be on the way to Tokyo in the Far East. After settling in, with the seat-belt sign off, David felt that he should justify his role, and suggested that they should review the case. Inspector Takata agreed, and they gathered around the bar at the rear of the first-class cabin. He asked, 'Can you tell me about bow and arrow? Is it like Samurai weapon?'

'Yes, indeed. Jim Marshall has prepared a briefing on the subject of modern archery. I have glanced at his notes, and perhaps I can paraphrase from them. I have to say, it looks as though the bow and arrow of today can be classified as a highly lethal weapon, although it does not have a history of extensive use for arson.

'First of all, its lethal potential is without question, as we know from the past history of the English and Welsh bowmen at Agincourt and other pitched battles. They were accurate, and the trained archers could be deadly at ranges of up to about 250 yards. They could sustain repeated draws of up to 50 pounds or more, and release as many as a dozen arrows in a minute, and of course in almost complete silence. Their arrows could pierce the light chain-mail armour of the time. Later on, the Turks, for example, perfected the skill to make laminated bows, using horn, wood, and sinew, and are on record as having shot up to 900 yards.

'Today, in competition, using powerful bows, with stronger draws up to 80 pounds or more, such distances can be achieved. Make no mistake, the arrows are like bullets. In the days of the longbow men, it is said that they could penetrate thick oak doors, and today a standard archer, with a typical draw of, say, 65 pounds, could pierce a telephone directory or an inch of wood. Or so it says here.' David paused, to make sure he had full attention and referred to his notes.

'Wood is seldom used for the bows today, apparently. In olden days, Spanish yew was favoured as the most resilient, or sometimes English yew or ash, or, in the Land of Our Fathers,' he glanced at Elizabeth, 'wych-elm. But wood soon deteriorates, and in any case the introduction of firearms made bows obsolete. Although the early muskets took much longer to fire and were less accurate, they did not wear out quickly, and could be kept in store, ready for the next battle. The bows simply dried up. Nowadays, bows have wood, usually maple or hickory, between layers of fibre-glass. It is also a precision instrument, with a sight that can be adjusted for elevation or horizontal correction, almost like a rifle sight, with prisms, rings, and cross-hairs. Even telescopic sights.'

'What about the arrows?' Elizabeth asked.

David consulted his file. 'Birch, fir, pine, or cedar – any straight-grained wood – is still used, but metal arrows, made of aluminium alloy, have become universal for competition. Ah, that is why our gang have been able to convert Walter Dudman's arrows for a special use. No doubt the heavier arrows will not fly as far, but long range may not be a problem for him in Kyoto. Presumably his bow- and his draw-strength will be enough, and he has perfected his technique at the various experiments that we know about.'

Elizabeth felt that David had made the point, and enquired: 'Is there any news from Copenhagen or Tokyo?'

David selected another report from his file. 'Not very much. Further questioning of Heinemann hasn't given us any clue to the four men's whereabouts. He is now on the spot: more frightened of disclosure than of a prison sentence – which is ominous. He claims that Eastwick is the only one of the four men whom he has met, and this may be true, as all his dealings were with Frank in pornography trading. He must have heard about the other three, but won't admit it.

'The Danish police say that he adamantly refuses to implicate the German-Danish Oil Corporation in this specific enterprise, but – as he knows the information can be checked – he admits that they gave him a generous budget to indulge in intelligence gathering generally, including clandestine efforts which he describes as "standard business practice", i.e. bribes. This accounts for his heavy cash withdrawals.

'The Corporation has put pressure on the police and they have had to release him, for lack of any evidence except for dirty postcards and magazines; but they are keeping a close eye on him, hoping that he may try to communicate with someone, and they have his telephone tapped.'

Elizabeth was shocked. 'I can't believe they've let him go! Can't they at least hold him on a pornography charge?'

'In Copenhagen? You must be joking. The Danish Government abandoned all censorship of sex literature in 1970. Not, I might add, that the incidence of sex crimes has increased as a result. Quite the reverse, I understand. They could charge him with having a false passport, and probably will, but in Danish law that is not enough to lock him up. In any case, the oil company will exert its influence. They have the best lawyers. And if you think about the situation, he doesn't need to make contact with Eastwick right now, as he has made the deal, and he knows that they are on their way.'

'But what about the big pay-off? The four men have only had the down payment.'

'Frankly, we have no idea. It might be another transfer of cash, but that is unlikely, if the sum is half as large as I think it is. It could be wire-transferred into a Swiss bank account, but I doubt that. I can't see our amateur arsonists getting involved in the world of high finance and offshore numbered accounts. But I imagine that, whatever method is used, it will be surreptitious in some way or other, if only to avoid a connection with his sponsors.'

'Anything about the Corporation that would be relevant?'

'Nothing. Norway has a minority holding, but they have plenty of oil of their own, further north. The large American oil companies are represented, but only nominally, and that is normal practice. They have been deeply involved in North Sea oil ever since it was first discovered, but they have far greater investments in British North Sea oil, so they do not stand to gain anything one way or the other.'

'Perhaps Inspector Takata has some news from Tokyo?'

He shook his head ruefully, and reported that a search in all the hotels in Tokyo and Kyoto had drawn a blank, but he felt that he should emphasize the gravity of the threat. He described Kyoto as the most beautiful city in the whole of Asia and one of the most beautiful in the world. It was the nation's capital for ten centuries, and still has hundreds of temples, castles, and pagodas of great historical interest and value. The old Imperial Palace is now used as a museum, and even the Emperor can only enter the throne room at the time of his coronation. During the war, many streets were made wider, to provide fire-breaks against the spread of fire if American bombs hit the suburbs and caused a holocaust as had happened in Tokyo. Even Japan's enemy in the war seems to have respected the cultural and historical importance of Kyoto. Today, there are no high buildings, as in Tokyo or Osaka, and every attempt is made to preserve the immortal soul of the ancient city.

'They say that most of the buildings are made of wood.'

'Yes. All wood. And many temples have thick roofs made only of straw . Burn easy. Beautiful Kinkakuji Temple burn down in 1950. Mad arsonist. We make new temple.'

'What about the singing nightingales?'

'Very special. Nijo Castle home of Tokugawa Shogun, ancient war-lord. He make floor with cunning design so that if spies walk on floor, it sings like bird. Made with special wood design to make bird noises. So when we read poem by Castleman-san, we think immediately of Nijo Castle.'

'But what a piece of luck that you knew abvout Eri's Cabin!'

Inspector Takata admitted that it was perhaps lucky; but as they often had meetings with the Self-Defence Force, just opposite, he occasionally tasted English fish and chips as a change from the local tempura.

Elizabeth yawned. The airline meal, coupled with the low hum of the aircraft's engines, was soporific. She excused herself, and returned to her now-reclining window seat. Even the stunning view of Greenland's snow-white ice-cap kept her eyes open for only a few minutes.

Chapter 20
Welcome to Roppongi

The welcome in Tokyo even exceeded the effusiveness of the departure from London. Haneda Airport was, as usual, thronged with a mass of humanity, but with the help of the airline staff, reinforced by special-force policemen assigned for the occasion, David, Elizabeth, and the Inspector were cleared through customs and immigration formalities in record time. They threaded their way through the human barrier outside the customs hall (approximately twenty relatives welcome all Japanese travellers when they return home) and soon they were in a police car, belting down the freeway into the city centre. Normally bloody-minded taxi-drivers gave the flashing light a respectful right of way, and in no time they were off the highway, and into the quiet street that leads to the Okura Hotel, one of the world's finest. Because of the peculiarities of the time zones, flying westwards with the sun, it was still late afternoon, with the exception that, having crossed the date line, it was already the next day.

Apparently forewarned of the arrival of two Very Important People, the hotel manager personally supervised the perfunctory check-in procedure, and the only slight snag was that he assumed them to be either man and wife, or good enough friends to need only one room.

David hastened to explain – remembering his experience at Tollard Royal, and not daring to look at Elizabeth – that two rooms would be required. Neither spoke as they were escorted to their rooms by the manager himself. Whether by accident or design, the Okura had covered all bets by putting them in adjacent rooms, with a connecting door. Possibly by this time completely washed out by the long journey and dog-tired, neither David nor Elizabeth spoke, except a whispered 'see you later.'

Nevertheless, as Elizabeth collapsed on the sheets for a brief hour's winding down, she mentally crossed her own private Rubicon.

* * *

David and Elizabeth both slept briefly, and by pre-arrangement met Inspector Takata in the convivial Orchid Bar at the respectable hour of 7 o'clock, to review the general situation. After the requisite bows, he reported that there were still no more new developments. The police were systematically double checking the guest lists of every hotel in Tokyo, the 1,400-room New Imperial, the 2,000-room New Otani, the giant Keio Plaza, the Palace, the Akasaka, and scores of others. They had located eleven groups of four Caucasian men staying as a group. Six of these had, on further enquiry, turned out to be unquestionably American, three had been French, German, and Italian, and the remaining groups, though impeccably British, were equally impeccable businessmen, vouched for by the hotels and their local offices, and readily identified by the passports recorded at the reception desks.

A similar story, on a smaller scale, was reported from Kyoto. The scope of the search would eventually be extended to the outlying suburbs and satellite cities – but that was a huge task. The metropolitan area of Tokyo alone housed more than 20 million people, and Takata had said wearily that they had decided to spread the net to include Osaka – another ten million or so – and then possibly Nagoya. Both of these latter cities were only half an hour's train journey from Kyoto. He asked for patience and, like honourable Marshall-san, he had faith in the noble cause of routine work. Westerners had to stay in a hotel somewhere and probably in a western-style, not a Japanese-style one. David confirmed this speculation, knowing that, just from his brief knowledge of the four men, they would be unlikely to stay in one with Japanese customs and Japanese food.

After a relaxing drink, the Inspector suggested that, as there was nothing else they could do at that moment, would the honoured guests be interested in a quick look at Tokyo by night, and perhaps even to visit Eri's Cabin? Elizabeth could hardly wait to finish her sherry, and did not even excuse herself for the normally statutory make-up. David almost forgot to sign the room bill, which in any case would have been irrelevant.

It was one of those unforgettable occasions when everything for the visitors was new and fascinating. Takata was a fine guide, showing them the fairyland of lights that is downtown Tokyo, point-ing out the big department stores for Elizabeth's future reference, and skirting the Palace perimeter before winding their way through the narrow streets in Akasaka, to pull up finally in a poorly-lit street in the district of Roppongi. Answering their unspoken question, he pointed to a small flight of stairs. The moment was electric. It was like discovering the Holy Grail, although the objective in this case was not exactly holy.

David put his free arm round the Inspector's shoulder. 'You've done us proud, Inspector.' He spoke with enthusiasm, almost excite-ment. 'Let us ask Eri if she has some English ale. Do you drink English beer?'

'Hai. Like good Kirin and Sapporo in Japan. Not like American.'

'Splendid, Let's go in. What about your driver?'

The visitors were given a hint of Japanese police protocol. 'He not allowed to drink on duty. Another time. We are not on duty.'

Sure enough, at the top of the stairs, a small inscription confirmed that this was indeed Eri's Cabin. Somewhat awed by the drama of the occasion as they entered, Elizabeth and David were uncharacteristically silent. Eri recognized Takata immediately, and poured out a Johnny Walker Black before he could hold up a reproachful hand. The Inspector did not wish to be given the reputation of a regular customer for the hard stuff. A whispered request produced four pewter tankards of Double Diamond. They all sat down in the same alcove which had been occupied by Frank Eastwick and his chums 48 hours previously.

Eri, a dapper and now middle-aged lady, quite obviously in charge, presided over the drinks. She promptly sat down next to Elizabeth and plied her with questions about Mary Quant, Mick Jagger, Jackie Stewart, and Miss Selfridge, and it was at least ten minutes before David could, as it were, bring the house to order, and get down to business.

'Eri – may I call you Eri? – I know the Japanese police have already asked you about the four men who came in on Monday night, but would you mind very much if I asked you some more questions about them? You see, I do not know them personally but I do know a lot about them, and I have seen some of them.'

'OK. What you want to know?'

'Did you overhear anything that they were talking about?'

'No. They not talk when I bring fish and chips. But they laughing at jokes. But I not hear anything. Honest.' She looked David straight in the eye, and he felt that she was telling the truth. He also noticed that, incongruously, she spoke not only with the familiar problem with r's and i's, but also with a slight Australian accent.

'But according to the Japanese police report, you did hear that they were staying at the Palace Hotel.'

'Not exactly. I hear Palace word in song they sing when praying darts. I ask Caserman-san for words of song, and he promise to send me L.P.'

'So the word Palace was irrelevant?'

'Prease?'

'Not important.'

'Yes.'

'It was?'

'Yes, not important.'

Takata interrupted quickly to explain: 'Japanese yes, English no.'

Eri asserted – and with her clientele, she was practised in dealing firmly to clear up any doubts – that she did not say that Palace was a hotel; but that perhaps the police thought so. She just remembered the word Palace. But she had been thinking. David was all ears.

'I think many things because Caserman-san good friend. I do not want to make trouble for him. Good customer. Always polite, not like some customers. Buy many drinks. Bring me presents. What has he done? Anything bad?'

David glanced at Takata, who nodded approval. 'Eri, before I answer your question, let me try one more. Did you hear any of them mention the word Kyoto?'

'Definitely not. And I would remember. I from Kyoto.'

'You are!'

'I born there, went to school. All my ancestors from Kyoto. I go there sometimes to visit mother and father.'

This time, after another glance for Takata's approval, it was David's turn to look Eri straight in the eye. 'I have to tell you, Eri, that your friend Caserman-san and his three friends are planning to make trouble in Kyoto.'

'Oh my goodness. Why they do that? He not hate Japan. He love Kyoto, go there many times. He study it, almost like special student.

He even visit my family.'

'I cannot tell you the reason. But I must ask you not to mention our meeting tonight, and you must forget our conversation. We are not trying to deceive you. But we are very worried. Isn't that right, Inspector?'

Takata nodded vigorously. He spoke to Eri in Japanese for a few moments, and translated for the guests, and continued. 'Yes, we very worried. They could damage your city. We must try to find them before they do terrible damage. Can you help us find them?'

Eri's face had changed from curious to horrified, possibly remembering Hiroshima. She paused, then said, 'You try all hotels in Yokohama?'

'Are you sure? Why there?'

'Caserman-san in navy in war. All navy people like Yokohama because it big port. He stay in Tokyu Hotel but not now. I do not know which one. But in Yokohama. He say he have girlfriend there.'

Inspector Takata was already on the telephone. 'Thank you Eri. You big help. We search all Yokohama hotels immediately.'

David concurred. 'I promise that we will do everything to save damage to your lovely city.'

Eri looked pleased. 'You take care of mother and father. I help you.'

'Good girl. If you think of anything else, you telephone Takata-san.'

'OK. Good on you, cobber.'

With which startling words of encouragement, they rose from the table. Except Elizabeth. She was sound asleep. The jet lag had caught up.

* * *

The police car deposited two sleepy arson investigators at the Okura Hotel. The Inspector assured them that, as soon as any news came in from Yokohama, he would telephone immediately. David and Elizabeth collected their keys and followed the Okura peculiarity of going down to their rooms, the lobby being on the fifth floor. David wondered if he should dare to kiss her goodnight when he guided her gently to her door. He was saved the trouble. 'We can dispense with the connecting door,' she said, 'I need some help with my zipper.'

Chapter 21

Nice Day for a Fire

Next morning, having rendered the necessary assistance to a recalcitrant zipper, together with a totally unexpected sequel, David sat on the edge of the bed and pondered on the joys of spontaneous seduction. If this was women's lib, he thought, he was in full support. He could hear splashing sounds, and realized, to his great joy, that this momentous occasion of their first intimacy had come easily, naturally, and with only a trace of embarrassment, mostly on his part. It crossed his mind that Haydn Lloyd, about whom he had heard so much both from his superiors and from Elizabeth herself, might not have approved. Ought he to have a conscience? Well, it was too late now, and after all, he had not been the initiator of their first night together.

His gaze wandered away from the bathroom and rested on Elizabeth's suitcase, which lay open on the rack provided. He was astonished to observe a most un-Elizabeth-like garment. He got up to look more closely as she emerged from the bathroom, to see him bearing down on her case.

'What are you looking for? We didn't need my pyjamas, if that's what you're looking at.'

'I wasn't thinking of that. I was looking at this monstrosity.' David held up Walter Dudman's sweater, hand-knitted by his devoted wife, in all its ghastly green, with yellow stags and Robin Hood at the ready. 'What the hell did you bring that for?'

'Don't you remember? I promised Mrs Dudman that I would take it to her Walter, and when you get to know me better, you will realise that I always keep my promises. You may think that I'm too sentimental. Perhaps I am. But I feel genuinely sorry for Mrs D. I'm trying to keep my sense of values. Unless you can think of a legal reason to stop me, I'm going to give Walter his sweater.'

'We've got to find him first. And what's more, I don't give a damn about his sweater, and certainly not now. While we're waiting for Inspector Takata to call, I can think of better things to attend to.'

'Only when you've showered first.'

* * *

At 10.30, the telephone rang. The Yokohama police had located a small Japanese, non-tourist-style hotel where the four Englishmen had stayed, but had checked out the previous day. The hotel porter had thought they were going to catch the Kodama train, maybe to Osaka, but was not sure. Yes, could be Kyoto. 'Meet me in lobby in twenty minutes,' Takata said. His mood had changed from the genial guide of the night before to sharp professional efficiency.

This time, David reversed the zipper procedure. Elizabeth looked radiant, well rested – quite surprisingly, under the circumstances – and dressed for a fashion parade. David wondered if the Inspector had tried his room first, and concluded that he would not ask. Perhaps his check-in protestations at the front desk had fooled nobody.

They were mobile within half an hour, cutting through the morning Tokyo traffic to the Central Station. Takata told them that, at about 4 a.m., one of his men had found the hotel in Yokohama where the four Englishmen, answering to the precise descriptions, and with their confirmed names in the hotel register, had arrived on Monday afternoon, and had stayed until early Wednesday morning. They had checked out soon after 6 a.m. and had probably caught the Kodama bullet train that stopped for a bare two minutes at 7.30. The hotel clerk thought it was that train because he had heard the name in their conversation.

'It must be Kyoto, because it's Thursday – to coin a phrase,' murmured Elizabeth.

'Pardon?' queried Takata.

David explained the allusion to the movie that satirized the multi-stop tourist program. 'Today is Thursday. All the previous rehearsals have been on Thursdays,' he continued, 'but the only reservation on the idea of keeping to that possibly superstitious routine is the dependence on good weather. Light rain would not matter, but if a heavy storm breaks, then they might postpone the effort, to be safe. But today, the chances look good, at least for them.'

It was a little too early for the cherry blossom. In the parks and at the roadsides of the broader avenues the trees still wore their hand-tailored straw jackets, soon to be cast off so that the hibernating insect parasites could be incinerated. Busy workmen tidying up the ravages of winter suggested that spring was on its way. Crocuses poked their violet and yellow heads above the ground.

As they entered the busy Tokyo Central Station, they all looked up at the sky to corroborate David's forecast. The skies were grey, but not the leaden colour that normally forbodes a heavy downpour. There was a slight dampness in the air, not unlike the kind of monotonous mistiness that characterizes the notorious English weather. Like the English, the Japanese delight in a fine day, but this Thursday morning was one of pale slate-grey, short of gloom.

The three were met by two other plainclothes policemen who bowed appropriately and then did their best to escort them unharmed to the exact place on Platform 16, marked with precision to line up with the doors of the train. Elizabeth had been used to the London

Underground crowds but she was grateful for the police escort for the sake of her dress and voluminous handbag, They were protected against the great tide of humanity that packs Tokyo Central, up to three-quarters of a million every day.

They climbed the stairs to the elevated platform. To serve a total of some 50 million energetic and industrious people in the southern part of Honshu Island, the Japanese transport planners had had the foresight to replace the old narrow gauge line with a meticulously accurate straight-and-level line to begin a new age of high speed railroads. Takata proudly told his guests that in a single year, the Tokaido Line, as the Tokyo-Osaka Shin-Kan-sen (or High Speed Line) was named after the traditional route, carried about 30 million passengers in a single year.

Sure enough, the train doors opened at exactly the right spot as the sleek sixteen-car train drew smoothly to a stop, and they took their seats in the first-class Hikari express, which would cover the 300-mile journey to Osaka, with only two stops, in three hours. A minute later, the train moved quickly up to speed, and the visitors studied the panorama of Tokyo's rooftops, the Tokyo Tower, and the docklands. Gathering momentum up to the 140 mph cruising speed, they passed Shin-Yokohama Station, where the Four Just Men had boarded the Kodama on the previous morning. With Elizabeth at his side, David wished that all police work was like this, especially after they emerged from a long tunnel and rounded a shallow curve to admire Mount Fuji, snowcapped, an almost perfect cone rising to more than 12,000 feet, with no intervening foothills to spoil the scene. The weather had become fine, the sky was clear, their spirits were high.

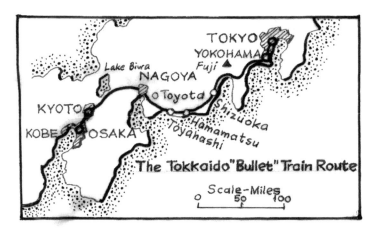

The pioneering high-speed Tokkaido line from Tokyo to Osaka.

Elizabeth whispered 'a nice day for a fire', which took the smile off David's face, as he realized that they were probably getting close to the zero hour for trying to forestall a catastrophe, possibly a holocaust, of no little dimension or consequence. He voiced his concern to Inspector Takata. He enquired why, in the circumstances, it was not possible to take strict precautions and close off the sections of the city where the precious historic buildings were located.

Takata produced a map of Kyoto, unfolded it, and with infinite patience explained that Kyoto had more than 1,200 temples and 600 shrines, in addition to the Imperial Palace and Nijo Castle. 'Old buildings all over Kyoto. Every corner. Everywhere.' He traced his fingers in a wide arc over the map to emphasize the point. 'Would have to clear whole city. Cannot do. Maybe spread panic.'

David and Elizabeth both nodded, appreciating the enormity of the task that would confront the authorities were such a course of action attempted. Kyoto had a population of one and a half million.

'So you accept the risk that perhaps the arsonists will have some success, even if we manage to stop them from doing the worst

184

damage?' Elizabeth showed her concern, and Takata seemed slightly hurt at the implied suggestion that the Japanese police were indifferent to the human tragedy that might ensue. He explained further that, with rare exceptions, all the treasured buildings were not immediately close to dwellings, and that mostly there were high walls all around them.

'Therefore danger to people not serious. And we watch like hawk.'

'But danger of damage to many buildings?'

'Probably. But loss of building not so important as loss of person. Also, we can forgive.' The Inspector smiled and looked directly at the two British guests. 'Perhaps you think we Japanese not concerned. You have bad memories of war. We also. Japanese and British peoples friends for one hundred years and recent war unforgivable. You not forget conduct of Japanese soldiers in China. We also not forget firebombing of Tokyo and atom bombs on Hiroshima and Nagasaki. One day we hope time will destroy all bad memories. Both sides.'

The possibility of a difficult silence in the conversation was rescued by a tap on Takata's shoulder from one of the uniformed girls who periodically dispensed green tea and the Japanese savoury equivalents of cake and biscuits. He was wanted on the telephone and went off to the booth in the buffet car.

When the Inspector was out of earshot, David suggested that they ought to side-step any reference to the war-related motives of the Four Just Men. Elizabeth concurred.

'Back to my psychology again, but has it occurred to you that, whatever the commercial or diplomatic fall-outs from this firebombing, assuming that they pull it off, the individual brutality of Japanese individuals has far outbalanced any impartial analysis of statistics? The total number of actual casualties suffered at the hands of the Japanese was not on a grand scale; but the individual crimes were headlines. The news that some Englishmen had set fire to some buildings in Kyoto would hardly produce a sense of shock in London's East End or in Coventry. I could see letters to *The Times* recalling the River Kwai or the Bataan Death March and comments in the pubs on the theme of "serve 'em bloody well right".' David agreed. 'That would play neatly into the hands of the oil company. It would pour salt into old wounds, and the consequent controversy that would be generated would help to jeopardize the discussions, if not the success of the proposed Anglo-Japanese long-term oil agreement. I can't quarrel with your psychology. Odd, isn't it? The Nazis herded children by the thousand into gas chambers, starved millions of Jews to death, massacred at least ten million in Russia, yet they still have their apologists. But the Japanese are never allowed to forget the cruelty of the sadists in their armed forces. I suppose Kipling was right: "east is east and west is west and never the twain shall meet".'

'Well, I hope he was wrong.'

Takata returned to his seat, effectively putting an end to the debate. He confirmed that rooms were booked in Kyoto at the Miyako Hotel, and security precautions had been intensified. But there was no trace of four Englishmen booked into any hotels.

David tried to answer this cold logic. 'As far as we can ascertain, when they left Copenhagen, the men did not know that they were being followed, or searched for, or even suspected. We picked up Heinemann before he had any chance of further communication with them. But Eastwick may be smart enough to take absolutely no chances. Yet he is unlikely to have stayed anywhere except in a hotel, especially with Bill Castleman's local knowledge. They must be somewhere that would normally be available to any traveller.'

'May I ask a question?' David looked alarmed as he thought Elizabeth might be bringing up the subject of wartime enmities and war guilt. She ignored his glance.

'You may think this a silly question, but why did they catch the train at Yokohama?'

David thought that this was the wrong end of psychology and his comment was patronizing. 'Because, my dear, they were in Yokohama?'

'But, correct me if I'm wrong, Inspector, from the hotel where they were staying, they could have just as easily gone to Tokyo Central and taken advantage of the Hikari, as we did, because it was top class.'

Takata demurred. 'No, they not save much time, as Shin-Yokohama station is quite near. Even with extra stops, they not save time by going back to Tokyo.'

Elizabeth was not convinced. 'I am not being explicit, and I seem to be rambling off the point a bit. I am trying to explore the possibility that the train they caught was taken especially because it was the multi-stop Kodama, and with Eastwick taking precautions, he may have asked Castleman not to book in to Tokyo, and that they could still catch the train at Yokohama to some place near but not at Kyoto. As a travel agent, Bill could have arranged both ends of the journey to put the police off the scent at both ends.'

Takata looked worried. 'Like looking for pin in haystack. We now have little time. Other stations before Kyoto are Maibara, Gifu, and Nagoya. Big job.' Nevertheless, he was seriously impressed, and went to the telephone again. David also noted the easy telephonic system from the train, and found himself wondering if a tie-line between H Division, Scotland Yard, and the Flying Scotsman might not be a good idea.

The Inspector returned, looking even more disturbed than when he departed. 'Bad news,' he said, 'Tokyo Chief of Police have call from Asahi Shimbun, biggest newspaper in Japan, and maybe world, with international syndicate. They receive letter, in English, claiming all Kyoto destroyed tonight as revenge for Bridge over River Kwai and *Prince of Wales* battleship. Say many bad things about Japanese. Letter ends with insult to Emperor and Long Live Queen Elizabeth, and is signed by Four Just Men.'

Chapter 22
Last Calls

'Did you post the letters, Bill?' The Four were at breakfast in Frank Eastwick's room at the Nagoya Castle Hotel, in the shadow of the castle in the city of that name, about 50 miles from Kyoto. Frank was carefully reviewing the plan of attack.

Bill Castleman confirmed: 'They should reach the news desks this morning.'

'I still think that is asking for trouble.' Walter Dudman shook his head, pausing after some mysterious maintenance work on his bowstrings. 'Suppose they surround the city or send a special detail to patrol the streets?'

Frank was assertive. 'They must arrive before the news of the fires, to gain maximum effect. Nobody would believe them if they arrived after Kyoto was burning or had burned to the ground. They would put it down to one of those nutcases who always likes to seek some kind of notoriety, just for kicks.'

'There's another factor,' Big Jim interjected, 'I've been studying the map of Kyoto very closely. They don't stand a hope of covering every access to the city. They would need a whole army. Think of the troops in Belfast a few years back, and how easy it was for the two private armies to keep up the action. So don't worry. Kyoto's a much bigger place than Belfast, and it has fewer police, if what I hear about the law-abiding Japanese is true. And remember that that place opposite Eri's was only the Self-Defence Force. The Japanese are no longer aggressive. Their armed forces are quite passive.'

'Pity they weren't so bloody law-abiding in 1942,' gritted Frank.

'All right, keep your hair on. You're the one who keeps telling us to control our emotions and set about this thing methodically, remember?'

Frank snorted. His hatred for all things Japanese bordered on the obsessive.

Dawn was breaking and they could see through the window the magnificent view of Nagoya Castle. The weather was clear and crisp. Walter observed with quiet confidence that right then, with the window open, he could drop half a dozen arrows directly on to the castle, almost in medieval fashion, one on each tier of the traditionally shaped tower, with its gracefully-curved parapet roofs.

Big Jim returned to his theme. 'I can't see how they can stop us. Look at this.' He pointed to the map in front of him, much in the same way that Inspector Takata was to do about three hours later on a fast-moving train, only a few miles away from where they were sitting. 'I've counted 83 temples and shrines and this map is on quite a small scale. And as we agreed last night, the Kyoto tramcars are going to be our allies.'

In this respect, Big Jim was right. In 1975, Kyoto was one of the few major cities in the world which persisted in operating single-deck tramcars, on a grid network covering the chequer-board pattern of streets aligned in parallel north to south and east to west, in a uniform, oddly uncharacteristic style, compared to that of most Japanese cities. These public transport vehicles, admirable for carrying hordes of people very cheaply, albeit uncomfortably, in the rush hour, were at the same time perfectly designed to cause traffic jams at the slightest pretext. Which is one of the reasons why most major cities in the world have dispensed with their services.

Kyoto, however, being obstinately Japanese, loved its tramcars as San Francisco worships its cable cars. Hong Kong has preserved its ancient double-decker trams, and kept them running long after other cities have consigned them to the scrapyard.

Frank Eastwick took charge. 'Whether you like it or not, I'm going to go over the plan again. We have to play this out with absolute precision. Jim, you have obtained the letter of introduction to the commercial vehicle department of the Toyota works. Any trouble in finding the place again?'

'None. When I went out to Toyota yesterday afternoon, I memorized the route exactly. I'm used to doing that, looking for car auctions all over England.'

'Good. And you made arrangements for two of us to pick up the truck this morning. Is there any more paperwork?'

'Not that I know of. Their salesmen were so delighted at the prospect of a new outlet in England for their heavy vehicles that they are bending over backwards to help. My dealer's licence, and some showroom photographs, convinced them that I was out for business. One or two souvenirs of car races that I've been in seemed to reassure them that I could handle the driving without a chaperone. Remember that they drive on our side of the road. They even offered to advise me of a road circuit to take in some mountainous stretches, to test the trucks severely. Naturally, I didn't tell them that we're going in the opposite direction.'

'Are you sure you have the route to Kyoto correctly plotted?'

'Quite sure. Following our agreed strategy, I shall avoid the Meishin Expressway, and follow the former main road, through Ichinomiya, Gifu, and alongside Lake Biwa. That takes us through the low mountains which will be chock-full of commercial traffic Our truck will be one of hundreds. According to Bill, it even has tramlines along it when we get into Kyoto. Right, Bill?'

'Strictly speaking, they're not for tramcars, it's a street railway, a limited-stop system that runs out into the neighbouring countryside, rather similar to the ones they used to have in Holland and Belgium. But basically, you're right.'

'Amounts to the same thing. Anyway, it's less conspicuous than the motorway. On the other hand, if we tried to avoid traffic by approaching Kyoto by one of the lesser roads, we might stand out just as obviously as if we were on the motorway, simply because the trucks avoid the narrow roads. In any case, there aren't many of them, as the city is surrounded on three sides by hills and mountains. Better to get lost in the crowd.'

'Right, that's settled. Jim will drive, and Bill will navigate. And Jim, you will return the truck to Toyota next morning, then go back to join us in Yokohama. Nobody will know where you've been on your test drive. Now, what about our chief marksman? Are you all set, Walter?'

The archer fingered the grip of the powerful bow which he was just packing carefully into its case, and pointed to the bow sight, a precision instrument attached to the middle part of the bow, just above the grip. 'I was toying with the idea of a telescopic sight, but I shan't need it. In the old days, I used to say a target would look as big as a house. Now I've got castles to aim at. In fact, I shall hardly need this sight, but I'll keep it on from force of habit. But in the twilight, I shall need my clicker.'

'Your what?'

'Clicker. Wouldn't be without it. Simple device here,' Walter indicated a small piece of spring steel attached next to the sight. 'Look, when I pull the arrow back, with the shaft underneath the clicker, the click tells me when I'm at the correct pull, and warns against preliminary release. I also have this gadget to hold the tension until the exact moment when I want to shoot.'

'Have you checked the arrows since we arrived?'

'This year's model, the new slim-fit pipe-bomb, you mean? No. I already checked them in my workshop back home. The fewer times they're handled, the better I like it. Thank our lucky stars that the customs men didn't get too nosy at the airport. Don't worry; they are snug in the box, exactly as I packed them, and no less fire-worthy.'

'But I thought Jim took you out yesterday afternoon for a practice shoot?'

'Yes, he did. We went out to some waste ground in the hills near here. I used blanks, identical arrows, same weight, same centre of gravity, but without the gunpowder.'

'So you're all checked out then?'

'Absolutely. Give me direction of target, range, direction of wind, and I'll hit the target, dead on.'

'That seems to be it then. Meet in the lobby in ten minutes. I'll pay your bill, Jim, while you get the car. Are you leaving it at the Toyota place?'

'Yes, I shall simply park it in the visitors' car park, and pick it up tomorrow morning, when I return the truck.'

'Fine. There is just one more thing, and I'll allow Bill to have the closing shot in this final briefing, as he's the one with the local knowledge.'

Bill Castleman looked around his colleagues in crime and spoke seriously. 'There is a remote possibility that, in spite of this meticulous planning, something may go wrong. In the event, it would be advantageous to split up, even though this would place you three at some slight risk, because you are in unknown territory. Listen carefully. If any one of you is stranded alone, find your way by some means or other to Kyoto railway station. You all have pocket maps of the city, so memorize the general layout, and above all, orientate yourselves so that you know instinctively which streets go east-west and which go north-south. All you have to do is to head south, on foot preferably, and you're bound to come to the railway track sooner or later. Finding the station from then on is only a matter of a short time. Just make sure that you mingle with the crowds.

'If the slightest thing goes wrong, we shall have to split. Then we shall meet on the Tokyo-bound Bullet Train platform, at the far end to the east, that is, towards Tokyo. Wait until the last train, if necessary, in the hope that, if we have to split, we can all join up again. There will be hundreds of people boarding the trains during the evening so, I repeat, you should be able to lose yourselves in the crowd.'

'I don't fancy my chances if you don't turn up, and I have to find my way alone,' grumbled Walter.

'If you can't make the last train, you will have to use some other initiative. But that is only in an extreme emergency. I am just explaining what to do in the unlikely event that we are forced to split up. Remember that nobody is expecting us. Nobody knows we are in Japan, except Eri. And nobody is going to connect a passing truck with a fire in the Castle.

'Incidentally, Frank, when we all get back to Yokohama, are we still agreed on the final payoff at Eri's Cabin?'

'We shall meet, never fear, tomorrow night in Eri's. While Kyoto's burning, the Four Just Men will be singing our song and collecting our just reward.'

Chapter 23
Closing In

The Hikari express glided at a steady and smooth 140 mph through the urban areas that line the southern coast of Honshu Island. Inspector Takata finished jotting down a few rapid words on a tiny note pad. One thing to be said for Japanese calligraphy: it is extremely economical of space. He looked up to David and Elizabeth, who were given once again a distinct impression that the alleged inscrutability of the oriental depended on individual definitions. Takata was extremely worried, and looked it.

'Must call Kyoto,' he declared with some agitation. 'Officials will meet train, but we must ask for reinforcements, maybe bring in help from Osaka. Must call every hotel in whole industrial area of Osaka and Kyoto Kansai district, Nagoya also. We may have luck to find something.'

When he had gone to the telephone booth at the end of the Green Car section, David unfolded the map of Kyoto which Takata had left on the seat. 'I don't suppose we are going to glean anything from this,' he said, 'but we must prepare ourselves for any eventuality. There is one small consolation: unless Eastwick or whoever wrote the letter to the newspaper was deliberately trying to throw someone off the scent – and that is unlikely because they do not know that anyone is on the scent – we now know the approximate timing. As you surmised,' he glanced at Elizabeth, 'with your behaviour analysis, they are aiming for consistency, whether through superstition or through some kind of pride in sticking to a timetable. They always experimented on a Thursday, and so today is the day for the strike, and it will probably be tonight. The last fires all occurred in the evening, so the chances are for a mid-evening fire tonight. What do you think?'

Elizabeth looked vacantly at the map. 'About all I can think of is that Kyoto isn't the same as Tokyo or Osaka, with bright lights and high life into the night. Probably quietens down towards the middle of the evening, and therefore the arsonists would perhaps run a greater risk of being observed, because the streets will not be so crowded. It is terribly important for them to get away afterwards, because by the letter to the press, they have put themselves at risk.

'I suppose that's one reason why the pay-off is a big one, and another reason why they didn't waste time after setting foot in Japan. The sponsors of the project want the havoc to be created to coincide with the oil negotiations in London which are taking place.'

David nodded assent. 'Equally, it follows that the letter had to be sent before the fire, or it could have been dismissed as some impostor trying to gain cheap notoriety. Half a dozen copycats frequently own up to a crime, once one has been committed.'

'Do they really?'

'Oh yes. And the more gruesome the crime, the more people own up.'

'So it was essential that the Japanese press got the letter first?'

'Yes. According to Takata, the Asahi Shimbun demonstrated a commendable sense of responsibility by informing the authorities immediately. Much as the news editor would no doubt have welcomed the opportunity of an exclusive scoop, he must also have been horrified at the enormity of the threatened crime. He would, of course, be aware of the implications of an international political incident, including an investigation of his newspaper's possible compliance.'

'Don't you think, then, that they will make their attempt during the busy part of the evening, on the well-known grounds that the safest place to hide is in a crowd? That's just common sense, and you don't need me to remind you of that.'

'In one way you're right. But four Caucasian foreigners, including two tall men, would stand out at almost any time. So why wait for the evening?'

'That's fairly obvious. A bow and arrow may be a silent weapon, but it isn't the easiest to conceal. Walter Dudman would stand out like a circus clown. No, it has to be in the evening, in the late twilight at the earliest.'

'We're not going to have a lot of time when we get to Kyoto, then – which, if I'm not mistaken, should be very soon now.'

David was right. The train was slowing down appreciably, and at precisely 11.21 drew into Kyoto station. They were met by the customary escort of plainclothes policemen, and the usual police car, which whisked them off to the Miyako Hotel. By 2.15 they were seated in a private room provided by the management, for a briefing on tactics from the Chief of the Kyoto Police, assisted by the Chief of the Kyoto Fire Department, with whom Inspector Takata had exchanged bows, and courteously handed over the command to the local experts.

In introducing David and Elizabeth – more bows – he was careful to stress the part that they had played in identifying the nature of the probable method to be used in the arson attempt, and was most complimentary in expressing the trouble they had taken to come half-way round the world to assist in preventing a potential disaster. The Kyoto Police Chief, Superintendent Sasaki, began with a short speech of welcome, translated by Takata, but wasted little time in getting down to business. He began, however, by handing an envelope to David.

It was a telex message from the British Embassy to say that the matter was being urgently reviewed and monitored at the very highest level. The Prime Ministers of both countries had been informed, and permission granted to suppress all publication of any news whatsoever pertaining to the attempt. Strict security must be observed at all times, and the criminals must be apprehended as inconspicuously as possible. The Embassy was to be informed immediately of any significant developments. The attempted conflagration must be stopped at all costs.

David snorted. 'England expects...' he began. 'This is disgusting. I don't think these politicians and bureaucrats have the faintest idea of what we're up against. They think that four arsonists are going to march up to the Imperial Palace, aim their bows, and then we shall step in and say, "You can't do that, chaps," and that will be the end of it.

'They haven't a bloody clue that all the details have been carefully planned, most probably down to the minute. The ingenious method chosen may yet defy all our efforts at detection until it's too late. It will be of little satisfaction to catch them after the crime has been committed. If they can set fire to either the Imperial Palace or Nijo Castle, that alone would be enough to discredit the British. They have an odds-on chance of getting both, as according to the map, the two places are less than a mile apart, and not too much mobility will be required. Anything else that they can manage will be a bonus. Typical Foreign Office. Not a bloody clue.'

The local police had pinned a large-scale map on the wall, and they grouped around it. In full relief colour, it vividly portrayed the city of Kyoto's position, snuggling into a southward-facing valley surrounded by a group of mountain foothills. To the south was a broad plain, containing the continuous build-up of residential and industrial areas which reached right to the Osaka metropolis. Kyoto itself was shaped like an egg standing on its pointed end, with a river flowing almost due north to south. The pattern of streets was remarkably like the grid common to almost any American city, endless rows in parallel, criss-crossing at right angles. Every half -dozen streets or so, there were wider boulevards, those that had been specially widened to form fire-breaks during the Second World War.

Along these, marked with distinctive red lines, were the tramway routes which the citizens of Kyoto loved so well and filled up every day.

And standing out clearly against the tastefully-chosen colours showing residential. commercial, or industrial areas, was a random polka dot pattern of black symbols of various sizes and shapes. They denoted the historical places of interest in Kyoto, the 1,600 temples, palaces, shrines, and castles which constituted a substantial propor-tion of Japan's fascinating national heritage of unique architecture. Many of them, including some of the larger symbols, appeared to be uncomfortably close to each other. In some cases, however, there were protective surrounding areas of green, indicating park land or gardens.

David pointed to the congested area of streets, on both sides of Marutamachi Dori, one of the broad highways running east-west, and which bisects the city into roughly equal halves. It was a busy district, with three of Kyoto's main hotels in the vicinity. The Palace Side Hotel actually overlooked the Imperial Palace grounds, and, David observed grimly, the Hotel Kyoto and the International Hotel were similarly placed in respect to Nijo Castle.

'I would suggest,' he said diffidently, not to appear to be trying to take over the local case, 'that you should concentrate maximum security right here. This area seems to be particularly vulnerable. I expect you have that already under control, but this is where I should perhaps go on the slender chance of my recognizing someone.'

Takata obliged, translating simultaneously to his colleagues. Sasaki nodded and conveyed the message that he was trying to organize protection for more than 1,600 buildings of architectural or historic importance with about 4,000 men. He had hastily conscripted them from every city around Kyoto, and had managed to spread them a little more densely in the vicinity of the Palace, the Castle, the Heian Shrine, and the Nishi-Honganji, Higashi-honganji, and Kinkakuji Temples. But the order of priorities of these sacred shrines was difficult to decide. Also, he dared not spread the cover too thinly elsewhere, for fear that the arsonists might get in some free practice at the lesser shrines and temples. On the other hand, if the police made themselves too obvious – not too difficult in this law-abiding city – then not only would the good citizens of Kyoto become alarmed, they would start to ask too many questions. The extra police presence might also alert the criminals to possible impending danger of discovery. This could cause a postponement, and they might vent their spite on another night. He did not know the reason for the absolute secrecy, but those were his orders: not to give the impression that anything was happening out of the ordinary. He was in a difficult position: he had been asked to deploy many extra police without appearing conspicuous and without anyone noticing.

The Fire Brigade Chief assured them all that his full force was alerted. In a city of wooden houses, fire drill was a way of life, but he was not happy about the prospects of a big fire during the rush hour. He had had many a fracas with the city transport authorities in the past, trying to persuade them to re-route some of the tramlines to make way for the fire trucks to get by, but all to no avail. The tramway stops stayed obstinately in the middle of the road in some of the main streets, and even in some of the side streets. He despaired of seeing any sense of priorities in determining the protection of Kyoto from a catastrophic fire.

The image of frustrated mobility during the Kyoto rush hour sparked off the germ of an idea in David's mind.

'It may be no consolation, if one of your lovely old buildings is set on fire,' he began, waiting for Takata to translate, 'but I would like to throw in an idea. If, as we all seem to believe, the most likely time for the attack is during the rush-hour – say, about 5.30 or so, just as dusk is setting in – then we have to concede that it could be extremely difficult for us to stop the first arrows being shot. But by the same token, it could be difficult for the arsonists to move about after the first fire-raising and the alarm being set off. There is bound to be a mad scramble of police, fire-engines, bystanders, and although they don't know it, there will be a lot of us on the look-out. As soon as the first flames are seen, we should be able to close in, in ever-decreasing circles.'

For the first time, Elizabeth volunteered an opinion. 'I wish I could share your confidence. But I have a nagging fear that these fellows are too clever to endanger themselves that easily, or to have come all this way simply to walk around more or less casually with archery equipment at the ready. You just can't conceal an archery bow. There must be something else in the plan. To start with, Walter Dudman must have a clear arc of fire, which means that, to a certain extent, he will be exposed. On foot, as four western foreigners, they will stand out in a crowd, or even worse, stand out where there isn't a crowd. Even if Walter does succeed in firing his salvo, he has to get out immediately, possibly to another firing point. The problem seems to be one of movement, mobility, logistics, getting around. To make sure of a complete conflagration, they have to set fire to more than one priceless architectural work of art. They have to be completely mobile.' Elizabeth emphasized the last word by thumping David's knee. She had made her point.

'By which you mean that they have to have a vehicle of some kind. What do you suggest, one of Toyota's Land Rovers?'

'I suppose it would have to be a utility vehicle or a small pick-up truck of some kind and it would have to have an open top, to allow Walter a clear arc of fire. Doesn't that narrow down the options?' Elizabeth's comments commanded attention, and she continued. 'But he would still be conspicuous. He would have to stand up to draw the bow. Technically, he could lie down or crouch but his aim would be terrible. So assuming that they have the approach route well mapped out, and they have surveyed the target area, measured the ranges, and so on, they could simply pull into a side street, or even into a back street, or mews, almost anywhere conveniently away from direct public observation. Walter could fire his first arrows, then move off to the next target.'

David had to concede.

'When you put it like that, it all sounds so easy. What do you think, Superintendent?'

The Japanese hosts had been listening with polite attention to the two visitors as they voiced their thoughts aloud. Inspector Takata had become so involved himself as he translated the trend of the conversation that he indulged in the curious Japanese custom of grunting at the unspoken commas, to indicate interest and approval, a habit that can be disconcerting to the uninitiated.

Superintendent Sasaki's grave expression told them exactly what he thought. His shoulders sagged and he spoke disconsolately to the Inspector, who passed the message on to David.

'We think best, maybe only chance is for Inspector Thomas to recognize men in street. He will tour city to observe and coordinate forces. Meanwhile we will issue special report to all police cars and to many policemen in street who have two-way radio and tell them to look for open truck with four Englishmen in the back.' But the Inspector obviously had little hope of their chances.

David was still smarting from having been upstaged by Elizabeth's penetrating analysis of the arsonists' logistic essentials, realizing that he should have thought of it first. He tried to divert the conversation by demanding to know what the hell Elizabeth thought she was doing by stuffing Walter's old green sweater into her voluminous carry-all bag.

'More psychology?' he asked, with a grin.

'Get stuffed,' she said, also grinning. David did not translate the remark in answer to Inspector Takata's quizzical look.

The guided tour was strangely like one of the lightning affairs beloved of one-day visitors who, having spent six daylight hours in Kyoto, return home armed with box loads of slides to prove that they have "done" all the places of interest in the city. With a few detours, and with frequent stops, the party drove from shrine to shrine, shrine to palace, always on straight roads, and turning at right angles at street intersections. Occasionally, even though it was in the middle of the afternoon, they had to slow down or even stop to wait for passengers to alight or to board the tramcars. In the broadest thoroughfares, these had special tracks which left a clear way for other traffic; but too often they occupied most of the available road space.

David noticed that there were quite a few policemen at every street corner, standing nonchalantly in shop doorways, and by British standards, there seemed to be an unusually large number of traffic cops on duty, even extra ones assigned to pedestrian crossings. The latter, meanwhile, many of them wearing white hygienic masks customarily worn by Japanese suffering from the common cold, and used to taking their lives in their hands while crossing the street, found unaccustomed protection from the official escorts, and even from plainclothes policemen disguised as kindly strangers.

At the fire stations, it was apparently inspection day, as gleaming fire trucks were to be seen in front of, rather than inside, the stations, with what appeared to be the entire crews, including extra help, vigorously cleaning and polishing. An unusual number of fire department vehicles were cruising along the main boulevards, although they did not seem to be going anywhere in a hurry.

The populace was oblivious to anything strange. In fact, David reflected, there was not much really unusual about the scene. Had he not been aware of what was going on, he supposed the extra few policemen, or the occasional cruising fire truck would not have looked particularly odd. It was only because he was primed, and that he was touring potential trouble spots with a guide that made their presence seem obtrusive.

He mentioned the point to Elizabeth, who observed that, with luck, perhaps Frank Eastwick and Co. would not realize that a small army was lying in wait to apprehend them.

It was just after four o'clock, close to dusk. As they reached the southern end of Horikawa Dori, he realized that his map-reading had been only too correct. One single drive along Marutamachi Dori would put Walter Dudman within archery range of the Heian Shrine, the Imperial Palace, and Nijo Castle, plus a few minor shrines and temples. Only five minutes' drive to the south, the Nishi-Honganji Temple and the Higashi-Honganji Temple were coming within range, even from the same possible firing point on Horikawa Dori.

He noticed too that almost across the street was the main railway station, where, in the rush hour, tens of thousands of people catching scores of trains would provide an effective cover for a getaway.

He asked Inspector Takata whether there was any chance of visiting some of the approach roads into Kyoto, but was forced to agree that this would probably serve little purpose. Desperately aggravating though it might seem, there was realistically nothing they could do but wait.

Although they had discussed the subject with Takata before, Elizabeth asked if all the policemen had been briefed with a full description of the four men, and was assured once again that portraits had been despatched from Scotland Yard by picture-wire almost within minutes of the disclosure in Jim Marshall's office on the Monday earlier in the week, actually at about 1 a.m. Tokyo time. Five thousand copies had been printed and distributed within hours. They suspected that the Englishmen might be disguised.

Elizabeth disagreed, on the grounds that they still did not know that they were suspected. They both looked at David. Much would depend on his being able to spot Eastwick or Dudman. Her suggestion that they might all cover their faces with hygienic masks, thus obscuring their national identity, Caucasian or Japanese, did not cheer them up.

They had just swung northwards from the congested area in front of the railway station forecourt, and were about to turn east across the Gojo bridge towards the Kiyomizu Temple, when there was a crackling on the radio and the Superintendent exchanged some agitated words with the source of the message. The time was just 5.15 p.m.

Takata looked stunned. 'It has started,' he said grimly. 'Nanzenji Temple on fire.'

Chapter 24
Reach for the Sky!

The Chief Inspector and Superintendent Sasaki did not waste time speculating. The locality of the first arson target, itself a minor casualty compared to the main objectives, was identified immediately as the most probable fire-raising route towards the old Imperial Palace. Sasaki gave the driver rapid instructions on the most expeditious way to cut across the arsonists' tracks. The car sped northwards up Kawaramachi-Dori at a velocity which any kamikaze-style taxi driver would have envied. The police radio intercom was working feverishly; and along the route dozens of uniformed men had miraculously materialized out of the woodwork. Kyoto citizens who happened to be on course, whether on foot, bicycle, or in cars, were unceremoniously brushed aside, allowing a clear path for Sasaki's car.

But one miracle that the Kyoto police could not perform was to remove the tramcars from their tracks. There they stood, or rumbled along, right in the middle of Kawaramachi-Dori, and there was no shifting them. Where two tramcars passed, a minor traffic jam built up, as usual during the rush hour. Sasaki made an instant decision. The radio became a babble of voices, and the driver swung to the left and sped up Teremachi-Dori, the tram-free street that runs parallel with the main boulevard.

Sasaki turned to Takata, who translated to David and Elizabeth. 'We will concentrate on Marutamachi-Dori.' He pointed to the map.

David was not so sure. 'What about these streets?' he said, pointing to other routes.

'Possible. I have given instructions for deputies to pay special attention. Meanwhile, we go for Marutamachi-Dori.' The Superintendent knew his city well.

Elizabeth looked up from the map, and asked quietly 'What exactly are we looking for? Are we to keep an eye open for four men in a car? Or a van? Or a pick-up truck? Would they be on top of a bus, are they on foot, or are they riding bicycles? I don't wish to sound facetious, but somehow I feel that locating the route is still not the most important problem.'

David nodded. 'We have to get back to earth, even if this driver tries to avoid it.' Without the danger of bouncing off tramcars, they were now approaching Mach 1.

'Let us try psychology again,' he looked purposefully at Elizabeth, who looked purposefully straight back. 'What is inside their minds right now? What is the most logical step for them to take next? Assume for a start that they are not on foot. If they had been, they would have been spotted, and would be in the bag by now. Walter couldn't shoot arrows from a bicycle. They must be on an open truck. Walter has to have a clear arc of fire.'

Elizabeth was far from satisfied. 'We know all that,' she said impatiently, 'you are simply repeating yourself. Can't you go further than that?'

David was not amused. 'All right, Elizabeth, let's have some of your psychology then.'

She glared, paused, and went on. 'If Dudman is in a truck, he would hardly be in a much better position for firing his bow than if he was on the ground. More mobile, but in no better a firing position. And the vehicle would have to stop. And they have to be close to their main target, and if not in sight, at least to know exactly where it is.

207

The gang cannot simply drive up without hindrance to a concealed point elsewhere, otherwise Walter won't have a clear shot. His arrows could fall anywhere, and he would be depending on luck.'

'But how can he improve his chances? Are you trying to say that he has to see the target, or at least have some ranging or reference point to obtain accuracy?'

'Yes, I am.'

David was sarcastic. 'So Eastwick is going to stop the truck, and like a post office engineer, Walter is going to get out, climb a telegraph pole, sight his target, and fire off a few rapid arrows?'

'Very funny! Work it out yourself.' The frustration, and the urgency of the moment, with the realisation of what was at stake, were combining to rasp a few nerves, and the irritation was beginning to show.

Takata had been listening solemnly to this heated exchange, and tried to keep up with the sarcasm of David's jibe about the telegraph pole, but did not wish his honoured guests to think that Japan was still in the Dark Ages of telecommunications technology. 'Japanese post office engineers no longer climb pole,' he said seriously, 'use special tall truck, with special inspection tower. Americans call "cherry picker,' he smiled, 'we call "cherry blossom picker".'

David was about to explain to his Japanese colleague that he did not wish to cast doubts on the Japanese telephone service, when Elizabeth suddenly clutched David and they first stared at each other, then at the astonished Inspector, who thought he had committed a faux pas.

David turned to Takata, and gripped his arm, so that there could be no mistake. 'Send out immediately an order for all your men to apprehend every mobile vehicle in Kyoto with an inspection tower.'

The Inspector caught on instantly and acted with alacrity. More excited gabbling on the multi-channel radio. They careened across Oike-Dori and the driver threw out his anchors to draw to a screeching standstill at the important crossroads at Nijo-Dori.

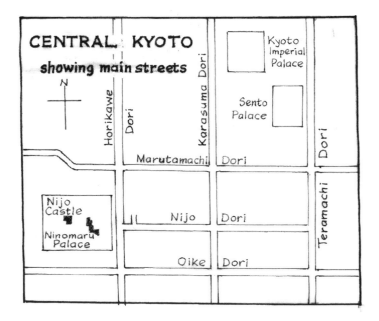

The Target: The Palace's old timbers?

Suddenly, all the accumulated psychology, logic, dedication, analysis: all came abruptly face-to-face with cold, dramatically-menacing reality. For there, about a third of a mile to the east, along Nijo-Dori, approaching at a deliberate, measured pace, close to the curb, with other traffic respectfully making way for this essential public service, was just such a mobile inspection/repair tower as Inspector Takata had proudly described.

It was the Toyota Commercial Vehicles Division's latest model, a tribute to the ingenuity of their hydraulic engineers, who had produced an apparatus capable of extension vertically to the height of a five-storey building. Some cherry-picker indeed.

At that distance, it was impossible to discern any details of the occupants of the vehicle; but whether they recognized the police car and took avoiding action, or because they were following a pre-determined route anyway, they turned right, that is to say north, up a small road running parallel with and only a block away from the outer wall of the old Ninomaru Palace in the grounds of Nijo Castle.

The police driver, apparently using water-methanol, screamed round the corner into the side road, just in time to see the now half-extended inspection tower turn again into an even smaller alleyway, the Japanese equivalent of a London mews.

If there was any doubt as to the fortuitous perception of the use of a mobile inspection truck as the fire-raisers' modus operandi, this was dispelled by the final turn taken by the vehicle. Why else should such a piece of equipment be directed down a small alleyway where not a pole, not even a tall building, was within a hundred yards? And why, on the platform at the top of the now fully-extended inspection tower, should a man be perched, equipped with a bow and arrow?

As they drew within close sight, the Toyota stopped abruptly. One man, of small stature – he could easily have been mistaken for Japanese – who had just got down from the cab, stared at the police car in disbelief for a brief moment, and with commendable presence of mind galvanized himself into action, and vaulted over an adjacent wall into the back yard of what appeared to be business premises. The police party could see only that he was wearing working overalls and a white hygienic mask; but David was quite certain that the fleeing man was Frank Eastwick.

Simultaneously with this disappearing act, two other white masks peered through the back window of the cab. Big Jim had spotted the police car in his rear view mirror, just as he turned the corner, and had passed on the unexpected information to his cab mate navigator, Bill Castleman. Just a little slower off the mark than Eastwick, they took to their heels to the other end of the alley, and disappeared into the crowded main street adjacent to the castle walls.

Walter Dudman was left stranded, five stories high in his crow's nest, from which point of vantage he had now attained the main objective of the entire elaborate plan. He had a clear sight of the thatched roofs of the old Ninomaru Palace, silhouetted against the dimming red and yellow streaks of a fast-fading sunset, and within range of his powerful bow. The target, however, was now far from his mind as he looked down at the small knot of threatening figures around the police car, with its blue light flashing in the gathering gloom.

Dumbfounded, he saw Frank Eastwick disappearing into the back door of a nearby building and Jim Smith and Bill Castleman already almost out of sight at the end of the alley. He was now exposed without any visible means of support except the fully-extended hydraulic tower that provided a precarious platform some fifty feet above the ground, with no-one except an obliging policeman to press the button to let him down.

Something had gone desperately wrong. Double-crossed? Faulty planning? Fatal timing error? There was no time to consider such details. One absolute certainty was that he was not going to escape from arrest. The dream of quick riches had evaporated. He would never be able to face Gladys again.

Some long dormant repressed spirit took over in his desperation to seek salvation, no matter how tenuous. He decided to gamble, on the spontaneous assumption that he had some bargaining strength to gamble with.

He turned suddenly from facing the Palace and, drawing his bowstring, aimed his bow directly at the nearest figure beneath him, who happened to be Inspector Takata. 'If I turn King's Evidence, will it get me a light sentence?' he shouted, forgetting in his panic that it was unlikely that he would be understood, or even if the Japanese police understood English, that they would have little notion of the King, much less his Evidence.

Takata turned towards David for interpretation, and took a half step towards him. 'Don't move,' Walter shouted, his voice now charged with belligerence. Takata stopped in his tracks – he understood that command well enough. Sensing that he had gained a slight tactical advantage, Walter turned once again towards the Palace and went on: 'My bow is half-drawn, I can set fire to the whole area. Don't move a muscle or I'll fire off a couple for luck to cut off your retreat and show you what these things are made of.' He crouched low behind the metal protective guard rails, realising that, in the twilight, it would take a lucky shot to immobilize him. He was playing the only card he had. 'I have drawn the bow and am holding it. If you try to shoot me, there is nothing to hold the first shot, except this clicker, and I might get off a couple more.'

The note of panic, mixed with desperation, was evident in the tone of Walter's voice. Caught completely by surprise, all semblance of reasoned thought had deserted him. Indulging in a wild display of brinkmanship, on a thousand-and-one chance that some unlikely solution might emerge to save him from utter disaster, he was dangerously trigger-happy, if such an adjective could be applied to a man with his finger on the releasing device of a taut bowstring.

David Thomas decided that he had to gamble too.

'Walter Dudman,' he shouted, with as much authority as he could muster, 'this is Detective Inspector David Thomas, of H Division of the Metropolitan Police Force in London. I want to discuss the situation.'

Walter was silent for a long moment, mainly in sheer disbelief. Japanese policemen were one thing; but a London policeman? It must be a bluff.

'I don't believe you, but go ahead. Remember that any wrong move and I can start the Great Fire of Kyoto.'

'Believe me. The joint police forces of Britain and Japan have

212

been tracking you down for the last few days. We know most of the story, possibly more than you do yourself. We think that you and your friends have been deceived into a senseless act of vandalism under the promise of a rich reward. Because of your money problems, your judgement has been badly affected.'

He paused to see if his words were penetrating. There was no sound from the crow's nest.

'We know exactly what you are up to, with your ingenious arson kit, with the incendiary arrows and everything, ever since the Wood Lane and the Ashmore trial experiments. I want you to give yourself up. I cannot promise anything. I can only say that your conduct from now on will have a considerable influence on the judge. I would also ask you to be very careful with that lethal weapon you have in your hands.' David could just see the crook of Walter's withdrawn right arm, and the left arm extended.

This remark only seemed to give Walter some false courage, reminding him that he still had the power to invoke fear.

'If you can't promise anything, what have I got to lose? I want a better offer than that.'

'Walter, don't provoke the Japanese police. They are being very tolerant of your horrifying and extraordinary behaviour. But don't push your luck too far. They are armed, and might chance putting a bullet in your arm or leg, or even worse, anything to try to stop you setting fire to a precious part of their revered city. They have complete jurisdiction and might even take a chance and kill you.'

'They weren't very tolerant in 1942. They are the ones to lose. If they hit me, this bowstring goes. With the clicker, I don't have to use much strength to hold on at this range.' Walter had a point. The effect of shooting him would simply trigger off the incendiary arrow.

This bizarre conversation was getting nowhere. The flash point of Walter's pent-up and panic-stricken anger was imminent. Rational persuasion was useless. David decided to ask for help. 'Elizabeth, if ever there was a time for a slice of psychology, now is the time. Any ideas?' Ignoring the satire, she did indeed have an idea, and after an animated whispered wrangling, she apparently won the argument. David returned to his shouting match.

'Let me make you that better offer. Although a Japanese Inspector here has some knowledge of English, there are only two people here who understand everything that is going on between us right now. The other person is British and she is someone you know and she is in the car.'

'She?' Walter was confused.

'I shall consult her. You may think we are trying to trick you into submission. Well, in one way we are. But I guarantee that this is completely well-intentioned. So don't shoot me with your arrow if I approach the police car.'

'All right. But be quick. And don't open the door of the car.' Walter suspected some subterfuge. Perhaps this "she" business was just an excuse to retrieve some extra artillery from the police car. In the darkening twilight, he did not notice Elizabeth creep around the back of the car and carefully get into the back on the other side.

David played his wild card, gambling that Walter's confused mind could give credence to the incredible and would not be able to work out the practicalities.

'Walter, you won't let us open the door, but the lady wants to speak to you.'

'Who the hell have you got there?'

'The lady says her name is Maid Marion, so you should know who I'm talking about. She says that, for her, nothing has changed, that you are not to worry about money, and particularly not to be a bloody fool. Those are her exact words.'

At the mention of the words "Maid Marion", and already beginning to weaken in his resolve, Walter imperceptibly relaxed the pull on the bowstring slightly.

The tone of his voice suggested that defiance was giving way to self-doubt. 'I don't believe you,' he said. 'Prove it. But don't open that damned door.'

'Very well, Walter, take a look at this.' Under Walter's watchful eye, through the door window, Gladys's hand-knitted green sweater, unmistakable even in the fading light, was displayed. Walter stared unbelievably at the two yellow stags and Robin Hood at the alert. He relaxed his pull on the bow, and slumped against the safety rail of the platform. The break in concentration gave the Japanese police the chance they had been waiting for, and several rifles were aimed at the lone, silhouetted figure in the crow's nest.

'Walter, it's all over. You have no more cards to play. One move from you to pull back the string, and you're a dead man and Gladys here is a widow. Give up now while there's still a chance of leniency. I meant what I said about turning King's Evidence.'

The bubble burst. The bravado evaporated. The play-act ended. Walter Mitty Dudman, champion archer, avenger of Japanese prisoner-of-war camps, was engulfed by Walter Judas Dudman, betrayer and deserter of his Maid Marion of happier days long ago.

'Drop the bow, down here.'

It clattered to the ground. Deflated in spirit and stamina, the strain showed as he slouched dejectedly in his metal eyrie while one of the policemen pushed the button to lower the inspection tower. The hydraulic tubes slid neatly into place, the apparatus folded up, and Walter Dudman came back to earth in more ways than one.

He looked expectantly towards the car, from which Elizabeth was just emerging. For one fleeting moment, her red hair, added to the vision of the green sweater, combined into a momentary image of Gladys Dudman in the flesh.

Elizabeth just said, 'I'm sorry, Walter,' and gave him the sweater. After a while, the policemen led him quietly away.

Chapter 25
Life or Death

'Two down, two to go,' observed David later that evening as they sat drinking green tea and saki in the Kyoto Police Chief's inner sanctum. 'Where do we go from here?'

The Anglo-Japanese arson prevention squad had returned to the local headquarters, having caught Jim Smith en route. They were moderately satisfied, if not complacent, over apprehending the archery equivalent of the hit man in a fatal shoot-out. Little damage had been done, and even the Nanjenzi Temple had not been irreparably burned, as the Kyoto Fire Brigade, already alerted to the expectancy of an alarm, had beaten all records in putting out the fire. The fire engines had converged with such alacrity and enthusiasm that it would take until the following summer for the Temple to dry the place out, such was the volume of water that had descended on the place.

Walter Dudman's mini arsenal of incendiary pipe-bombs, together with the launching apparatus, had been carefully removed, and gingerly stored in a protected place of safety. The relief amongst the Japanese authorities was immense. Orders were given to reduce the thousands of supplementary policemen to a small skeleton force, which in turn would be dismissed if nothing untoward occurred. There was much drinking of saki and Suntory in high places; Superintendent Sasaki and Chief Inspector Takata spent the evening beaming like oriental Cheshire cats, and dispensing good-will to all, especially to honourable Thomas-San and honourable Elizabeth-San, the Saviours of Kyoto. The Government authorities had been informed, and the British Embassy given a full account. The Ambassador himself telephoned David. 'Jolly good show,' he said, 'you have both saved us an awfully desperate pile of embarrassment. The Foreign Office is very satisfied. Knew you'd do it. Do drop by for a chat before you go back to Scotland Yard.'

The Ambassador had omitted to mention that, acting on a tip from the Tokyo Police, they had discovered two nasty-looking incendiary devices in the Embassy visitors' waiting room. They were wrapped up in cardboard tubes, and tucked into a corner where a member of the public could see them and perhaps report them, with incriminating deductions, to the Japanese police. He also omitted to mention that the Foreign Office had been in constant communication every half-hour for the last two days, and that he had concentrated on preserving the traditional stiff upper lip, not only to prevent any suspicion of apprehension spreading in London, but also to keep his own staff at ease. The prospect of selling a third of Britain's North Sea oil for the next quarter of a century had been teetering in the balance, and he had felt that somehow he might have been held responsible if Kyoto had gone up in flames.

'More to the point,' said Elizabeth, accepting a slightly different beverage than that offered during her previous visit to the police station. 'Where have Frank Eastwick and Bill Castleman gone?'

This was indeed the 64-yen question. Frank had shown a clean pair of heels when he disappeared over the backyard fence; while Bill, using his local knowledge, had strolled down Teramachi Street, feigning symptoms of the common cold, and heavily masked with a white face pad. He had walked in to a yakatori bar, sampled tidbits of skewered meat, fish, and vegetables, and waited until all seemed clear.

Jim Smith, on the other hand, like a fish out of water, had been gaffed immediately, and now sat in a small room with Walter, strictly supervised by two Japanese constables, awaiting questioning. The Kyoto police, meanwhile, having inspected the incendiary pipe-bombs, had placed them all in a box, and despatched them to a piece of waste ground where, with detonators removed, they were retained as evidence.

Preliminary questioning of the two in custody had not revealed much that could not have been guessed anyway. A very subdued Walter, clutching incongruously at his Robin Hood sweater, had confirmed that, apart from the name and address given to him, he knew nothing about any Copenhagen connection except that it seemed a safer place to assemble than at London Airport. Jim Smith, questioned separately, claimed that the source of the pay-off, as far as he knew, was an English organization of ex-prisoners of Japanese war camps who had come into some unexpected funds from the legacy of one of their deceased members.

Both were convinced that they had been caught because some-body had informed against them. They had planned to complete their fire-raising, return the mobile truck to Toyota and simply catch the train back to Yokohama. Then, on the following day, they were going to rest up, and repair to Eri's Cabin in the evening where, Frank had told them, they were to collect the remainder of the money that was to have solved all their separate financial worries for the rest of their lives.

Walter was demoralized. His disillusion was complete. Not only had he been caught in a criminal act which was his first real encounter with the Law, but the enormity of the crime which he might have committed was beginning to dawn on him. Sitting in a Japanese police station, in the hands of the people who had every right to be infuriated – to put no finer point on the situation – he was at his wits' end, no more the Life-and-Soul of the Party. There was no Life and only a very poor Soul at Walter's party that night, as he sat with Jim and the two constables. He clutched his sweater as a drowning man clutches a straw.

Big Jim just sat sullenly in the corner, resigned to his fate.

'Hey Walter,' he rasped, 'who was this Hineyman bloke in Copenhagen? Was he the bastard who split on us?'

'Don't know,' said Walter doubtfully, 'Frank gave me the name in case Gladys wanted to get in touch with me urgently while in Copenhagen. She worries about me when I go away on archery shoots, which this was supposed to be, as far as she knew. Frank gave me the name, and said only to use it in case of dire emergency, if that would keep Gladys from getting panicky. His friend Heinemann would stall her off with a story to get me off the hook.'

'Was he anything to do with this caper?'

'Might be. I had to swear not to mention his name to anyone, not even you.'

'Damned queer.'

David and Elizabeth had been listening to this dialogue through a monitor next door, hoping that something might emerge that might be of interest. A Japanese policeman came in, bowed deeply, and handed a note to David.

'Hell's teeth,' he exclaimed, 'Copenhagen has allowed Heinemann to slip their surveillance. He had some bags locked up in the luggage storage at Copenhagen Airport and bought a ticket under an assumed name, with a false passport, which must have been in the bags. They think he's gone to Frankfurt, under the name of Ludwig Bornburg, slightly but effectively disguised, dark moustache and spectacles. Copenhagen police want to know if he should be apprehended by the Frankfurt police.'

Elizabeth looked puzzled. This was an uncalled-for infringement of the expected order of things, according to her psychological analysis. She had subconsciously put Heinemann to one side as being out of harm's way, as he had no further part to play in the active part of the arson plot. He could have been followed up later.

'There's something odd about this development,' she said, 'surely he has no reason to make things worse for himself by risking a connection and identification.'

By now, David had learned to recognize the signs. Elizabeth had the habit of brushing her auburn hair back when she came up with some inspirational thought, and her track record had been extremely good so far. He tried to follow her thought process. 'All right, what is the situation from Heinemann's viewpoint? He has never admitted to any connection with Eastwick beyond dealing in girlie magazines and dirty postcards. If everything goes according to plan, he simply pays them off, and nobody is any the wiser. But if they are caught, one or more of them might blow the whistle on him.'

Elizabeth warmed to the train of thought. 'He must have been expecting dramatic news about a Palace fire in Kyoto, but only heard about the early minor one and that the culprits had been apprehended. If we hadn't caught anyone, we would have had no way to prove a connection with Heinemann and therefore no idea of any underhand business with the oil company. Just war veterans seeking revenge. His connection with them is only through Eastwick, and the money paid to him so far is only the down payment. If Eastwick doesn't get the rest of his money, he could squeal; and even if the plot fails he could squeal anyway. So, whatever happens, or whatever has happened, isn't there the possibility of a pay-off assignation?

'As things stand now, Eastwick has to get his money, otherwise he is going to spill Heinemann's beans. If this affair gets publicised, and if he is implicated, Heinemann could finish up in jail for ten or twenty years.'

David pursued this speculation. 'It's not a prison sentence that he's worried about. A huge industrial conspiracy of international proportions is at stake. The German-Danish Oil Corporation is not going to let Heinemann off the hook. The only reason he is alive today is because neither he nor the oil company thought that anything could go wrong. But when his employers know that the plan has failed, and that, under questioning, the perpetrators might leak the source of their sponsorship, their reputation would be that of a criminal organization. So they have to shut Heinemann's mouth, and he must know this, and so he has to shut Eastwick's mouth to save his own skin.'

'You're not suggesting…?'

'Yes, murder. Under the circumstances now, and he'll soon find out, he has to get rid of Eastwick.'

'Suppose he thinks that Frank is already in custody now, or at least the subject of a widespread "all-stations" call?'

'The point is, he doesn't know. And until he does, we can leave nothing to chance. Until the game is up, he has to assume that Eastwick can still be silenced. I bet he's on his way right now, with the sole objective of killing Frank. If he succeeds, we can never implicate the oil consortium, however strong the circumstantial evidence. If, however, he finds that we have caught Eastwick, he will have to disappear, lose his identity, and probably end up as a farmer in Argentina, or a travel agent in Brazil.'

David asked Inspector Takata to telephone the Copenhagen police and ask them to keep a watchful eye on Heinemann at Frankfurt Airport, but at all costs not to apprehend him. Just follow his movements, almost certainly to take a plane to Tokyo, and to keep us informed.

'Don't you see?' he said, with an air of triumph. 'If we can keep a close tab on Heinemann, he may lead us to Eastwick, and we'll catch them all, red-handed.'

'A bit of a long shot, surely?'

'Well yes. But Eastwick has disappeared, and we haven't caught Castleman yet either.'

'Where do you think they have gone?'

'My bet is Eri's Cabin.'

Chapter 26
The Pay-Off

And so it was. The Four Just Men's emergency procedure had worked a great deal better for the two survivors than had their master plan for setting fire to Kyoto. Bill Castleman, with his previous experience in organizing group travel to Japan, had had no more difficulty in finding his way to the railway station in Kyoto than finding Waterloo Station in London. Frank Eastwick took a little longer, but his sense of direction had guided him to the railway tracks and then to the station without any trouble en route. They had met at about 8.30 on a fairly crowded platform. They had separated, bought tickets separately, caught the late Kodama Bullet train to Yokohama, where they sat the night out in a bar, drinking their sorrows, and wondering what had happened to Walter and Jim. Temporarily and quite fortuitously, they did not go back to their hotel, where they would have been apprehended. They drank too much, collapsed, and spent the night almost literally under the table, thus extending their hours of freedom.

Alcohol, they say, loosens the tongue. Frank had confided in Bill to the extent that he had not chosen to do hitherto. Life was beginning to feel a little lonelier, and his thoughts were somewhat mixed. He had explained that the arrangements for collecting the final pay-off from his principal – he did not specify – was to meet them in Eri's Cabin. 'You really suggested the ideal rendezvous in your song, Bill,' he admitted. He did not know what was going to happen exactly, now that the police had miraculously appeared on the scene in Kyoto, at the very instant when Walter was about to administer the coup de grace. He supposed that the meeting with Heinemann would still take place, but he was apprehensive of the outcome when he had to admit total failure. The thought that Heinemann himself might have been on the police agenda did not occur to him.

Nevertheless, he had to go through with it; the consequences of not meeting his previously potential benefactor might be worse.

* * *

David Thomas and Elizabeth Lloyd had basked in the glow of their mutual success, and the word psychology was never mentioned. David had asked Inspector Takata to telephone Eri and insist that she should act quite normally if her friend Bill came in with any friends. She had been relieved to hear that her beloved city had not gone up in flames, and promised to be discretion itself. Her assertion was fortified by the hint that her bar could be closed down because it was a clearing house for illegal imports. She was also to show no sign of recognition if the Inspector came in with David and Elizabeth for some late fish and chips.

Next morning, Friday, after a totally relaxed and uninhibited night together, the two representatives of the British anti-arson team were picked up at the Miyako hotel. Still suffering from the light-headed morning-after condition, they were given a ceremonial send-off by Superintendent Sasaki and an impressive assembly of senior dignitaries, led by the Mayor of Kyoto. He gave an altogether charming speech, in which, by the semantic process perfected by the Japanese, he conveyed his sincere appreciation without making the slightest reference to the subject. He gave them each a traditonal souvenir: wonderfully embroidered kimonos.

Inspectors Takata and Thomas, with Insurance Investigator Elizabeth Lloyd, then took the return journey to Tokyo, sleeping most of the way, in preparation for their blind date in Eri's Cabin.

* * *

Herr Ludwig Bornburg, alias Gerhard Heinemann, watched his single suitcase come through customs, and submitted his smart black brief-case for inspection. 'Just business papers,' he said, and was pleasantly surprised when the customs inspector waved him through. Even if he had not, there was little danger of anything being found, either in the cases or on Herr Bornburg. He never carried a firearm, while any small metallic mechanism that might be part of a lethal device was shaped to appear above suspicion by any X-ray equipment.

What Bornburg did not know, however, was that while the cooperative customs official was giving him an easy passage, another customs man was on the telephone. The immigration authorities had done exactly the same, having inspected his passport, and welcomed him graciously to Tokyo.

Heinemann had congratulated himself that he had slipped through the meshes of a European net. He should have been on guard against being ensnared in the invisible gossamer of a delicate Japanese silken web.

* * *

Early on Friday evening, a smart-suited Inspector Takata and an equally smart Mr David Thomas re-visited Eri's Cabin, playing the part of two business friends taking an informal respite from the slog of a business day, together with an elegant Miss Elizabeth Lloyd, Mr Thomas's travelling secretary. The three found a corner table, already reserved, where they could observe the whole premises, including the bar, and particularly the entrance. Nobody could come in or go out without their seeing them.

After the second drink, the door opened and Frank Eastwick and Bill Castleman came in. There was no mistaking them. They had thrown away all pretence at disguise, as indeed, there had never been any apparent need in the comparative safety and serenity of Eri's Cabin. They exchanged a few pleasantries with a forewarned Eri, and sat at a table only a few steps from their pursuers. A young Japanese and his apparent girlfriend came in shortly afterwards. The man had one drink, bought a packet of cigarettes, asked Takata for a light, said 'It's a chilly Friday evening,' in Japanese, and went out again with the girl.

Elizabeth gripped David's hand under the table. She could feel the hidden tension, in spite of the outward equanimity of her two companions, now trying to outdo each other in a show of imperturb-ability. She found it difficult to make flippant conversation, and was relieved when David launched into a detailed explanation of the complications of the laws of cricket, and that Lord's cricket ground had nothing to do with British aristocracy. She played her part of the dumb blonde, or in her case, the dumb redhead. 'You should play cricket,' she said to Takata. 'After all; you drive on the left, like we do.'

They did not have to extend the flippancy very long. The leading actor in the play about to be enacted entered quietly at 7.30. 'Good evening,' said Herr Bornburg, alias Heinemann, to Eri, 'do you have such a thing as a Tuborg lager?'

Eri apologised. 'Sorry, only English, Australian, and Irish beers. And Japanese, of course. Maybe you try Harp lager?'

Bornburg frowned, as if to cast doubt on all non-Danish beers, accepted the offer, and sat down with Frank and Bill. He carefully

227

and conspicuously deposited the black briefcase he was carrying on the seat beside him. The case was also conspicuous to the trio at the nearby table.

David realized that this was the first time that he had seen Heinemann in the flesh, although he presumed that this was not his normal appearance. The Dane had added some sideburns to his moustache and horn-rimmed spectacles. Bornburg or Heinemann, though, he was a typical Saxon, tall, blond, fresh complexion, the sort of face that would readily burn in bright sunlight.

David and Elizabeth strained to hear the conversation, but could only hear snatches; but knowing the subject, they could interpret the occasional word and the gestures. Frank went into a detailed explanation of how a shower of fiery arrows had been replaced by a shower of policemen who had appeared from nowhere. 'We must have been betrayed,' he declared with some heat. 'We were lucky to get away. And the Japs have got Walter and Jim.'

His tone suggested that his erstwhile colleagues were now languishing in a Kyoto jail, having barely survived a murderous beating, were now wrapped tightly in barbed wire, and being subjected to various forms of oriental torture. He also seemed to be suggesting that the betrayal might have originated in Denmark. He had decided that the arrival of the police had been partly luck, partly because the Nanzenji Shrine fire had put them on the alert, and that the Toyota company might have reported the unusual loan of the cherry-picker. He did not know that the three of them were now under close scrutiny.

But he did know that the briefcase was supposed to contain the final pay-off for a job well done. Regrettably, the job had not been well done. It had not been done at all, and he feared the wrath of Heinemann, who had already paid out a tidy sum, and had received nothing in return.

He was agreeably surprised and enormously relieved, therefore, when the Dane patted him affectionately on the back, told him not to worry about a thing, and would Bill kindly order another round of drinks.

'Look here,' said Heinemann, all amiability, 'you four have been under great strain. You made a brilliant attempt to pull off one of what some would regard as a major crime, but in reality was a good try at getting justifiable revenge for past crimes. The risks were incalculable. We sympathize with you in your disappointment, but the police got a lucky break. My principals have asked me to salute you for your brave efforts, and some payment was guaranteed, whatever the outcome.'

He raised his glass, and the others, slightly bewildered but enormously relieved, touched theirs with his. 'I salute a gallant failure,' he declared dramatically.

Frank was suspicious. 'Do you mean that you aren't going to ask for the money back?' he demanded, more in hope than expectation.

'Not only that,' beamed Heinemann, 'my principals have considered the matter and realized that they had underestimated the enormous risk you were taking, and have asked me to make an appropriate adjustment in the event of a mishap. Bearing in mind especially the sad loss of your two colleagues, therefore, it gives me great pleasure to make a supplementary contribution to your personal expenses. It is not, you understand, as much as if everything had been achieved, but you will find that we have been generous, and also we may need you again.'

'How generous?' demanded Bill Castleman.

'There is a sum of money in this case.' Heinemann nodded towards the black briefcase between him and Frank.

'How much?' Frank demanded.

'Three hundred and fifty thousand pounds. How you divide it is your business.' There was the faint unspoken suggestion that if Frank and Bill wished to split it between them and disappear into the wild blue yonder, that was their affair.

'I thought English pounds would be most convenient for you. Don't ask me how I got them into Japan. It is sufficient to know that they are all here, in reasonably disposable denominations, in this case. Why don't you open it and check? I haven't locked it.'

Frank did so. He furtively raised the lid, and turned it away from the trio at the other table who just might be watching, and who he had observed to be glancing in his direction once or twice.

He extracted a bundle of notes at random, and flicked through them professionally, much in the same way that he might have checked a large betting pay-off to a lucky backer of an outsider at the White City. In the shadow of the lid, there was no way to tell if the notes were genuine; but they looked all right, and even if they were not, he could find channels for converting them.

Heinemann excused himself. 'If you don't mind,' he said pleasantly, 'I would like to get back to my hotel; the jet lag is setting in. Here, let me shut the case for you before too many eyes might see what's in it. Remember that the combination is 9867. That should be easy, it's your telephone number. Just spin the numbers, 9867, but do it privately or in a quiet corner so that no-one can see what's inside.'

Heinemann very carefully clicked the case shut, handed it to Frank Eastwick with, 'Don't forget, 9867,' and strode out of Eri's Cabin. He was astonished to find two Japanese policemen barring his way at the top of the short, open, flight of stairs that led down to the street below, opposite the Self-Defence Force. He did not argue. Many years of industrial espionage and other shady activity had given him an instinct of when to talk and when to act. When one of the policemen produced his badge, he chose the latter, having suddenly realized that his cover had somehow been blown. He put his head down, and charged. That was a bad move. Japanese policemen, especially in

Tokyo, have been trained to take care of a particularly insidious form of mass demonstration which includes masses of humanity forming human "snakes" designed to break down protectively-shielded police "walls". One man charging, especially when he was expected to charge, therefore presented no problem. Almost as if carrying out a set piece of gymnastics, they used Heinemann's own momentum to upend him and help him on his way down the stairs, with the slight modification that they deprived him of the use of his feet.

He landed on the third step from the bottom, partly on his head, partly on his shoulder, and subsided into an unconscious heap beside the sign which said "Eri's Cabin Upstairs". Two more policemen deposited him in the waiting van.

The noise of the commotion on Eri's stairs was audible in the bar.

'What the hell was that?' said Frank, realising that the noise coincided with Heinemann's exit.

'He must have slipped,' said Bill, rising to see what had happened . 'Hope he's all right.'

'Hang on, I'll come with you,' said Frank, keeping a tight hold on the black briefcase.

They went out, closely followed by two men from a nearby table. At the top of the stairs, Frank Eastwick and Bill Castleman sustained the second surprise of the evening, as they found themselves firmly secured front and back by what felt like eight pairs of hands, and what, quite definitely, were two pairs of handcuffs.

Totally bewildered, they joined the still-unconscious Heinemann in the van. Frank was still desperately gripping the black case, as a drowning man clutches a straw.

Chapter 27

An Open and Shut Case

If ever a gang of criminals languished – as the term goes – in jail, Frank Eastwick and Bill Castleman languished abundantly. Frank was in a bad way. This was his first acquaintance with Japanese detention procedures since he had been released from a prisoner-of-war camp some thirty years previously, and he was quite sure that the correct, almost courteous treatment which his present captors meted out was merely a sadistic prelude to positively ghastly things to come.

Unfortunately, a circumstance which might have helped to put his mind at rest, namely the companionship of his fellow arsonists, was denied him, as the jailers insisted, at least for the time being, on their solitary confinement. He need not have worried, as the last thing that the post-war Japanese authorities wanted to do was to bring back any memories of those wartime excesses.

Frank was not to know this. He suffered the tortures of the damned, and had even lost interest in the precious black briefcase, which had been taken from him. Under David's explicit instructions, the case was securely wrapped and secured, and locked safely away in the Tokyo Police Superintendent Nakamura's safe, and to everyone's disappointment, David was adamant, almost obsessively so, that it should not be opened, even if Frank told them the combination. They had asked, but had received the reply 'Find Out', which was one reason why he was alone in his cell. With the combination, the police could have sprung the lock, or prized open the case, with the greatest of ease. Elizabeth was taken aback by the vehemence with which David objected, threatening (quite falsely) that there might be repercussions involving regulations of international jurisdiction.

They had discussed the intricacies of international law and responsibility. Quite clearly, the four Englishmen could be charged with arson under Japanese Law, on at least one count – the Nanzenji Temple – and on a second count, attempted arson – the Ninomaru Palace. Equally, they could be summoned under English Law, for the destruction by fire of various deserted sheds and huts at various spots in southern England.

But what about Heinemann? The Danish authorities would have a stake in him also. His role was now proved to be an intimate and critical one, possibly the leader of a well-planned conspiracy of grand arson on an unprecedented scale. Nakamura observed that, had the arsonists succeeded, the conflagration could have been as terrible as the Tokyo holocaust during the War. This, he was clearly implying, was not a common case of arson, not even like setting fire to a warehouse full of billions of yens' worth of merchandise. This involved the pre-eminent architectural achievement of the Japanese heritage, symbolic of the national pride of Japan.

Elizabeth listened to these discussions in uncharacteristic silence, as the reaction to the intense activity and tension of the previous few hours set in. She could see that David was still as alert as ever, even expectant, and his contribution to the discussions of police protocol seemed to be superficial.

'Why don't you relax, David?' she said, a little impatiently. 'After all, the villains are now safely in custody, and we can leave it to the lawyers to sort out the allocation of responsibility to the police here and in London.'

David's reply was surprisingly serious. 'It's not quite over yet,' he said grimly.

'What on earth do you mean? Surely these matters can be settled amicably.'

'You don't understand. This is much more than a case of arson.'

'You mean there was a threat to human life, if the fires had been started and proliferated, as in Tokyo and Hamburg and Dresden?'

'We have to overcome the lack of evidence against Heinemann, and I want everyone to know that he came here with murder on his mind.'

The two Japanese sat upright. David had everyone's attention.

'Consider the situation. At the moment, we have nothing on him, except that he was offering money to Eastwick. He could – and probably will – claim that this was a transaction involving some petty pornographic literature, and that they were in Japan to set up some trading here. Remember that he was nowhere on the scene in Kyoto, and the meeting in Eri's Cabin was the first time we ever saw him. The case against him is tenuous. And he is not going to reveal the identity of his mentors. The oil company is not going to permit any revelation of their involvement, as the Danish Government would close them down. Heinemann has to save his skin, and he can only do that by ensuring that Frank Eastwick – his only direct contact and potential informer – is eliminated. The other three know nothing about the oil connection. So Frank Eastwick is vulnerable, but if we can get the two together, we may be able to nail him. I believe I can make him confess, but it will be something of a risk.'

David took Takata and Nakamura to one side and an animated conversation ensued, while Elizabeth went out to powder her nose. When she returned, she was astonished to be invited to be taken back to the Okura Hotel in Nakamura's personal police car.

She was not pleased.

She appealed to David. 'You must be joking,' she declared with warmth. 'I was part of the success of the whole case, and I'm damned well not going to be eased out of the last act, whatever that is.'

David endured a look that could have stopped his circulation.

'Sorry, old girl,' damn it, the man was positively patronizing, 'but there are times when a woman's presence makes no contribution whatsoever, and this is one of them.'

'What the hell are you going to do, strip him?' Elizabeth was very angry.

'Not exactly, but I don't want you to be here.'

'You bastard, you double-crossing bastard.'

She turned to the Superintendent and said, icily, 'It will give me great pleasure to accept your offer. And don't be in a hurry to bring Inspector Thomas back. In fact, you needn't bring the bastard back at all.' With which parting demonstration of occidental passion, she swept out, with the Japanese exchanging slightly bewildered glances. They even forgot to bow.

* * *

Gerhard Heinemann glared at David, now accompanied only by Inspector Takata, in what, in Her Majesty's Forces' parlance, was good for three days C.B. for "silent contempt". He had been invited out of his solitary cell, handcuffed, to be interviewed by the two detectives. He made no attempt to conceal his intention to be uncooperative.

David opened the questioning. 'Herr Heinemann, or Bornburg, or whatever you happen to be calling yourself today, I'm going to ask you some direct questions, and I would advise you to be careful how you answer them. You are already incriminated up to the hilt, and you could get yourself in deeper.'

The reply was predictably truculent and sarcastic. 'All so correct. Everything you say will be taken down and used in evidence routine. It won't work, because you don't have any evidence. Incriminated in what?'

Gerhard was proud of his fluent English, which included the colloquial and idiomatic. He had to be something of a linguist, in his professional clandestine activities.

'Do you deny, then, that your meeting with Frank Eastwick in Eri's Cabin had no ulterior motives, such as a substantial pay-off for services rendered, that is, setting fire to the Ninomaru Palace in Kyoto?'

'Pull the other leg. I know nothing about a fire. Frank was paying me.'

David raised his eyebrows. 'Please explain.'

'I supplied Frank with a lot of literature from Denmark, and he owed me the payment. He wanted to visit Japan, where a friend was distributing his magazines. I had to visit the country too, on official business for the oil company. It seemed a mutually convenient place to meet, and in pleasant circumstances. Nothing illegal in that.'

'But I saw you bring the case in, and Frank took it out.'

'Ah, yes. Now I understand your confusion. It was my case and I brought it in, empty. But Frank put the money in the case, and as there was so much, I was going out to get a taxi and Frank was going to come with me, as an escort for protection, after he finished his drink. But your strong-armed thugs got in the way.'

That was something of an understatement. Gerhard had one arm well bandaged, and his normally smooth cheek and forehead bore several lacerations and bruises, caused by Eri's third step from the bottom.

'You're a smooth one, Gerhard. That's a load of bullshit. We were at the next table, and Frank only looked at the money that was already there.'

'You can't prove anything.'

David stood up. 'I'm not going to prolong this farce any longer.' He and Takata escorted Heinemann into an adjoining room, far more austere, no windows, and walls of bare concrete, with no embellishments. Eastwick was brought in, and joined the Dane behind a simple table, facing David and Takata. Behind the two policemen, a wide door had been left open.

David addressed Frank Eastwick. 'Frank, your friend here alleges that you met in Eri's Cabin last night so that you could pay off your debt for the supply of what we could call artistic literature; but that we intervened just before he was going back to his hotel, and you were going to go with him.'

Frank had had all he could take. His experiment with grand arson had gone so disastrously wrong that, even if he could have made any sense of this volte face, he was not going to go any further along his career of crime. He had already decided to cooperate with the police, in the hope of getting a lighter sentence. So his reaction was prompt and to the point.

'Pack of bloody lies.'

David caught the eye of the constable at the door, who nodded, and slipped out, and returned with Exhibit A, the black briefcase. David placed it on the table between them. 'Now, Gerhard, you know the combination of the lock. You said it was Frank's telephone number. Perhaps you can open the case for us, just so that we can check the magnitude of your trading activities.'

The silence that followed could have been cut with a knife. Heinemann had stiffened. David watched his eyes carefully as they flitted back and forth to Frank Eastwick.'

'I've forgotten the combination.'

Frank spoke up. 'Why don't you ask Bill and Walter? They'll tell you who's lying.'

David and Takata stood up, and took a couple of steps back toward the open door behind them. 'We can do that,' said David pleasantly, 'but there is no need. Why don't you open the case, Frank? You do know the combination. Mr Heinemann emphasized it several times you know – 9867. You don't need us to count the money. We'll wait outside.'

Frank Eastwick started to spin the numbers, first one, then a second. Gerhard Heinemann's demeanour changed abruptly, apparently having a panic atack. Without warning, his nerve cracked. He lunged across the table, and with his handcuffed arms, bandages and all, knocked Frank's hands away. He grabbed the case, awkwardly because of the handcuffs. His voice was now hysterical.

'It's mine,' he shouted. 'If anyone opens it, I'll open it.' He clutched the case to his chest.

'You really shouldn't interrupt, Gerhard,' David's tone from behind the door was almost oily. 'Frank, why don't you try again?'

'No!' Heinemann's panic was now extreme. In spite of his handcuffs and his damaged arm, he was nursing the case like a baby. Meanwhile David had unexpectedly retreated further through the open door, and spoke from a distance.

'My dear chap, you must contain yourself. All this fuss over a few thousand pounds, or marks, or kronur. What was the combination, Frank?'

'9867.'

'Right. Off you go.'

'For God's sake, stop!'

David emerged from behind the door. He took the case carefully from Heinemann's now limp arms. His next words were deliberate.

Heinemann slumped back in his chair.

'Gerhard Heinemann, alias Ludwig Bornburg, I formally charge you with the attempted murder of Frank Eastwick, and warn you that anything you say will be used in evidence. Do you have anything to say?'

Gerhard had nothing to say. Nor, for that matter, did anyone else. The constable took the Dane out first, then Eastwick, who continued to stare back over his shoulder, unbelieving and uncomprehending. David Thomas just smiled a satisfied Welsh smile.

Chapter 28

Just Routine

'This had better be good.' Elizabeth Lloyd's manner left no room for compromise.

'Calm down, darling. I can assure you that, to coin a phrase, I can explain everything.'

'Inspector bloody Thomas, I am not your darling. You can address me as Miss Lloyd. And you're a pompous two-timer. You've got one hell of a lot of explaining to do. You're lucky to find me here at all.'

'Please bear with me a bit. And thank you for still coming here.' David's tone was restrained, almost humble. He had despatched the worthy Inspector Takata as a diplomatic envoy between the two warring Welsh factions. Elizabeth had already been half-way packed, and preparing to leave. The ever-helpful Okura management had provided an attractive tray of coffee and canapés, with a courteous note written on a smart card, and this had soothed her down a little. Then Takata had brought her to the Police Headquarters.

He had done his best, assuring her that the last chapter had been unfolded in the case, and that David desperately wished to see her, to explain away the outstanding details, and more to the point, to explain his apparent arrogance. Her curiosity had overcome her pride, and she allowed herself to be graciously conducted, with full Japanese protocol and motor cycle escort, to the Headquarters. David had asked for special treatment, and by the time Elizabeth arrived, to be greeted with many low bows, her anger had subsided to a more rational level.

Confronting David in Superintendent Nakamura's office, his serious demeanour took the sting out of her indignation. She repeated her command that the explanation had better be good, but her language became more measured, and she agreed to bear with him a bit.

'You see, Miss Lloyd, if I may be permitted to address you as such, things were about to get a little dodgy, even a little bit rough, and, at worst, positively dangerous.'

Elizabeth was sarcastic. 'To life and limb? You're not only a two-timing bastard, you're a lying s.o.b.'

'I'm quite serious. To limb, probably, and even to life, perhaps, if things had gone wrong.'

'Bloody Codswallop. Explain.'

'The long and the short of it is that that black case was a bomb.'

'Pull the other leg.'

'I know that this sounds far-fetched. But you must remember that we speculated that Heinemann might be planning to get rid of Frank Eastwick, because he could spill the beans, and Heinemann's career would certainly be ended. He might end up in jail, be knocked down by a car, or be found in bed after an overdose of something.

'I noticed that when they met, Heinemann produced the case and after showing Frank the money, he just clicked the case shut. He did not go through the combination himself but emphasized it more than once to Frank Eastwick. In fact, he seemed to make absolutely sure that Frank could not forget it. And he was being too friendly. I expected him to be bringing bad news at least, annoyed that his arsonists had failed and worse, that they might, as I said, reveal all to the authorities. So he was out to silence Eastwick. But why not waylay him in a dark alley? Always a risk of being caught. Much better to allow Frank to blow himself up, with no trace whatsoever of any explanation, except accident or suicide.

'I put two and two together – and now I admit it was an inspired guess, a long shot if you like – and guessed that when Frank Eastwick next opened the case, his dialling the combination would set off a detonator that would trip off a bomb. All reminiscent of booby traps used in the War, when troops retreated, but left these things behind. Also, if I could prove this, we would have the evidence we needed not only to connect Heinemann with the arson attempt, and lead to intensive enquiries of the origins of the plot, but to prove attempted murder as well.

'So I called his bluff, assuming that he was not suicidal, and invited him to watch Eastwick open the briefcase. The risk was that, if he was suicidal, or if anything had gone wrong, Inspector Takata and I would be ready to dodge through the door behind us, and behind a solid concrete wall, to avoid the shrapnel. But all that routine would have been difficult to explain to you, even more difficult to involve you in the action. We had to rehearse our athletic retreat behind the wall, and three would certainly have been a crowd.'

Elizabeth was silent for a while. Her confrontational attitude subsided. There had been a great deal more to the meeting that morning than had met the eye. She remembered the austerity of the stony surroundings of the interview room, and remembered too that she had wondered why a wide door had been left open, when the circumstances normally demanded the reverse. And then she realized that David had been remarkably intuitive in achieving this denouement. Furthermore, he had been gallantly protective in despatching her back to the hotel. She looked at David in a manner that suggested the withdrawal of the recent characterization of her travelling companion, even the promise of restored amicable relations.

'What can I say? And I thought I was the psychologist of the party.'

242

'No need to say anything, Miss Lloyd, or may I call you Elizabeth? You could take back the bastard bit, and refine your analysis of what constitutes codswallop. But that will have to come later. I have to see the British Ambassador. I would like you to come as well.'

'Why us?'

'I need your presence.'

'You mean that even now I may be of some help?'

'I think so. I have to tackle the problem of which country should make an attempted murder charge on a Danish national, travelling on a German passport, trying to murder an Englishman in Japan, and being apprehended by the Metropolitan Police of London. I understand also that the whole thing is going to be classified in some way so that the press do not turn this into a diplomatic incident and even now jeopardise the big oil deal between Britain and Japan. And there's another thing.'

Elizabeth seemed suspicious. 'What's that?'

'Not codswallop, I assure you...' David paused for effect. 'I want to enquire about how to obtain a special marriage licence for two itinerant English persons of legal age. And I think you should be there – just in a psychologically advisory capacity, of course.'

* * *

Detective Inspector Michael Bridgeman of the Arson Squad accepted a cup of H Division's tea from Constable Marsh, and passed back the file of the Case of the Mysterious Fires to Detective Superintendent Guy Sanders.

'That seems to wrap it up,' he said pleasantly.

Guy Sanders was not so sure.

'That bloody Thomas,' he expostulated. 'He'll be impossible to live with. Look at this cable that's just come in.'

243

Bridgeman read the cable, which certainly did seem to be slightly presumptuous. But perhaps there were extenuating circumstances:

MR AND MRS DAVID THOMAS SUGGEST CONGRATULATIONS ARE DUE TO CONSTABLES CHEESEMAN AND MICHELMORE WHOSE ROUTINE BUT PERCEPTIVE OBSERVATIONS HAVE PROBABLY SAVED A WHOLE CITY FROM DESTRUCTION, MAINTAINED ANGLO-JAPANESE CORDIALITY, AND REINFORCED BRITAIN'S PROSPECTS FOR A POSITIVE OVERSEAS TRADE BALANCE FOR THE REST OF THE CENTURY.